Enchiladas, Rice, and Beans

DANIEL REVELES

ONE WORLD

Ballantine Books • *New York*

A One World Book
Published by Ballantine Books

Copyright © 1994 by Daniel Reveles

http://www.randomhouse.com

Library of Congress Catalog Card Number: 94-94309

ISBN: 0-345-38426-1

Text design by Holly Johnson

Manufactured in the United States of America

First Edition: September 1994

10 9 8 7 6 5 4

This is for Harriet-Nicol,
recordar es volver a vivir.

CONTENTS

ACKNOWLEDGMENTS

I especially want to thank Valerie Ross—kin, friend, and confidante—whose priceless insight influences every page I write. I can never repay the debt I owe the people who saved my life: Brenda and Mark, Gary and Andrea, Mike and Val, and Sandy Carty Fitzgerald. And Ralph Brown, who didn't even know it. He just showed up at the villa, unannounced, with a warm embrace and 1.75 liters of Scotch. *Gracias* to Bertha, Carmen, and Gloria, my *antología enciclopédica* here in Tecate, who often share my corner table at La Fonda. *Un abrazo para* Denise Paccione for every time she took me to lunch and listened to me grumble about a writer's life. A very special thank you for Jane Dystel, my agent. Were it not that she saw what others failed to see, I wouldn't even be writing this page. And then there is Cheryl Woodruff, *mi editor inspiradora, amiga y paradigma* at One World/Ballantine.

—D.R.

Tecate, B.C., Mexico

APERITIVO

I live behind the adobe curtain and I bring you a plate full of *chismes*. In your country you call them tales. As the teller of these tales it is my duty as a *caballero de palabra* to warn you that what follows may appear some distance from the truth. It is said that in Mexico we defy all the natural laws of physics—what goes up stays up, and water runs uphill.

Tecate, Baja California, is a dusty little border town stippled with Easter-egg-colored houses where two sovereign nations meet *panza-to-panza*. They are separated by four thin strands of rusty barbed wire. On Mondays, Señora Mendoza uses it for a clothesline. On a windy day I've seen her crawl through the wires and retrieve her underwear which has entered the United States illegally. At six in the morning I watch armed border guards raise the Stars and Stripes and unlock the tall gate—and the two nations become one. Mexicans drive into the U.S. to get to their jobs, Americans drive into Mexico to attend to their businesses and factories. Mexico is "business friendly." This means cheap labor and no IRS. By eight o'clock a small herd of giggling school children who attend the Mission School in the U.S. begin to walk through the gate. They carry their passports in their lunch boxes. They take them out and show them to the grim guard at the gate. I see little Juanito will be late for school this morning. He forgot his passport. He'll have to go home. His mother will scold him.

It would give me great pleasure to show you around the pueblo of Tecate. Join me—at my corner table at La Fonda—and watch the human drama unfold while mariachis garnish the air with music. Later, we can take a shady bench in the main plaza. Look, here come the hawkers . . . the balloon man, the awesome fire-eater. Pay no attention to that man walking toward us. Do you see what's in his hand? He's holding a jar crawling with bugs. For a small donation he'll take out a caterpillar and eat it. See that little yellow bird flirting with us from his wire cage? He earns a good living telling fortunes.

Tecate's pageant of characters is endless. Listen to a young woman explain why in Mexico she is far better off as "the other woman." And you just have to meet Doña Lala, the village witch who sees more patients than the local doctor. But you must also be prepared for a few surprises. Culture shock, like mumps and measles and other childhood diseases, is probably more severe in adults.

Only a few months ago I was sitting in El Taco Contento, a small but popular twenty-four-hour eatery on Tecate's alleged main boulevard. It was packed nearly to capacity. This means about eleven people (all men). But you could hardly improve on the scene this warm Saturday afternoon. Everyone was in party spirits. Linda Ronstadt, the sweetheart of Mexico, was singing "Por Un Amor," and the tacos were delicious beyond all praise. The door opened, and an American couple breezed in. They were dressed in high fashion shorts, she in Dockers, he in Bugle Boy. They were fortyish, the color of milk glass. I caught only the last line of a conversation that no doubt had its beginning on the sidewalk.

"We're on vacation, Harry, lighten up."

Harry showed no signs of doing so. His face was that of a man who had just bitten down on an unripe lemon.

Mrs. was clearly in charge of the tour. She marched up to the young man behind the counter. "Two tacos, please." No, that isn't quite accurate. She spoke in Dayton, Ohio, Spanish. *"Dos tacos, por favor."* She held up two fingers, for her benefit or his wasn't clear.

The exuberant brown face gave her a luminous smile the width of the Republic. *"Sí, sí,* señora!" and he removed a white cloth with all the pride and flourish of Antoine of Paris, revealing a neat row of leering calf skulls. The eye sockets were dark and empty, but the huge heads seemed to be smiling, and they had rosy cheeks. He didn't say "Voilà!" he said, "Scalp, cheek, or tongue?"

"Aaauugh!"

"Brains if you prefer, señora. We still have a few eyes." "Aaauugh!"

No sound issued from her husband. He appeared to be in a coma.

"Harry, do you see that?"

Harry found his voice. "Let's get out of here, Martha."

I recall another recent incident during a colorful two-day festival in Tecate. The stadium was packed with locals and tourists. It appeared that municipal police (in tan) and state police (in green) could not agree on who was in charge. Their discussion began with just some name-calling, which, we all learned as children, can break no bones. But soon they were at it with sticks and fists, and these we know can cause major damage. When negotiations reached a stalemate, the two branches of law enforcement decided to shoot it out. At this point someone thought it advisable to call more cops. In a matter of minutes the Federales (in khaki) arrived on the scene, and hauled all the policemen away. If you find this anecdote puts undue strain on your limits of believability, I understand. I wouldn't accept it myself if I hadn't been there that Sunday afternoon in July, cowering under the bleachers to avoid the cross fire.

Then there is Obdulio, to give you another taste of what I mean. He's my nearest neighbor, from a rancho two miles or so down the road. He comes by on occasion to exchange news, and pauses for a sip of José Cuervo. But when dusk comes, and we see the first owl flutter clumsily into the tall oak with its mournful hoot, he tells me that it is Lola Santa, a wicked sorceress who bears him ill and transforms herself into an owl. "To what end?" I ask. And he says, "To put a curse on me," and he leaps on his horse and bolts for home.

Rattlesnakes are abundant in these parts, and prudent people go to great effort to avoid their society. Salvador Ramos, the local wood-carver, sees them as a blessing sent by heavenly agents. Judging from the age of his children, Salvador is probably in his mid-fifties. I have watched him snare a rattlesnake, sever its head, and tilting the headless serpent to his lips like a bottle of tequila, drain it of its blood. I claim it's disgusting. Salvador claims that the fresh blood of a rattlesnake inhibits the aging process. The interesting thing is that Salvador looks to be about twenty-five.

The reader who expected to find in these pages common clichés and stereotypes, those exaggerated caricatures of Mexicans that don't really exist except in popular parodies, will be disappointed. I want to introduce you to *real*

Mexicans, people you might not otherwise have the opportunity to meet. I want to take you into their homes, their offices, their cafés. You'll meet the rich and powerful as well as the poor and humble. You'll catch them all in the very acts of everyday life.

One more thing. If you are an American reading this, you may find the chauvinism of the men and the submissiveness of the women somewhat exasperating. I do too. That is when I have to remind myself that all societies do not develop in parallel. Mexico abolished slavery before America, but didn't get around to giving its women the right to vote until 1953. Can equality be far behind?

Like life itself, these stories have their moments of laughter, irony, and sometimes tears. They are as unalike as tacos and toast. And yet they seem to go well together; thus I have served them on the same plate as Enchiladas, Rice, and Beans.

—*Your Servidor*

Of Time and Circumstance

"*Kee-kee-ree-kee!*"

I was still safely behind the gates of sleep where cares cannot gain admittance. I parted my heavy eyelids and listened again.

"*Kee-kee-ree-kee!*"

Everything I really needed to know about roosters I learned in kindergarten years before I could understand Fulghum's uncommon wisdom. And that was that roosters always say "cock-a-doodle-doo." Open the pages of any storybook and confirm the fact for yourself. It's always been "cock-a-doodle-doo." But El Gato was right. Here in Mexico the roosters definitely crow in Spanish. And if it weren't for El Gato, I wouldn't even be here.

"*Kee-kee-ree-kee!*"

Time? It didn't matter. It was still dark, still cool. Soon night would yield to day, the sun would warm the edges of the morning. The date? That didn't matter either. There was no calendar here. And even if there were, it would be blank. This day belonged to me. I was in paradise.

The entire episode really began several years ago when I went to David with an urgent errand. I ran up the three flights of rickety-rackety stairs two at a time. The crumbling Hollywood Producers Building on the boulevard of the same name had an elevator, but you'd have to film it in time-lapse photography to perceive any motion.

I had three months of my life and countless sleepless nights under my arm in two reels. We had shot 25,000 feet of film in a dozen Turkish towns and villages from the magnificent ruins of ancient Troy to Mount Ararat, where Noah ran his ship aground. It was my job now to put all the elements together and produce one hour of television entertainment. I had scenes that ran too long, others I couldn't extend to accommodate narration, great music and no place to put it.

I saw David's door as soon as I reached the landing. David Zimmer, thirty-one and single, was one of the best film editors in Hollywood and one of the busiest. The sign on his door read:

POST PRODUCTION TRAUMA CENTER
EMERGENCY ENTRANCE

David, whose crazy blond hair and zany mustache made him look like a blond Groucho Marx, turned off his Moviola and looked up at me through thick lenses. "My God, you look wasted! What did she *do* to you?" He vibrated his eyebrows.

"I'm exhausted, I worked all weekend."

"Yes, I recognize the symptoms of postproduction syndrome. There's what you need." He rolled his eyes to direct my attention to the wall behind his editing bench, a collage of wholesome erotica, nudes adorned with cherry blossoms, summer flowers, and autumn leaves. One brunette was dusted with snowflakes. "I scored a music track for my artwork. Listen to this." He hit a button and the luminous strings of Vivaldi's "Four Seasons" poured into the room from four giant JBL speakers.

"I don't think that's what the good father had in mind, but it does seem to work." I returned to the subject at hand. "I had to rewrite the whole show. But you can now cut a final to this." I handed him my mutilated script.

"What's this? Tearstains!" He laughed at his own joke. "When do you go on the air with this?" David went to a calendar on his wall. It was the size of a bed sheet and displayed every day of the year at a glance, courtesy of Hollywood Film Laboratories. Every square representing one precious day of life of an unknown number was marked with X's and scrawls and circles and notations. It looked like a bus bench in the ghetto.

"Look at your calendar, David! It looks like mine. The deadlines are killing us! We're pawning our future, we're selling away our very lives! Why do we do it?"

"Car payments." David wiggled his eyebrows up and down. "I thought you were going to buy that little piece of paradise down in Baja and get away from all this."

"Believe me, I am. I just can't find the time to stay down there long enough to find what I want. You'll know when I do, David—you won't see me!"

"Hey, I've got a friend in Tecate, he's a lawyer. He could probably find something for you."

"Really?"

"I'm sure of it. He's got connections all the way to Mexico City. I've got his card here somewhere." He shuffled through scripts and film cans and finally produced it from his wallet. It looked like a very used Kleenex cut to the size of a business card. "Here it is, Felix Fernando Espinoza Gil. Geez, look at all those names! They call him El Gato in Mexico. The cat?"

When George Herriman conceived Krazy Kat and named the protagonist Felix, he couldn't have known that long after his comic strip would be forgotten, little Mexican boys baptized Felix would forevermore be known as El Gato. "You really think he could do something?"

"Oh yeah, I'm sure he can. And he's a helluva nice guy. Tell him you're a friend of mine. He's a million laughs. Ask him if he's still delighting the pretty ladies."

That same afternoon, I put the wilted card in front of me and picked up the phone. I was born, raised, and schooled in Los Angeles by my Mexican parents who had fled the bloody revolution of 1910. And like so many Mexican-Americans that I know, suffered an irrational sense of insecurity in the presence of a "real" Mexican. My language was badly rusted from many long years of disuse and abuse. I didn't want to sound illiterate or ill-bred. I put the phone down and did a quick rehearsal. Satisfied, I dialed again and listened to the phone ring in Mexico. It was more a nervous beep, rapid beeps, coming two at a time.

"*¿Bueno?*" A female voice.

"Is Señor Gil in the office?" It's pronounced "Heel."

"On whose behalf?"

I gave my name and she said, "*Un momento.*"

"*¡Bueno!*" A masculine voice this time.

"Señor Gil?"

"Felix Fernando Espinoza Gil, your *servidor.*"

It was the carbide steel voice of the headmaster with hemorrhoids and a migraine on the way. It was not the voice of a man who could evoke a million laughs. Even the obeisant *your servidor* did nothing to ameliorate the case-hardened edge. Sweet Jesus! I recognized my error at once. I called him by his mother's maiden name. His surname was the first one, Espinoza.

"*Gracias,*" I replied to the courtesy.

The frosty voice continued. "Perhaps if you would have the kindness to state your needs, I could tell you to what extent, if any, I could lend my assistance."

I didn't like him. I didn't object to the formality, it wasn't that, but his elitist manner was too cold, too severe for a project so near my heart. Now I chose my words carefully so as not to commit some horrid grammatical error. "I'm calling from Los Angeles. I'm a friend of David Zimmer, who suggested that I give you a call."

"Well, señor, you are not too selective of the society you cultivate, but I will not hold that against you. How can your *servidor* be of assistance?" The steel voice didn't soften, but I caught a glint of humor.

Maybe he wasn't so bad. "I'm planning on building a modest vacation home near Tecate, and I thought, that is, David thought you could help me locate something suitable since it isn't easy for me to get there."

The tight voice now loosened perceptively, but without loss of social precision. "It would be an immense pleasure for me if I could help you succeed in your endeavor. What are you looking for?"

"Just a few acres where the phone doesn't ring and I can have some peace and quiet."

"*Sí,* I understand perfectly." Warmer now, and sunny as a morning in May. "Where you can keep a horse perhaps, a big sorrel with flaxen mane, a noble beast who comes galloping to your side when you give that special whistle. And you can ride through endless valleys scattering your cares along the way . . . in the arms of your mistress, the wind."

The brittle formality laced with doilies of poetry made me 'smile to myself. I was beginning to like him. "*Sí, sí,* you have the idea."

"You'll need a few chickens to deliver the morning eggs, of course. And a rooster to command the sun to rise and shed its soft pink promise of the new day—and summon you to life itself!" Was this the same man who answered the phone?

"You've got the picture. A big red rooster that tiptoes on the fence and cries cock-a-doodle-doo!"

"Cock-a-doodle-what?" The voice tightened.

"Cock-a-doodle-doo." Now I felt silly.

"Is that what roosters say in English? Down here they sing *kee-kee-ree-kee.*" He put everything into his imitation and I'm sure I heard the secretary giggling in the background. "Our dogs say *guau guau.* What do American dogs say?"

"Woof woof."

"Now that we have that important piece of business addressed and set aside, let's put down some specific guidelines. About two *hectareas?*" He must have concluded that my education was not complete, and he added, "One *hectaria* equals two-point-five American acres."

"Yes, that would be perfect. I suppose we should discuss fee. I also expect to cover your expenses."

"It is much too early to speak of that now, so please, you must put that thought out of your head. By the way, how are things in that great world power to the north?"

Was he serious? "Oh, fine, just fine."

"Do you still have traffic jams in Los Angeles?"

"There are three and a half million cars here. Even finding a place to park is a nightmare. That's one reason I want to go down there."

"You may be too late. We have only four thousand cars and you can't find a place to park. We have a fixation about copying Americans. It gives those of us in the third world a feeling of equality."

This man definitely had a sense of humor. So I felt safe in delivering David's message. "David told me to ask you if you still amuse the ladies."

"Tell David I still keep the ladies well-entertained. When I pull off my *calzones* they burst into fits of laughter." I heard mixed laughter in the background. Doubtless a visitor in his office was enjoying his end of the dialogue.

"Well, Señor Espinoza, I appreciate your attentiveness and your courtesy." I'd kept the entire conversation carefully contained within the formal third person form. My language might falter, but he couldn't think I had no manners.

"Please! I leave the *usted* form to the deities and the peasants. I prefer to be addressed as *tú*. Now I'll see what I can do for you."

"*Gracias*, should I call you in about a week, would that be convenient?"

"Convenient? Your servant is available whenever you need him, whether it is twelve noon or twelve midnight."

We rang off. What an extraordinary character. In twenty years of traveling and meeting people at every artificial level of society, I couldn't recall anyone to compare to the *licenciado*. I could hardly believe the project was actually on the way to becoming reality. I was definitely going to enjoy working with him.

I immediately wanted to give the voice a face and form. Was he young, was he old, short, fat, tall? I decided then and there to form my own composite picture of this unusual man and square it with the facts when we met. I made myself one rule: I couldn't ask him or anyone who knew him a direct question. I would have to do it all with my powers of observation and perception, which I believed were equal to Mrs. Hudson's tenant at 221B Baker Street.

I took out a yellow legal pad and began. His voice was tuned at a lower pitch than most Mexican men, but it was not deep. His elocution impeccable, uncontaminated by colloquialisms. Obviously well-educated, well beyond law school. His social procedure was consistent with the Mexican concept of good breeding. The poetry was all his own. I put him between forty and fifty, dark face, neat black mustache, meticulously groomed. Probably a little portly, considering his sedentary occupation. I added glasses.

A week later I dialed the number. The señorita answered.

"*Buenos días*, law office." It sounded like a song.

"May I speak to *licenciado* Espinoza." This time I got the surname right.

"Ah, *sí*, you are the gentleman who is looking for property, *sí*? I'm afraid the *licenciado* isn't here, he flew to Mexico City early this morning."

"Oh." My voice was gray.

"But he'll be back in the office tomorrow. He just went to see his mother for Mother's Day."

"But Mother's Day was last Sunday."

"In your country you put holidays where it's convenient. In Mexico, Mother's Day is the tenth of May whatever the day of the week." She had acquired the *licenciado*'s form of expression, probably from years of exposure, much as the limbs of a tree incline alee. "And every tenth of May the *licenciado* drives to San Diego, buys a dozen Weenchel's doughnuts and catches a flight to Mexico City and delivers them to the sweet old lady."

"Winchell's doughnuts?"

"*Sí*, the dear lady has some very singular ways. She's lived like a princess all her life. She's been all over the world, but during a visit here, she discovered Weenchel's doughnuts."

"It's fortunate her fascination wasn't with Baskin-Robbins. I'll ring him up the day after tomorrow. Is that all right?"

"We love to hear from you any time."

Two days later I called. She recognized my voice instantly, and I liked that. Her voice was soft and feminine, warm, and the color of buttercream. "El Gato is back." It was the first time I'd heard her call him anything but *licenciado*. Should I make a description of her too? No need to. It was safe to say she was the typical Mexican legal secretary, all bosom and thighs mounted on two pins. "I'll have him on the line in a moment."

"*Buenos días*." The voice resonated. "How are things on the Other Side?"

"Getting better every day. How are things in Mexico?"

"We are making steady progress in our effort to emulate everything you do up there. We admire your efficiency. We only have two intersections with traffic lights, but the municipality has just installed left-turn-only arrows."

"Why, that's marvelous, you'll see a big difference."

"We already do. You see, we don't have left turn lanes." We both laughed. "We're also building a new road to alleviate traffic. It might even be finished by the time you get here."

"Does that mean you have something?"

"A couple of properties, but I don't think they'll do."

"What have you got?"

"I found two *hectarias* of rocks and gullies. If you level a section, you might be able to stand on one foot."

"Well, that's out, what else?"

"There is a beautiful piece of land just south of town. Level, lots of oak trees, a little stream—"

"I'll take it, I'll take it!"

"It is downwind and contiguous to the municipal dump."

"Oh."

"There is talk of relocating this indispensable monument to man's existence to the new state prison."

"Did you say the state prison?"

"Yes, it was started a few years ago amid a great deal of publicity. But they ran out of funds halfway through the project. It stands useless and abandoned today. I suppose they could burn trash in the guard towers, but that's light-years away. Don't start interviewing roosters yet. I think I better keep looking. Can you call me next week? If I'm not here, Graciela will have the information."

"*Sí*, absolutely." I made a note of Graciela's name.

"Tell me, is it true that every American home has a microwave?"

"It's a safe bet."

"I think I will drive into San Diego this afternoon and buy one."

"What do you want with a microwave?"

"It is a wedding present for my sister. I told you, all Mexicans want everything Americans have."

"Does that mean you're going to import smog?"

"We couldn't afford it. We're a debtor nation, you know, but we haven't lost our ability to laugh at ourselves. Even our jokes have now taken on the American format of good news/bad news."

I couldn't help but wonder how an army trained to introduce cultural change could conquer a nation without firing a shot.

"I was at a Rotary Club meeting last night and the speaker told us that if inflation gets any worse in the next six months, we'll all be eating garbage."

"My God, that's terrible. What's the good news?"

"That is the good news. The bad news is we'll have to stand in line for it!"

We were both laughing when we said adios and agreed to touch bases in about a week. I took out my profile and made a single change. I made him younger by ten years. He was now forty.

"You're a little early." Graciela's voice was like fresh flowers when I called a week later. It was nine-thirty. "He plays tennis every morning. Could you call back about ten?"

It was nearly eleven when I got my call through. "Did the *licenciado* get back from his tennis game?"

"*Sí*, but he has someone in his office. I will get his attention."

"No, no, you mustn't." I pictured a heavy-duty client in the office and myself an unprofitable intrusion on the phone. "I can always call him back when it's more convenient."

"Oh no, that's all right. It is not a client. It is one of his tennis colleagues, and they talk only the nonsense of all men. Besides, I know he will want to talk to you. You put him in manageable humor. He really enjoys your calls, you know."

"I know I certainly do. You've all been so cordial to me, a total stranger."

I didn't hear the click of the hold button, I heard her say, "*Teléfono, licenciado*, it's the voice of the Other Side."

"*¡Buenos días!* How are things in El Norte?"

"Getting faster every day."

"No one can say that about Mexico."

"I think I'm ready for life in the slow lane."

"You know, your country is the epitome of efficiency. How we envy you! Someone told me you can actually do all your banking transactions on a slot machine without ever walking into a bank. Is this really true?"

"Oh yes, it saves a lot of time."

"*¡Magnífico!* And what do you do with all the time you save?"

"I wish I knew."

"We are so backward down here. We didn't give women the right to vote until 1953." He was interrupted by some unintelligible but animated comments from Graciela. He resumed his speech with an exaggerated chauvinistic tone. "We still have to look at the pretty bank teller in her swirly skirt and frilly blouse. We lose so much precious time lusting for her while she asks how we are, and then we are obliged to inquire after her. We are so inefficient!"

He was having so much fun with this theme I could see the wink and the grin a hundred fifty miles away. "Well, we're the drive-through capital of the world," I said.

"We may never catch up with our neighbor to the north. I know you pump your own gasoline, but tell me, is it really true that when you go to lunch, you remove your own dishes and clean your table?"

"I can't deny it."

"Then is it also true that your whole telephone system is run by robot recordings? You know what someone told me? That if you dial 911 a recorded voice says, 'If this is a fire, press one; if you're reporting a burglary, press two; if rape is imminent, press three . . .' Tell me this is not so."

"They claim it's efficient. It takes less people."

"Of course, you live in a throwaway society. And what do you do with all your discarded people, recycle them like plastic cups and disposable razors? I notice everything in your country is disposable—friends, colleagues, even parents, simply use and throw away. That would never work down here." I heard the shuffle of papers.

He returned to the present. "I'm glad you caught me today because tomorrow I go before the tribunal and that will take all day."

"Tribunal? Don't you plead your case before a jury of the accused's peers?"

"We don't have juries here. We go before a judge."

"But what if you don't like the judge's decision?"

We said it at the same time. "The tribunal!"

"Now that's curious."

"Your judicial system or ours?"

"There it is again."

"What are we talking about?"

"Did you notice those two words we just used—*tribunal* and *judicial*—are exactly the same in English and in Spanish?"

"I never thought about it. I suppose it occurs only rarely. The only other word I can think of offhand is *general*."

"Well, there's *invasion, dental, radio* . . ."

"And now that I think about it, *doctor*, and *indigestion*, and *colitis*."

"You've got the idea—ah, that's one for me, *idea*!" He paused for a moment, fully pleased with his new find. "But I suppose you would rather have a progress report."

"Do you have anything?"

"The truth is, I have nothing definite."

"But you're optimistic."

"Oh *sí*, everybody was hurt by the devaluation of the peso against your dollar, and many people want to sell what land they have."

"That bad."

"Many enterprises have gone bankrupt."

"You don't have Chapter Eleven down there?"

"Oh no, we tried that back in 1864. At that time France was our biggest creditor, and that's when Napoleon sent Maximiliano down here to repossess Mexico." I heard the squeal of his swivel chair. "History is queer, no? Diplomatic relations between America and Napoleon were not cordial. And yet none other than his nephew, Charles Joseph Bonaparte, ends up Attorney General of the United States."

"Can that be true?"

"Oh yes, it was during the reign—excuse me—during the term of Theodore Roosevelt."

Where did the man get all this? "Why don't I check back with you in a week or so? I'm looking forward to flirting with the pretty tellers and dealing with real people once again."

"As always, I look forward to the pleasure of our next visit."

"*Gracias*. Oh, I nearly forgot, how is that new road coming along, nearly finished?"

"*Sí*, they just have to make the potholes and they can cut the ribbon." We rang off.

A week later I called his office. "No, the *famoso* Gato has not returned." Graciela's voice was as sweet as ever. "He has an office full of people waiting. I would pull his *bigotes* if he had them!"

So, no mustache! I made a note. "Why don't I try again late this afternoon?"

"That would be perfect. I know he has something very interesting for you."

It was late in the afternoon when I connected. "It's me, Graciela, did the man get back?" We were on familiar terms now.

"He just now came in from an arduous drive to Ensenada and back. He's exhausted and a little ill-humored."

"I do understand how that is. I can call another time."

"Oh no, he actually looks forward to your calls. You brighten his day. I'll take him a cup of coffee and you cheer him up."

I heard him lift the phone, and before he could say anything, I sang, "How are things in Mexico?"

"Life is a heap of *mierda* with tinsel on it!" It was the sound of a man in pain. I wanted desperately to give him comfort, but the right words ignored my summons. "We try to bribe Fate the same way we try to bribe our government officials, only to find that the difference is that Fate is *incorruptible*. Well, never mind all that, life goes on. I do have news for you."

I tried to keep it light. "Good news or bad news?"

"You can start auditioning roosters."

"Really! I'm excited, what did you find?"

"Four *hectarias*, mostly level with gently rolling pastures. A cool breeze scented with wild sage ruffles through giant oak trees and a million leaves applaud! I even noticed a little stream that murmurs a love song all day long. . . ." All the color was back in his voice now.

"Stop it, stop it, this is it! How much?"

"The family wants four thousand American dollars."

I couldn't believe what I was hearing. "Taxes?"

"Excessive."

I knew it! There's always a catch. "How much?"

"About fifteen U.S. dollars per annum."

"I'll take it, I'll take it!"

"¡*Magnífico!* And I will bring the wine and we can christen the new land. *Sí.* I will have a bottle of Sangre de Cristo and it will be my honor to offer you the first toast!" He was himself again, and that made me feel better.

"I'll be there before you can put down the phone!" When I regained my composure, I said, "By the way, what do I owe you?"

"A cup of coffee."

"Did you say a cup of coffee?"

"Following a lavish dinner, of course."

"Please, be serious."

"I am. You have achieved the rank of friend."

"¡*Gracias, un millón de gracias!* I can be there next week. Will that work for you?"

"Unfortunately I will be in Mexico City all of next week. My sister's wedding, remember?"

"Did you buy the microwave?"

"*Sí*, I went to one of your large department stores and met one of your recycled people with a dormant soul, a woman with the look of defeat on her lifeless face. We conducted the entire transaction without exchanging a single word. So, just to see if she might be human, I said, 'The microwave is for my bedridden grandmother.' And do you know what she replied?"

"I can't imagine."

" 'Bedding is on the second floor, have a nice day.' I suspect she operates on two C-type batteries and a diet of microchip cookies."

"I'm sure your sister will love the microwave. Look, I'll come down in two weeks, how will that be?"

"*¡Perfecto!* I am looking forward to your arrival in our poor and humble pueblo with eager anticipation. You may even be installed in your rancho in time for my wedding."

"Wedding! You're getting married?"

"A tangible contingency."

"My very best wishes, *felicidades!*"

"*Gracias.* And even bigger *gracias* for making me see the tinsel."

A strange remark, I thought as I put down the phone. What could have been bothering him? I took out my yellow pad and completed my picture. He was now dark, lean, tall, no mustache, and if he was getting married, I took his age down from forty to somewhere between thirty and thirty-five. I took his glasses off. I could pick him out in a crowd!

It was Saturday morning, and I realized nearly three weeks had evaporated since El Gato found the very thing I wanted. On sudden impulse I decided to drive south and appear in his office. Yes, of course, I would take him to lunch, he would show me the property, we would drink the wine under the oaks, and we'd all live happily ever after.

I had no trouble locating the office. They were located on the second floor above the bank, reached by way of an outdoor iron stairway that came down to the narrow side-walk. It looked like an afterthought. I was carrying two small packages with me. I slipped them under my arm, walked directly into the office and looked around for Graciela, the fat secretary with the sweet voice. There was no one at the desk. The office was empty. I could hear movement down the hall, and assumed that she may have gone to the ladies' and would soon return. I stood waiting quietly. Almost immediately I heard footsteps approaching.

In a moment a pretty young woman made her appearance. She had the sweet face of a Dresden figurine and luxuriant black hair that fell to her waist. She couldn't have weighed more than ninety-five pounds. At birth. Two-twenty was a conservative and charitable estimate. A star is born for the wide screen, I thought, and congratulated myself immediately for my perspicacity.

"*Buenos días.*" A pleasant voice, but uncertain.

"*Buenos días,*" I answered, but before I could begin to introduce myself, the enormous young lady turned toward the hall.

"You have a visitor, Graciela," she called out, and floated toward the door. "I'll see you tonight," and she was out the door. I could have sworn I felt earth tremors as she descended the stairs.

Graciela walked into frame at that moment and I lost my audio track completely. The girl who stood before me must have been made in collaboration with the angels. David would have said, "A *knockout!*" The face, an exquisite cameo. Black fire in bright onyx eyes. Her raven hair was swept back and held off her neck with a strand of narrow ribbon.

"*Buenos días,*" she said. The curve of her lips was enough to make you see visions and dream dreams. My mouth must have still been ajar because she added, "*Sí, señor,* what can I do for you?" She was not smiling.

"You must be Graciela, I've been talking to you on the phone."

I watched the pretty face brighten as all the light bulbs went off in her head. "And you must be our friend from the Other Side, of course!" She made a sudden little jump as though she had just seen a mouse. She recovered quickly, gave me her hand and continued. "It is a privilege to meet you," and she recited all her names. She retrieved her hand to brush back a strand of disobedient hair away from her face.

"The pleasure is all mine, believe me." There was a short, awkward pause. "Oh, I brought this for you." I handed her a two-pound box of See's chocolate cremes. I noticed that she was tall and willowy. She was wearing black gabardine stretch pants that couldn't lie and a simple salt and pepper jersey that failed to keep its contents a secret.

"How thoughtful! *Gracias.*" Then, as though prodded by an invisible mother, she said, "Where are my manners! Please, let me get you some coffee."

"Oh, you needn't bother."

"Bother? It is no bother!" And she was on her way down the hall. She returned with a ceramic mug filled with black coffee in each hand. She was graceful as a dancer. There was a subtle movement within the jersey as the spike heels made contact with the floor. I'd directed so many magazine layouts for lingerie clients that I automatically began to speculate as to style and model: black, white, nude, front closure, soft cup, underwire?

"I am so sorry! I should have asked if you used cream or sugar."

I wanted to send her back down that hall again for sugar, for cream, and once again for no reason. "Oh, like this is just fine, *gracias.*"

She walked behind her desk and removed a carton full of files from her chair before she sat down. I noticed more cartons on the floor. I must have caught her at Saturday housecleaning. "I am afraid the *licenciado* is not here. Was he expecting you today?"

"Oh no, I told him I would be down in a few weeks. But I didn't know exactly when."

"I am so sorry."

"I'm disappointed, but it's my own fault. I should have called first."

She looked into her cup without comment, when her eyes caught sight of the package still in my hand. "I brought a little *regalo* for El Gato," I said with the familiarity of an intimate friend.

"How very thoughtful—what a nice thing to do."

"Just some tennis balls."

I followed her into the main office. It was a large room with highly polished old-fashioned hardwood flooring. I smelled leather and cedar oil. The wall behind the walnut desk was a floor-to-ceiling mosaic of red, green, blue, maroon, and black book spines embossed with gold titles. On the side wall was his law degree from the University of Mexico, standard equipment in a law office. It was the document in the frame below that brought the man into sharper focus, a Ph.D. from Harvard. There was the usual portrait of Benito Juarez. But then I saw a man I never expected to meet in Mexico: Abraham Lincoln. The two isometric champions of freedom at the same moment in history meet for the first time on El Gato's wall!

When I put my gift on the desk, I noticed a pad by the phone with his list of words ready for my next phone call. *Rifle, laudable, inexorable, particular.* There was a bottle of Sangre de Cristo with a scarlet satin sash around its neck. A green tennis ball sat idly in his in-box.

The phone rang at that moment and Graciela went to her office to answer it. A small bulletin board caught my attention. It was full of old newspaper clippings held in place

25

with colored thumbtacks. They looked like editorial columns from the local paper. I browsed with amusement.

City Hall Furious!
NEW TREES BEAR BITTER FRUIT

The citizens of Tecate have come to accept the enormous potholes in their roads that serve no purpose other than to break an axle or a spring. But this morning the boulevard looked like a park. Flowering oleanders were growing in every pothole. We counted over 75 trees in three blocks. But city hall denies it is a municipal project. "We do not consider this funny," the mayor was quoted as saying. "And if I find the culprit, I'll have him arrested!" It has been suggested that this might be the work of El Gato . . .

CITY HALL PROMISES NEW MUNICIPAL POOL

The mayor of our town dove into his swimming pool this afternoon only to find himself in the company of 400 schoolchildren in swimsuits. The mayor was not cordial. He called the supervisor of schools, who claimed that an invitation for all the children was received in a letter from the municipality last week. The mayor denies any knowledge of the letter, and a search of the files has failed to turn up a copy. However, the mayor said, "We have approved funds for a public pool and construction will begin next month." This reporter suspects that perhaps El Gato . . .

I wandered to the other end of the room. It held an enormous couch of soft leather the color of honey. A white sweater lay crumpled between a cushion and the arm where it was tossed; a pair of tennis shoes, one lying on its side, sat on the floor. The coffee table had a clean ashtray and a tennis racket in its frame.

Graciela returned from her phone call and, with a wistful sigh, bent down and began to pick up. Like a weary mother who does it all day long, she gathered first the sweater, then the shoes, then the racket. The nape of her neck was covered with soft baby ringlets of black silk.

She almost laughed. "I wonder why it is? Girls grow up to become women and men grow up to become boys." She placed everything neatly in the armoire.

My eyes came to rest on that enormous sofa and all the implications. Was there intimacy here? She was wearing a ring. His? El Gato had said he was getting married. I wondered. Perhaps my eyes stayed on the sofa too long. Maybe she could read my thoughts as they traveled across the wall like a TV news ticker on election night. Abruptly she walked back into the outer office, and I followed.

"I am so sorry you have come all this way for nothing." Her voice was almost crisp. "I know he would have loved meeting you very much. He really enjoyed your phone calls—we all did."

"I have only myself to blame." No reply, so I added, "Do you think he will have reason to come by today?"

"No—I'm afraid not."

"You won't see him then until Monday?"

She made no immediate reply. She pursed her lips in the form of a kiss. No doubt some thought process was in progress. Finally, "Today is his birthday. Friends are giving him a fiesta tonight. You are invited if you should care to go."

"*Sí*, I would love it! I must meet him before I leave. Where is it to be and what time?"

27

"Where are you staying?"

"The Tecate Motel."

"I will pick you up at eight." With that she offered her hand and I left.

I wandered around the town without purpose. I found the intersection with the new left arrow signals. El Gato was right. The installation was ludicrous. Busy Saturday traffic was a wild free-for-all. Cars would become hopelessly snarled and in the next minute magically unsnarled. I have never seen such chaotic harmony. Pedestrians with absolutely no understanding of lights, crosswalks, and other aids to navigation darted in and out among the cars with the insouciance of the blessed. Bicycles and taco carts squeezed between the cracks to give the scene an element of suspense. I was prepared for screeching brakes, the blast of horns, and rude signs. The scene was silent. Occasionally a driver would stop and hold a brief conversation with someone he knew, and traffic in both directions would again come to a halt. No one blew a horn, no one called out an obscenity. Back in L.A. they would have been lynched on the spot—shot, more than likely.

The little plaza was spotless. No beggars, no grizzly derelicts to step over or around like we have downtown. I sat on a lacy wrought-iron bench to watch the human parade. I got my shoes shined (twice) and sampled a cantaloupe popsicle. There were no strangers in this town, myself included. Everyone who passed my bench said *"Buenas tardes"* or gave me a nod and a smile. This was no anonymous society. These were not recycled people. They were *alive!* This was the town for me.

I left the plaza in search of a place to slake my thirst, and I recognized the iron stairway to El Gato's office. A

28

man of ample girth and florid countenance was on his way down. We reached the bottom step at the same time.

"Don't bother to make the dangerous journey, señor, the *licenciado* is not there. The office is locked." He was mopping his bald head with a soggy handkerchief. His clothes were wilted and he looked to be about two heartbeats away from cardiac infarction.

"He's not in today," I offered. "I was here earlier."

"It's no surprise. The man is always someplace else." Either the climb had left him giddy or the fact that I had been there qualified me as one of the intimates. He gave me his damp hand and his names. "Perhaps you will join me for a refreshment. I need immediate restoration."

We walked back to the plaza and took a pleasant table in the shade. Almost immediately a young man was at the table. "Send an ambulance with two beers immediately— seconds count!" The waiter disappeared instantly without comment.

"You are a friend of El Gato? How is it we've never met?"

I began to explain when we heard the siren. *"Wooo, wooo, wooo!"* The waiter, doing a credible imitation of an ambulance, arrived with two amber bottles of Corona dripping with dew. My new friend didn't bother with the glass. This was first aid. The ambulance brought him another. This one babbled into the frosty glass with a spew of bubbles that cheered the man visibly.

"I've known El Gato all my life," he told me after the first sip. "He's as eccentric as his father. His father was also a *licenciado*. He's been dead many years. God rest him. But El Gato is even more *chingón*. If he isn't in Mexico City pulling a lever, he's at the state capital putting sand in the governor's pants. Or he's making life miserable for the mayor. He's a firecracker, that Gato."

It occurred to me that I was learning a great deal about El Gato and I hadn't asked a single question. Anyone this lugubrious must be a salesman, I thought.

"I haven't seen him for months. I'm taking the evening flight to Mexico City from Tijuana and just thought, being that close, you know, I would stop by and give him my *saludos*. I'm just returning from San Francisco. I'm in sales. Wholesale liquor."

Bingo.

He took a long swallow and continued. "He has a lot of power for a young man. He hasn't seen thirty-five Aprils."

This was unsolicited information, I thought, honorably obtained. I stored it.

"But the man uses his power to help the people of this town."

"How does he do that?"

"The stories are endless. There was the time the co-mandante at the border confiscated a load of food and clothing that someone was trying to sneak in. Of course, the comandante thought he would either extort a generous bribe or he would take it home." Here he paused for a laugh to add an element of tension. "Mysteriously, the consign-ment disappeared from the customs yard without a trace. It turned up on the doorstep at the convent!" He drained his glass elaborately, giving the anecdote a dramatic finish.

"El Gato?"

"Who else?" He threw his hands to the side. "He is something of a Robin Hood down here. Call the ambu-lance?"

"Just one more."

The ambulance arrived without sirens this time. "The

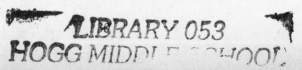

last time I saw El Gato he was babysitting a little girl, but that was several months ago."

"Babysitting?"

"*Sí*, it is very sad. There is a little girl, maybe ten, eleven, I think. And the poor little thing is dying of leukemia. Well, señor, you know what that man does? Every day—and I mean every day when he is not out of the city—he sits with her. He brings her toys and comic books and he reads them to her—every day!"

Suddenly I was moved. When he said "leukemia," I felt a thickening in my throat.

"I made the trip with him once. It's in Ensenada. And I watched the man, that big powerful *licenciado*, feared by all officialdom, playing Barbies with the little girl, and making funny voices for the dolls to make her laugh. I nearly wept."

He brought out his rumpled handkerchief and wiped his face. I didn't say a word. I didn't want to hear any more.

"I met the little girl's mother, of course. A very bitter woman, and understandably so, wouldn't you agree? Do you know what she said to me?" He didn't wait for my answer. " 'God has abandoned us, at least we have El Gato.' "

I began to understand some things about the man behind the voice on the phone. And now that I thought of it, Graciela did seem somewhat distraught this afternoon.

"Nothing keeps the man from his visit. If there is an important meeting, it waits. If the *gobernador*"—he emphasized the word—"has an important dinner, *it waits*! But then, of course, he comes driving back burning the road under him. Nobody who knows him will ride with him. Do you know what they say?"

I shook my head silently. I was still working on "leukemia."

"They say if you want to avoid the devil, get in the car with El Gato because even the devil will not ride with him!"

The conversation, like the shade on our table, drifted to other subjects more sterile in nature. We wrestled for the check like gentlemen. He won. We exchanged courtesies and parted.

By eight o'clock I was ready for Graciela. But remembering the Mexicans' meticulous attention to tardiness, I decided to wait for her in the bar. The bar was nearly empty but for a few tourists. I now remembered the frustration when my cousins visited from Mexico. We could never do anything on time. It must be in our DNA. At eight-thirty I began to wonder how they ever get a show on the air when Graciela glided into the room. She walked in her own light. She was wearing a cool summer dress of frothy chiffon with pastel lime, orange, and lemon panels in the full skirt. It was fitted at the waist, slightly scooped, with wide straps that tied behind her neck. She looked like a sherbet parfait in three flavors. Her black hair fell on her shoulders. A tiny gold medallion rested innocently in her cleavage. The tourists turned to stare and were still staring when we went out the door, her skirt swirling and rustling seductively.

I followed her to a red Honda. She slid behind the wheel, tugged her skirts up over her knees, and taxied to the street. I studied her beautiful face at close range in the pale light of the instrument panel as she contemplated her move. Eyes wide open and alert, the soft lips forming a kiss. I concluded this was a mannerism due more to preoccupation then affection. She seized the moment! We catapulted out of the parking lot, flew in front of a semi truck and trailer, close enough to smell the driver's breath had I my-

self been breathing. She zipped across three lanes of traffic
like Pac-Man gobbling up dots. I was expecting to hear a
horn concerto. A Hail Mary left turn at the intersection,
and we were on the main boulevard, where my heart resumed its normal function.

I had no idea where we were going. In a few minutes we
came to what appeared to be an enormous department
store. Every window upstairs and down was ablaze, spraying
the dark night above with an aurora of yellow light. It
looked like Sears during one of their forty-percent-off
sales. Cars were parked nearly on top of each other. But
Graciela had no problem finding a place to park on the
sidewalk.

"Can we do that?"

"The chief of police is inside."

There was no need to ring the bell. The front doors
were wide open. We stepped into a blizzard of colored
shirts, flouncy dresses, and shimmering stockings. The room
was a blur of arms and legs and faces fuzzing in and out of
focus through a split-image lens. There must have been
three hundred people in front of us. The roar would have
blown the eardrums of the celebrated deaf adder in the
Scriptures. Voices on top of voices, fragments of music, sudden spasms of laughter.

From somewhere came the gay melancholy ecstasy of
mariachis, music sweet as a kiss, painful as love. I could
hear guitars, a festive trumpet, violins weeping. Men and
women ran to us and threw their arms around Graciela as
soon as they saw her. Smiles went off like flashbulbs, kisses
were flying in all directions, here and there earrings sparkled in the crowd. I followed close behind her. There was
too much confusion for introductions, but it must have
been obvious that I was "with" her, and came dangerously

close to being smothered alive in the melee of hugs and kisses.

It must have taken the better part of an hour to get from the front door to the *estancia*. At some point in the journey I lost Graciela and I was on my own. I was carried off by a swift current of bodies, and it deposited me at the bar. Somehow, in that forest of outstretched arms, a tall drink was placed in my hand and I worked my way back against the heavy current. I squeezed my way toward a marble staircase and stationed myself on the first landing to survey the party. If I was as observant as I liked to believe, I should quickly pick out El Gato. After all, he was the guest of honor, that would certainly make it easy. I knew him now. I had to find, and meet, this cynical, irreverent, blasphemous, sensitive, beautiful man!

There was a sudden explosion of voices chanting, "GATO! GATO! GATO!" I looked up to see an entire baseball team of young boys in full uniform weaving their way through the crowd. They looked like small-gauge Red Sox. The chanting grew more passionate as the young boys progressed. "GATO! GATO! GATO!"

"What is a baseball team doing here?" I asked the man crunched next to me.

"You don't know Los Gatos?" He was cuddling a glass of unadorned and undiluted tequila. "*Pobrecitos*, every one of them is an orphan. But you should see the little *chavalos* play. They are *formidable*!"

"Los Gatos?"

"*Sí*, El Gato said he always wanted to own a baseball team. But he couldn't buy the Dodgers de Los Angeles, so he outfitted all the boys at the orphanage. I believe they are presenting some kind of trophy."

I excused myself and immediately went to follow.

"GATO! GATO! GATO!" the crowd roared. If I could get to the presentation, I would have found my man. But it was impossible. I was being crushed to death. There was a sudden cheer followed by a second explosion of applause. The throng loosened up and I saw the little boys come marching out, teary-eyed and flushed.

As long as I was on the ground floor, I decided to make another pilgrimage to the bar. I took my drink and worked my way into a large salon. Friendly faces greeted me as though they knew me. It took time but I finally worked my way to a safe corner and looked around.

"You are a friend of El Gato?" The question came from a distinguished old gentleman of noble dignity obviously mortified by his own realization that he had overestimated his capacity. His eyes were glazed. I couldn't see his mouth as this was concealed beneath snow-white handlebars. The hair on his head looked like carded wool. He held a drink that threatened to spill. "Forgive the impertinence of my question—you are here." He extended his hand. "Severino Epefinio Cadena Luz, your servant." He bowed to me like an ambassador presenting his credentials. "There is only one Gato," he said, and lifted his glass in salute. None spilled.

"*Gracias.*" I acknowledged the courtesy, shook hands, and recited my names. "You could say I know him, but I've never met him in person. I have hopes of meeting him here tonight, but that looks difficult right now."

"There you are! I've been looking all over for you!" We were interrupted by a stunning young woman in a red satin dress with thin spaghetti straps that aroused speculation. She embraced the dark man. He reciprocated with his free hand. "They're calling for the presidente municipal."

She stood on tiptoes and whispered in his ear. The venerable gentleman summoned all his pride, awarded me temporary custody of his drink, and with all the dignity that remained, fastened his fly.

The pretty girl looked at me from the shelter of his arm with a smile that contained more than cordiality. But what? An apology, a plea? Uncertain, I answered with a feeble smile.

"You'll excuse us?" She put her arms through his and led him away.

I watched her guide the mayor through the crowd. The sea of bodies moved almost imperceptively, like a restless tide, and I was now standing alongside totally different people. I could have sworn I hadn't moved from where I was standing. I searched the new crowd. My eyes immediately caught sight of a man who stood apart from the throng. Like a virgin bride, he was dressed in pristine white from neck to shoes. He was a head taller than the men around him. He had an interesting face of chiseled terra-cotta and coal-black hair, a tall drink firmly in his hand. The little man standing with him was soaking up every word. El Gato? No, the bushy mustache disqualified him. I worked my way to another room, replenishing my drink on the way.

I caught a glimpse of Graciela as I came away from the dining room. I squirmed my way toward her end of the room, but lost her by the time I completed the migration. I came to a set of French doors and stepped into a large courtyard fragrant with roses and jasmine and orange blossoms. Here was the source of all that wonderful music, poignant as memory, music that knew its way to that secret place where tears are stored. The mariachi wrung out a love song that brought a lump to my throat for no reason I could think of. Mariachis have that effect on most people I know.

The song ended with a sigh, and then, without warning, the thumping, throbbing beat of "La Bamba" shook the courtyard. The crowd went into a frenzy, and everyone who could find room for his feet picked up the infectious cadence. Near a fountain of carved pink stone I saw a pinwheel of color, Graciela, hair flying, eyes on fire. She was dancing with a man dressed in a pale blue shirt and navy trousers.

Could this be my man? I looked closer and reviewed all my clues on my yellow pad back at the office. He was taller than any of the other men around him, trim, and lean like a tennis player would be. So far so good. No mustache. It was looking better. His hair was dark, but not black, and his complexion was quite fair. Of course! His name was Gil, the Spanish version of Hill. He had an Anglo-Saxon mother, and that would account for his fair complexion. I had my man!

He danced with extraordinary grace; she, perfectly synchronized with his every move. Their eyes flashed surreptitious messages to each other as they moved together like body and shadow. Her sherbet skirts swirled deliciously when she turned, opened like a parachute as she came down precisely on the point of the beat.

I eased my way toward my quarry. I was quite near them when "La Bamba" ended with a double thump. A roar of cheers and vivas and bravos, and then applause burst all around them. I reached the winded couple just as they embraced and exchanged a warm kiss on the cheek. Here was my moment. I stepped forward.

"*El famozo* Gato, at last we meet, sir!" I extended my hand and gave my name. I caught a glimpse of the crowd staring at me through my peripheral vision. "I am your friend from the Other Side—and I want you to know, I brought my rooster with me!"

The tall man's eyes shined on me, the quick smile on his fair face making deep pleats in his cheeks. He gripped my hand firmly. "I am immensely flattered by your error, señor, I am—" and he rattled off a volley of names I made no effort to catch.

The handshake concluded, I turned to face Graciela and seek refuge from my embarrassment, but she had disappeared into the crowd. Mortified, I excused myself and returned to the first landing on the staircase, as I had done before. I now decided to abandon the absurd idea, just enjoy the party and look him up tomorrow. The mariachis began again and nearly everyone was now either dancing or singing. The ebb and flow of the human tide continued. I caught sight of the fat secretary, and just a quick flash of a woman with purple hair. I saw the mayor dancing with the stunner in the red dress, straps still in place. That interesting man in white made a brief pass.

"Who is that man in white?" I asked the man who stood on the landing with me, unable to contain my curiosity.

"You don't know El Fito? Fito Fernandez, we are in his house. The little man with him is the governor."

At that point three beautiful creatures were coming down from upstairs. I had to press against the balustrade in order to allow them to squeeze by me. It was not unpleasant.

I don't know how long I had been there watching the ceaseless movements of a restless sea when I felt a tap on my shoulder. I turned to see Graciela on the step above me.

"It's after three and this will go on for days. Shall we go?" She must have seen the question on my face. She did that adorable thing with her mouth again. "That was my brother."

It must have taken another hour to work our way back to the front door, stopping for long, ceremonious good-byes. I received firm embraces from the men nearest us, and tight almost tender hugs from the women. Occasionally I felt a kiss brush my cheek. I had never seen any of these people before in my life and yet their affection was spontaneous, and they gave me the feeling I belonged. I could hardly wait to be a part of all this.

We found the car on the sidewalk where we left it, though it was now in the company of several others. Even with the doors and windows shut we could hear the din of the crowd and bursts of music. The silence in the car was soothing and neither of us spoke. In a few minutes she was pulling into the darkened motel.

"I certainly enjoyed the evening. It was a great party, but I can't say I'm not disappointed. I was so looking forward to meeting El Gato. He's been such a good friend to me. You both have."

"I know for a fact that he was looking forward to meeting you too. He enjoyed your phone calls immensely. You know, he said he found you quite *simpático*."

I felt flattered. "Look, maybe tomorrow." She didn't answer. "Do you suppose?"

"When do you leave?"

"I can stay until noon. You think there's really a chance to meet him before I leave?"

"I'm so sorry. Look, I'll pick you up in the morning and take you to him." Her voice sounded strained. That, or she was tired. It *was* four in the morning.

"I'm a bother." I now regretted pressing her. Maybe there was a problem with that little girl in Ensenada who was so ill.

"You are no such thing! I'll pick you up at nine—make that ten—and take you myself."

"See you in the morning, then," and I offered my hand. Was I imagining something I wanted to imagine? Did she really hold my hand longer than necessary? *"Hasta mañana,"* I said.

For a moment I thought she was going to kiss my cheek, but all she did was whisper, *"Hasta mañana."*

Next morning I rose at nine (it was an effort), had breakfast in the coffee shop, and was ready at ten. She would be late, of course, I expected that, but how late? I went back to my room, packed, checked out, and returned to the coffee shop. I took a table by the window and toyed idly with a carafe of coffee. It was eleven when she came through the door.

"Buenos días." I smiled.

"Buenos días," she said softly, "I see you survived." She was wearing black leggings, boots with the cuffs turned down, and a long white shirt which she wore outside, thus hiding anything interesting the leggings might have revealed. She smelled like freshly gathered carnations.

"What have you there?" she asked as we got in the Honda. She had noticed my tape recorder.

"A surprise."

We headed south toward Ensenada. We said little. The noise from last night must have etched a groove in my brain. I could still hear the music! I was glad she was at the wheel while I sat mesmerized watching the scenes slip silently past my window: a vineyard, a cornfield, row crops, squash and beans, a boy leading a colored cow, more corn, a man walking behind a pair of sleepy horses cleaving furrows in the dark earth. A noisy crowd of crows in sinister black smocks followed the plow. A little white house drifted into view. I knew that at that moment there was a woman in there rolling out big tissue-thin tortillas in a rustic kitchen. I could smell onions and cilantro and red chile, and beans simmering over wood fire in a clay pot.

The faint smell of carnations brought me out of my fantasies just as Graciela pulled off onto a shoulder so narrow it barely held all four wheels of her little Honda. She got out first and walked to the front of the car. I followed.

"What are we doing here?"

She didn't reply, so I figured there had to be a plan and she was in on it. I scanned the entire scene. All I could see was hazy green pastures spattered with millions of miniature yellow flowers. They looked like confetti. The tang of wild sage made my nose tingle. Ancient gnarled oaks stood in deep pools of shade, talking in low whispers. Of course! This was obviously the property El Gato wanted me to see. He was probably preparing some kind of surprise. In a minute the incredible Gato would come ambling out from behind one of those trees holding a bottle of Sangre de Cristo with a scarlet sash around its neck. This man really knew how to do things.

Well, I thought, I've got a surprise for you too. Anyone who flies Winchell's doughnuts to his mother has got style. He was going to love this. I snapped on the taped recorder on full volume.

"*Kee-kee-ree-kee!*"

"You hear that, Gato? I brought my rooster!"

"*Kee-kee-ree-kee!*"

No answer, no response. Graciela too was silent, and at that instant I saw what Graciela had brought me to see. My mouth filled with brine, my eyes began to burn. Suddenly I felt a painful tightness in my chest, the ground going out from under my feet. I must have grabbed for something because I remember dropping the tape recorder. There, on the very edge of the road, surrounded by fluffy pink and red carnations, stood a plain white cross.

I looked into Graciela's beautiful face. Her eyes filled. God, I wanted to grab her and hold her close. "It happened two weeks ago," she said in a painful whisper, "he was on his way back from Ensenada. He was angry."

I couldn't control the stinging in my eyes. I did a quick flashback to yesterday. Graciela wasn't cleaning the office, she was packing the personal effects of a dead man. That strange look on her pretty face when she saw El Gato's gift in my hand was *pain*. That wasn't a fiesta I attended last night, that was a wake—all those people were in tears! "Graciela, Graciela! Why didn't you tell me?"

"We're just not ready to let him die." And she burst into tears.

Jeemy

"Popsicles ... fruity, sweet, and frosty!"

"Hot churros! ... The churros are here!"

"Brooms ... brooms ... I sell brooms! Clean house, pure heart!"

"Tweety tweety, kee—chip-chip-chip!"

Tecate had just signed the lease for three months of summer (with an option on an additional four), and the vendors were among the first things to emerge in the main plaza. The fragrance of a thousand roses sweetened the balmy air; towering *álamos* opened their parasols for the gentle citizens who were now streaming through the plaza on their way to their endless assignments or returning from their interminable errands. Here and there you could hear the hiss of lawn sprinklers. Fugitive whiffs of corn roasting over hot coals whispered irresistible bribes. The melodic voices of the hawkers encircled the plaza in an endless recitative, first rising then falling, coming in, going out, lilting, laughing, sighing, crying, like one of Scarlatti's madrigals.

"Shine ... shine ... Chiclets?"

"Balloons, balloons ... Meeky Mouse ... Porky Peeg!"
"Tweety tweety, kee. Tweety tweety—trrrrrri!"

This was the cry of a Mexican yellow-breasted sap-sucker, a highly motivated heavy hitter with mischievous eyes and Lee Iacocca charisma. Great and small, bright and beautiful, the Lord God made them all, but this charming little bird was also wise and wonderful. He was endowed with a special gift. He could look into the future and see coming events, and upon receipt of a thousand pesos, would willingly share this intelligence.

The little sapsucker could charm the thorns right off a cactus. He flitted and flirted from his small wire cage within a larger wire cage until he gained your attention. The only thing he lacked was the power of speech. *Dios mío!* If he could talk, he'd be selling time shares in Puerto Vallarta. But he was smart enough to recognize his limitation and took in a partner who *could* talk. His takeover man was Alvaro, a man so ordinary, further description is hardly necessary. Together the two partners dominated direct sales in the plaza, and the fortune-tellers enjoyed a majority market share.

I took possession of an iron bench in filtered shade and watched the pair at work. I observed a young girl of uncommon beauty walking across the plaza nearly at a waltz. A flutter of yellow wings and a sweet chromatic trill drew the attention of her dark eyes. As soon as the prospect came abeam of the wire cage, the takeover man came to life.

"Step right up, señorita, let the feathered oracle look into the future and reveal your fortune."

The señorita reached in her purse, withdrew a large coin, and put it in the T.O. man's waiting hand. Alvaro opened the small cage and the twittering prophet came fluttering out to her. *"Tweeky twee!"* he sang, and he cocked his little yellow head this way and that and blinked his shiny eyes in a most ingratiating manner.

"Tell me, little bird, will I ever meet Señor Right or am I destined for the convent of Santa Brigida?"

The little bird hopped over to a large bowl filled with little slips of colored paper and began to peck around, as birds are known to do. He tossed them around with his long beak, made his selection, hopped over to where the girl was waiting and dropped it in front of her. His work done, he flew back into his inner cage and Alvaro closed the gate. She then withdrew the paper, unrolled it, and read. The smile on her face implied that she would not be enrolling at Santa Brigida.

In a short time I saw an old woman swathed in a black shawl hobble painfully to the fortune-teller and pay the fee for hope. She was followed by a young man who didn't seem old enough to me to be unnecessarily preoccupied with tomorrow. Later came a stressed-out businessman carrying a briefcase. He appeared to be in a hurry. I got the impression that most of the people of Tecate were plagued with problems that could benefit from ornithomancy.

Just beyond the kiosk, I could see a man in a wheelchair weaving his way in and out between the benches. He would stop for only a brief moment, exchange no more than a few words, then push off abruptly and resume his rounds. I was too far to overhear his dialogue.

My first thought was that he was begging, but I quickly dismissed the idea. I've never seen a beggar in the plaza, no unsavory characters pleading in silence with faded eyes. No derelict was engaged in some form of inappropriate self-amusement. No one held up a sign claiming WILL WORK FOR FOOD.

There was, of course, no scarcity of other interesting denizens of the plaza. The human flamethrower had just arrived to work. But you can't consider him a panhandler. The fire-eater is a legitimate man of commerce. He opens his mouth as though to blow a smoke ring, and a three-foot plume of yellow flame gushes out with a roar. He charges a dollar for the performance, and the spectacle is worth the price of admission. The only real pervert in the plaza is Tecate's renowned entomologist, and his act is so disgusting he doesn't draw much of a crowd. He carries a Mason jar containing an extensive inventory of bugs *en vivo*—cockroaches, spiders, stinkbugs, crickets, and the like. For a dollar he'll take one out, pop it into his mouth like a bonbon, and eat it.

I returned my attention to the fortune-tellers. While the psychic avis maintains a rigid attitude toward client confidentiality, Alvaro is always good for an interesting anecdote. I exploited my advantage as an old client (I know everything that's coming into my life until the turn of the century) and I made appeal under the articles of friendship. That same afternoon (in various installments between cases) I collected the curious story of El Jeemy.

The events began in Los Angeles in 1979. Jimmy Weirgenthaler sat in the small office of Weirgenthaler Furniture Manufacturing Co., a sofa business he started eight years ago with a used Sears Skilsaw and five thousand dollars. He was writing up an order he had just taken over the phone. In a minute he would have to hand it to the orangutan who suffered from permanent PMS, and he would have to listen to her bitch and moan the rest of the day.

He walked the four paces with the zeal of a man headed for the scaffold and put the order in her box. "Would you process this this afternoon, Frieda?"

"I've already processed today's orders, you know," Frieda Fishman snapped back. "I haven't been just sitting around all day you know."

"I just wanted to make sure the boys started on it first thing Monday morning."

"I'm doing the mail, you want me to stop what I'm doing?"

Jimmy left the order and returned to his desk. Geez, why did I ever hire this broad?

Frieda Fishman sighed, and for a minute Jimmy thought he heard the air compressor in the shop release its air supply. "They've already gone home in the back anyway. I'll come in extra early Monday morning and put it in." This was intended to convey that office hours were from nine to five, but she would be willing to make the supreme sacrifice and come in at eight when the shop opened.

Jimmy made no comment, and she made her prerecorded political announcement. "I had to do the payroll today, you know, and go to the bank. God knows I never stop around here. I don't even take a lunch hour, you know."

Jimmy watched the clock hit five, but he knew the Martyr to Business would burn herself at the stake another ten minutes to make her point. At ten after Frieda Fishman closed her desk. "Good night, Jimmy."

"Good night, Frieda." The door closed behind her. "Bitch!"

Now that he was alone and it was quiet, Jimmy began to make his extortion payments. First, a check for the benefit of his ex-wife, beginning with this month's alimóny. He fell into conversation with himself.

"Why did you ever marry her?"

"I was in love."

"Bullshit!"

"All right, she had fantastic equipment."

"And?"

"All right, all right, she would do *anything*."

"Have you ever asked yourself why she married you?"

"Yeah, I had a twelve-inch—"

"Cut the crap."

"Okay, she married me to get back at her folks. They didn't approve of me."

"Great start."

"Get off my back."

Jimmy continued writing checks. Now that he himself had introduced the theme, he couldn't shake it out of his mind. He married Bernice right out of Beverly Hills High. Her school, not his. He went to Poly High. If he had never taken a job in her old man's plant, he never would have met her. Or married her. She as much as told him Lori wasn't his child. He should have had his head examined. When they tried for another one, the doctor told him he had a low sperm count. Or was it low motility? Who the hell cared. Geez, the kid was fifteen years old now, and a duplicate of her mother. He did his best. Tried to get her to work at his office so she could earn some money. These kids today. She could say *shit* and make it sound like a dulcet tone on a gold flute. She gagged on the word *work*. It came out of her mouth like a turd.

Jimmy looked at the checks as he placed them in their envelopes. He couldn't believe it. House payment, four thousand. Payment on the Mercedes, fifteen hundred, the BMW, another fourteen hundred. At least he didn't make a payment on Lori's Mazda. He didn't think a girl of fifteen should even have a car. Bernice's parents gave it to her for her birthday. Schmucks. Alimóny, six grand, child support four grand. Seventeen thousand bucks a month. This left him less than eight hundred bucks until the first of the month. It's a goddamn joke, he thought. I'm working fourteen hours a day, six days a week, to keep a roof over her meaningful relationship that moved in with her. Shit, I'm crazy.

Jimmy locked up, activated the fifteen-thousand-dollar security system, got behind the wheel of his six-year-old Toyota and started for his apartment. He always stopped at the Radisson for a beer on the way home.

"Good evening, Mr. Weirgenthaler." Arturo knew his customers. He placed a Michelob draft in front of Jimmy. "What's new, Mr. Weirgenthaler?"

"Hi, Arturo. Same old shit. Running a furniture factory, killing myself so everyone can live the American dream. The dream is a fucking nightmare. That includes FICA, the IRS, and the county. I guess they dream too. My orangutan earns more than I do."

"I don't know why anyone tries to do business here. It's an impossibility. You should move your factory to Mexico. That is the good life. I have a brother-in-law down there. He's in the export-import business. He lives like a king!"

"But I can't own property down there."

"You put it in a Mexican name. Or you marry a nice Mexican girl and put it in her name."

"Does that work?"

"Everybody does it. You run a good business, no IRS, nice Mexican wife who waits on you hand and foot—and a good-looking *chamaca* on the side. What else could you want—it's paradise!"

"Yeah, why are you here?"

"I've been here all my life. And my wife won't go for it."

"Well, there's nothing stopping me. Except, of course, I don't know any Mexican women, I don't speak Spanish, and I hate Tijuana."

"Not Tijuana, I'm talking about Tecate, it's a quiet little town. The language comes by itself. And there are thousands of beautiful Mexican girls who are hungry to get married. My brother-in-law, the one I was telling you about? He can introduce you to dozens of beautiful *chamaconas*. Look at this." Arturo pulled a sheet of paper from under the counter.

Jimmy took the cheaply printed flyer and read the ad.

MEET BEAUTIFUL MEXICAN LADIES!
Personal introductions $150.00
Satisfaction Guaranteed
Call Trinidad Contreras (619) 842-7556

"Who's Trinidad Contreras?"

"That's my brother-in-law. We call him Treenie."

"I thought you said he was in import-export business."

"He does that too. He was here just the other day. You should see the *chamaconas*. He brought me some pictures— really nice stuff." Arturo withdrew a stack of photos from behind the cash register, removed the rubber band and handed them to Jimmy. Arturo poured him another Michelob.

Jimmy shuffled through them casually. They were all young, attractive, and overdressed. On the back was written the girl's name and age.

"Nice, no?"

"Not bad. Look at this one." Jimmy turned the picture over. Elmira, age twenty-four. "Say, can I keep this?"

"Of course! Keep it. Give Treenie a call. Tell him I sent you. He's a good man to know, Treenie."

Jimmy had a third beer, paid, and left the Radisson headed for home and a downer. Three years of busting my

50

ass so that everyone can live happily ever after. Everyone but me. I'm supporting my ex, the kid, the boyfriend, seventeen employees, the state, the county, the federal fucking government. It's a goddamn life sentence with no parole is what it is. Maybe I should just blow my brains out.

By the time Jimmy got to his apartment, a seed had dropped into the fertile soil of his mind, where it would be nourished by anger, frustration, and loneliness. Ideal conditions for germination.

Jimmy started the rat race at seven-thirty every morning. He opened the office on Monday, supervised production, worked with suppliers, and talked to his customers. He wasn't even aware that the seed was taking root or that the photosynthetic process had begun. By ten after five, when Fat-Ass Fishman went out the door, the place was deserted, and that's when Jimmy realized for the first time that a new plan had burst into leaf. He picked up the phone.

"Treenie Contreras, please."

"Your *servidor* speaking." The voice suffered from laryngitis.

"I guess that means you're Treenie Contreras."

"Yes sir."

"Your brother-in-law Arturo suggested I give you a call."

The scratchy voice brightened. "Oh yes, what can I do for you?"

"You can introduce me to Elmira."

"Oh Elmira, yes, yes, an excellent choice. The photo fails to show her charming personality. She is an excellent cook and homemaker. She is the best in my book. Satisfaction guaranteed."

"You mean I can bring her back for a refund or exchange?"

Treenie was silent a moment. He got the line from the

Sears catalog. He didn't expect anyone to actually claim a refund, but it looked good on the flyer. And besides, it sounded better than "limited warranty."

"Yes, absolutely. Satisfaction guaranteed. When would you like to meet Elmira?"

"A week from Saturday. Where can we meet?"

"We can meet at La Fonda here in Tecate. It is the best there is."

"Twelve noon?" There was a heavy pause. "I'll bring cash, you bring Elmira."

For the next two weeks Jimmy was having trouble keeping his alacrity from leaping out of his body. He had to put his hands in his pockets to keep from doing cartwheels through the shop. On May 29, the day before the long Memorial Day weekend, Jimmy signed the payroll checks, accounts payable, including the checks for three governments. As usual, by ten after five the place was deserted. He sat at his desk and made out the monthly check payable to his ex for seventeen thousand dollars. Enjoy it, baby, it's the last one you'll ever see.

He then checked the company's bank balance: $37,451.84. He took the company checkbook from his desk, printed a check payable to himself for thirty thousand even, and put it in his wallet.

Jimmy took one last look at his manufacturing business. The shop was dark. It smelled of pine. Bolts of upholstery material were stacked in the lofts. The band saws that whined all day were silent. He walked back into the front office. There was the remainder of a Big Mac on the orangutan's desk. He shut off the lights. "So long, assholes. Tomorrow I start a new life." He walked into the night.

Saturday morning Jimmy walked into the Wells Fargo branch where Weirgenthaler Manufacturing had its account and presented his check. The teller gave him thirty thousand in cash and a plastic smile. "Have a nice day," she said. Jimmy smiled. You bet I will.

By quarter to noon Jimmy crossed the international border into Mexico. He was greeted with wide smiles. He parked, walked two blocks, found La Fonda, and pushed through the doors.

The dining room was full, noisy as Saturday market, and decorated with cobwebs of cigarette smoke. He went directly to the cashier. "I'm looking for Treenie Contreras."

The pretty hostess opened her mouth to answer, but the pharyngeal whisper came from behind him. Jimmy spun around to see a small, sinister-looking man step from behind a large palm. "Treenie Contreras, your *servidor*," he rasped.

Jimmy couldn't help staring. Treenie Contreras did not resemble most Mexicans in voice or visage. The voice was raspy as sandpaper. The face was dark Mediterranean. He looked like a Greek posing as a Corsican traveling on a French passport providing the Maltese Falcon with sensitive information. The heavy eyelids looked almost swollen when he lifted them to reveal his bulging eyeballs. Thick lips offered Jimmy a cordial sneer that somehow didn't fill him with a lot of confidence. He wore a white guayabera blouse. He made Jimmy think of Peter Lorre. The overhead fans spinning lazily added to the illusion. The only thing missing, Jimmy thought, was a dark man in a fez peering from behind a beaded curtain. He didn't see Bogart, but who could say he wasn't in his back office?

Jimmy offered his hand. "I'm Jimmy Weirgenthaler."

Now, Weirgenthaler is a name no prudent Mexican would ever attempt to pronounce for fear of dislocation of the tongue or other permanent damage to that organ. "I'm honored, Meester Jeemy. You are in for a very pleasant lunch," he croaked, and led Jimmy to his table and introduced him to Elmira.

Jimmy assessed and approved the boobs in the two seconds it took to shake hands. "I'm very pleased to meet you." He looked into a pretty face of polished pecan. She wore her eyes like ornaments. They were huge and seemed to give off sparks. He wanted to run his hands through the dense black mane. It reminded him of the deep pile plush fabric they used on one of their sofas. They called it Ebony Elegante. She had a mouth that must be kissed. She was wearing a navy-blue body shirt with a scooped neck, a fine gold chain adorning her throat. Gold earrings touched her shoulders. He took the chair next to her. Jimmy had not lost sight of his purpose.

Not bad for a blind bargain. If she can sign her name she'll do fine.

"Very much pleasure to meet you, Jeemy." Elmira liked what she saw. He was in all probability the tallest man in Tecate. The face was fair, and hadn't seen forty Aprils. The eyes reminded her of the intense blue of a Jalisco sky. His hair was wild and the color of ripe wheat.

I'll have to put some weight on him. If he is as gentle as he looks, I'll marry him.

Treenie pursed his lips and hissed like a snake. This universal summons, understood throughout Mexico, brought the waiter to their table. "Bring everyone a margarita," he rasped. "This is our American friend's first visit, we want him to experience the best our insignificant and humble little town has to offer."

Two margaritas later the food arrived. Treenie dissected a lobster, Jeemy wanted to try the carne asada, and Elmira ordered enchiladas, rice, and beans. She asked for *agua mineral.*

"Would you like to sample our local beer?" Treenie offered in a scrapy voice.

"You mean you have a brewery right here in Tecate?"

"Right after World War Two, Alberto Andrete discovered deep wells of extraordinarily pure water. He brought brew masters all the way from Germany. I knew old man Fleischman. I think you will approve."

They ate and chatted amicably to the sound of animated conversations and little gusts of gay laughter coming from the other tables. A balladeer came in off the street, began trolling for romantics, and a love song drifted across the dining room.

Treenie explained to Elmira in Spanish that his client was a gentleman of reputation *indisputable* who was here to establish home and business in Tecate. Elmira acknowledged all this with a demure smile. It was apparent to Jeemy that he and Elmira wouldn't be doing a whole lot of communicating. But maybe that was a good thing.

"A song, señores?" The balladeer was standing at their table. "A poem, or an amusing riddle?"

By way of charades, Jeemy conveyed to Elmira that she should fill her heart with music. Little sparks flew up from her eyes and she suggested a title. The balladeer began to sing the first line of "Cuatro Vidas." Treenie sent some invisible cue to Elmira, the balladeer moved in closer, and Elmira gave the poignant melody life and brought new colors to old lyrics. The man on guitar arranged a decorative fringe of harmony around her crystalline voice.

When the song ended, the final chord was overlapped by a clatter of applause from neighboring tables. Jeemy slipped the balladeer payment. The singer drew the sign of the cross with the five dollar bill, bestowed a kiss upon it, and stuffed it in his pocket. *"Mil gracias."*

By three o'clock in the afternoon the crowd began to thin out. Elmira excused herself and retired from the table. As she walked away, Jeemy admired the gorgeous brocade skirt, metallic threads on a dark ground. Nice piece goods. It would look terrific on one of his tuxedo-style sofas. Problem was, the cutter didn't line up the geometric pattern along the hemline. The hallmark of bargain-counter garments.

"Is it always like this down here?" Jeemy asked.

"Like what?"

"So, I don't know, so romantic, I guess. I feel like I'm in a movie. We don't have lunches like this where I come from. I could get to like this."

"Yes, it is always like this. We are never too shy to be ourselves, Meester Jeemy. We laugh, we sing, we cry, we express what we feel. We have no line of defense between us and our feelings. Sentiment does not embarrass us."

"By the way, how much will you charge Elmira?"

Treenie didn't answer. His eyeballs bulged as though he was trying to swallow a golf ball.

"C'mon, I'm a businessman."

"One hundred fifty."

Jeemy took out his wallet and counted out three hundred-dollar notes. "This covers both of us, you get lunch."

Elmira returned to the table. Treenie swallowed the remains of his beer. He scanned the dining room with cautious eyes and rasped, "I must be on my way. If you will excuse me, I will retire and leave you to each other." He rose and disappeared behind a palm.

It took Elmira a few minutes to compose a sentence. "Would you like me to show you around Tecate?"

"As a matter of fact, I would. What's this town got that's interesting?"

"The most eenteresting theengs about Tecate ees what we don't have."

"Huh?"

"You drive."

"I don't know the traffic rules down here and I don't have a Mexican license."

"That's okay, neither does anyone here."

They found the car and got in. "Okay, what's first?"

"Would you like to see the airport?"

"You got an airport? Yeah, I'd like to see it."

She directed him south on Highway 3. At about Kilometer 4 the sign came into view. It had a white silhouette of an airplane on a dark blue field. A large arrow pointed to the right. Inside the arrow was the word AEROPUERTO.

"You really do have an airport. I thought you were kidding me." He turned right onto a dirt road and followed it to where it perished against a chain-link fence.

In front of them was the runway, a strip of buckled asphalt where only flies could take off and land safely. It looked like the airfield at Corregidor after General Wainright surrendered it to the Japanese. At the far end the remaining shreds from what had once been a wind sock fluttered in the warm breeze. Trash piled high against the fence like snowdrifts.

"Jesus! What else don't you have?"

"A new state preeson weeth no eenmates, a coffee processing plant with no coffee, and a reever with no water. Want to see?"

"Pass. Let's go back into town and you can give me a walking tour."

They strolled all six blocks of downtown Tecate, looking in all the shop windows, stopping to browse here and there. They returned to the plaza to find a place to sit. Nothing attracts hawkers in the plaza like a young couple on a white wrought-iron bench.

"Roses! . . . Who will buy my red roses? Don't yield to jealousy, señor, let my roses meet your lady!"

"Popsicles! . . . Popsicles never fail to sweeten her disposition!"

"Even your hustlers are poetic down here." Jeemy bought all the roses the vendor was carrying and placed them in Elmira's arms. He tasted his first mango popsicle and the strange new flavor of a first kiss.

"*Tweeky-tweeky kee-kee-kee!*"

The musical bird song and a flutter of color attracted Jeemy's attention as intended. The little sapsucker then made eye contact and flirted outrageously. "What's with the bird?"

"He ees a fortune-teller."

"Are you serious? You're putting me on." Jeemy drew closer. "This I gotta see. You go first."

Alvaro's hand was already in position to receive payment. Jeemy obliged and Elmira spoke to the bird. "Tell me true, will I soon be a happy woman?"

Alvaro opened the enclosure, the little bird hopped to the dish, selected a little paper scroll, and delivered it to Elmira. He may have curtsied before returning to his place. Elmira unrolled the paper and read. " 'Beeg surprise coming your way.' Now you try, Jeemy."

Jeemy made payment. "Will my new business venture be successful?"

The bird went through his routine and delivered. Jeemy looked at it and handed it to Elmira. "It's in Spanish."

Elmira read. " 'You will soon have millions.' "

A week later Treenie Contreras escorted Jeemy and Elmira to the Juez del Registro Civil and presented them to the judge, an emaciated little man whose last rites should have been observed last week and ought to be arrested for impersonating a corpse. The little office smelled like someone's kitchen. The appetizing aroma of onions, red California chile, fresh cilantro, and crushed garlic made Jeemy's stomach growl from hunger. The source of these wonderful smells was the judge himself, who must have been unaware of his gastronomical emissions. Elmira felt her eyes burn from the onion fumes when he spoke to her.

"Los declaro marido y mujer."

"What'd he say?"

"He just pronounced you husband and wife," Treenie translated in his husky voice. They sealed the covenant with a loveless kiss.

The apocryphal bride and groom moved into a comfortable apartment and set up housekeeping. Jeemy could see that Treenie had been right in his assessment. Elmira was an excellent homemaker and a fantastic cook. He would have to watch that he didn't gain a hundred pounds. She was also an unremarkable lover. But not bad for a pig in a poke.

Jeemy now turned his mind toward his new life and what he would do with it. He was safe here. Nobody could touch him. He left no traces behind. And all his predators were on the other side of the fence. The first thing he'd have to do is get rid of all that cash he'd been walking around with.

Treenie introduced Jeemy to Alameda, general manager

of the prestigious Banco de Mexico. It smelled like a coffee shop when they walked in. Alameda's desk was surrounded with men in animated conversation laced with laughter. They stood under a veil of their own smoke, and all had a cup of coffee in their hand. There was a bag of sweet cakes on the desk from the bakery around the corner. Treenie introduced them. They immediately extended their hands and gave their names, but it went by too fast for Jeemy to remember them. They all seemed to have strange names down here. They called one man Teetu or Tootie, he couldn't quite get it. There was another older gentleman dressed in white from blouse to shoes. They called him Fito. There were other names he couldn't catch at all. Someone put a coffee in Jeemy's hand and passed the sweet cakes.

"What has you gentlemen so impassioned?" Treenie scraped.

"Raul was telling us about the gringos' ban on smoking."

Jeemy noticed they all had a cigarette in progress.

"I was in the Department of Motor Vehicles yesterday. I had to get my license renewed. I casually lit up a cigarette and you should have seen the riot this caused. I thought they were going to throw me in jail!"

Fito, the man in white, broke through the lusty laughter. "They're very strict about that on the Other Side. You're lucky they didn't deport you!"

"The gringos have been very successful at persecuting the cigarette smoker until they have driven him from their society. But they will share the streets with the criminal and send their children to school with them."

Jeemy was ready to defend the country he'd just defected. "Don't tell me you have no crime down here."

"Maybe even worse than in your country. The difference is that we have no jury. If the judge thinks he's guilty, the *cabrón* goes straight to jail. He does not pass Go and he does not collect two hundred dollars!"

"What if he's a school kid?"

"He gets expelled from school. I don't know where he goes, but he can't get back in school."

Treenie decided this could go on forever, and it was time to do business. "Alameda, I bring you a good friend of mine. He is new in town and wants to open an account."

The group began to break up. "I've got to get to the office," Teetu announced.

"So do I." The man in white got to his feet.

"I don't know what you're doing here anyway, Fito, you own a bank."

"He gets lonely at his bank." Alameda laughed.

The visitors shook hands again with Jeemy and cleared out. Jeemy accepted Alameda's invitation to a chair. "My first question, of course—is my money safe here?"

"Safe?" Alameda couldn't hold back a chuckle. "Americans are so suspicious. Banco de Mexico has never closed." He didn't add "as in your country," but it was implied. "Señor Jeemy, your account will be in U.S. dollars. This bank has never had a failure. Your money is as good as the government!"

"Second question. Do you report my account to the IRS?"

"Under no circumstances!"

Jeemy opened his account with twenty thousand and bought ten thousand in ninety-day certificates of deposit at fourteen percent.

The next day he was sitting with Treenie at La Fonda

with a glass of their vile vintage. He had a yellow pad, a ballpoint pen in his hand, and a look of determination on his face.

"What's the wage rate down here for skilled labor?"

"About a hundred and fifty pesos."

"In dollars."

"Six dollars."

"Wow! I was paying those jokers up there fourteen an hour." He wrote it down.

Treenie shifted his eyes left and right and spoke in a dark undertone. "No, Jeemy, not an hour—six dollars a day."

"Holy shit! I can't believe this. I should have come down here ten years ago—I'd be a fucking millionaire!"

Treenie refilled their glasses.

"Now, I'm going to need two band saws, a source for pine, and upholstery fabric, wire, webbing—all sorts of supplies."

"We don't have those things here, you will have to import them."

"How do I do that?"

Treenie gave him a slippery smile. "I am an importer, remember?"

"Will I have to pay a lot of duty to bring my stuff in here?"

"No, you will not pay duty."

"You mean it's duty-free? Hey, I like it!"

"No, Jeemy, not duty-free. We just will not pay the duty—we pay a little bribe to Comandante Pedroza." There was that sly grin again.

"Wait a minute now! You're talking about bribing high federal government officials. I don't intend to get involved in that. I've heard all about Mexican jails. In the U.S. I did everything absolutely straight. No funny stuff, Treenie, I want everything legal."

"When do you need all these things?"

"Next week, of course. I don't have time to waste. I am a man with a mission!"

"If we do it your American way, your goods will sit at the border for three months. If you give Comandante his candy money, I can have it here tomorrow. You see the difference, Jeemy?"

"Bribe the son of a bitch!"

Treenie's reply was a crafty smile. He braided his fingers and waited for Jeemy to continue.

"The first thing I have to do is find a small building for manufacturing. About twelve to fourteen hundred square feet. Electric power and telephone. Where do I find a reliable commercial real estate agent?"

Treenie massaged his earlobe, moved in closer and whispered. "I am a real estate agent."

"Oh shit!"

"What is it the matter?"

"I just thought of something. Taxes. The fucking taxes. Do I have to pay income tax down here?"

"Yes and no."

"Explain yes and no to me."

"Each month you go to the Treasury Office in person and report, yes? And each month you pay no taxes. Very simple, yes and no."

"How does that work?" Jeemy saw what he thought was the first glitch in the guacamole.

"You retain a certified accountant. He keeps your books. He, not you, goes in each month and makes the report and makes sure no taxes."

"Uh-huh. And what does this cost me?"

"A hundred and fifty dollars a month for this service."

"I don't believe this. Every business down here is run like that?"

"Oh yes, it is very simple, really."

"All right, where do I find a certified accountant?"

Treenie peeled back his eyelids. "I am a certified accountant," he rasped.

"You're hired."

"I am always at your disposal, Jeemy."

"By the way, do you have a big drug problem down here?"

"No, you have the drug problem up there, we simply act as distributors."

"I'll bet they catch a lot of them right here at the border."

"About six months ago the Americans broke up a drug smuggling ring. They arrested four Michoacanos and two of their own U.S. customs agents."

"I guess I just worry about crime. All that talk at the bank yesterday got me thinking. Do you have a lot of crime down here?"

"Tecate is too small, you have to go to Tijuana for major crime. In the history of Tecate we've never had a bank robbery, a holdup of a gasoline station or liquor store. I suggest you keep your car locked, but you don't have to worry about a lunatic walking into the post office or the school or the taco shop and gunning down innocents. The most serious crime here is homicide, and that invariably involves alcohol or a woman or both."

"At least you maintain your roads. I noticed you had workmen repairing the intersection when I crossed the border."

"They have been repairing that section of the street for the past twelve years. They will never finish it."

"Okay, Treenie, now that you're on the payroll, I want you to drive across the border to Tecate, USA, and open a bank account so I can look real and pay my suppliers with dollars. Put it in your name." He handed Treenie five thousand in cash. "Can you do that?"

"Yes, I can open the account. No, I will not drive. I will walk."

"What the hell's the difference?"

"The difference is that if the U.S. customs ever decides to search my car, they may find the money."

"I never thought of that. Is it against the law?"

"No, not against the law to transport money, but it must be reported on a government form. You would not like that, no? If I walk across, they never ask anything except to see my passport."

"Do you always think of everything?"

The reply was a scratchy whisper. "When you live between the jackal and the serpent, Jeemy, you must learn to survive by art."

This guy is no importer, he's a smuggler, Jimmy thought. He's okay, but I'll never get used to his sinister looks and that Peter Lorre voice. Maybe I should tell him I'd like to have him checked out. Naw, he'll just say, "I am a private investigator, Jeemy."

Jeemy made two phone calls to two of the biggest furniture retailers in L.A.—Sofa City and Discount Furniture Warehouse—two accounts he couldn't get into when he was up there. All he had to say was, "I can deliver a line of economy contemporary sofas and matching chairs for half the price you're paying." He cut his deals over the phone.

Jeemy installed his equipment and supplies. He hired two woodworkers and two upholsterers. Then he hired a big three-hundred-pound porpoise with a happy smile round as the sun and a sweet disposition as an office manager. Nothing was too much for Yolanda. Do this, do that, bring coffee. She did it all with a smile. *Sí*, Señor Jeemy. Always, *sí*, Señor Jeemy. If she lost a couple hundred, he might even play grab *nalgas* with her.

Jeemy appeared in person at the *Comisión Federal de Electricidad*, a government agency, and applied for electric power.

The girl looked at his application. "No problem, Señor, er, Señor . . ."

"Jeemy."

"Yes, Señor Jeemy. Will you be paying the outstanding bill left by the former tenant? Four hundred pesos."

She's got to think I just fell off the turnip truck, he thought. "Absolutely not. I only pay my own bills."

"I don't blame you one bit! But of course we cannot connect yours until the old bill is paid, and we don't know where the former tenants are."

Jeemy handed her four hundred pesos. In two weeks Sofas de Mexico was in operation.

Four months later Jeemy was selling one hundred percent of production and the money was rolling in faster than he could fill out a deposit slip. Before the first year was out, he enlarged the plant, hired four additional employees, and doubled production. He still sold everything he could produce. It seemed he couldn't do anything wrong. And the best part was, his money was resting comfortably at Banco de Mexico, safe from Nosy Parkers.

He could now afford to send Elmira down to Guadalajara to visit her family any time she got homesick. It was during this period of susceptibility that he caught a pernicious eroticomaniacal virus and met a carrier of the same affliction. Her name was Sarita. She was taller and thinner than Elmira. She looked to him like Cher with tits. It began as an innocent drink, escalated to a not so innocent weekend on the beach at San Felipe, where he discovered that whatever Elmira wouldn't do, Sarita would. He thought he could live very nicely with this arrangement and leased an apartment for her in Colonia Linda Vista.

Jeemy had no trouble adjusting to his newly adopted country. He quickly conformed to the contours of Mexican culture, like rubber pressed in a mold. This is my kind of town, he thought. I can do anything I damn well please. I can arrange anything with a couple of bucks in the right hands. It's like no rules. And down here, the man is the fucking *king*—I love it!

He became a regular at the Cafeteros table at La Fonda, he was known by name at every taco cart in town. Whenever he had occasion to take a shortcut through the plaza, he couldn't resist a peek at the future. Such was the case this fine morning.

"Tweeky tweeky trrrri!"

That goofy bird blew his mind. "What's around the corner for me, little guy?"

The yellow sapsucker performed his office with all the grace and charm typical of this species. Jeemy accepted the tiny scroll and brought it to Elmira for a more accurate translation.

"Beware a dark man will take your money," she read.

That's crazy, all the men down here were dark, and he didn't know a soul who could—Treenie! He'd have to keep a close eye on him.

It was fun to walk into the bank and withdraw forty or

fifty thousand U.S. dollars in cash for Treenie's deposit, and flirt with Maria. He always waved at Alameda when he came in, and stopped for coffee with the regulars on the way out.

"*Buenos días*, Mari, how was your weekend?"

"*Buenos días*, Jeemy. It was beautiful, I was at the beach."

"Just you and sweetheart?"

Maria dropped her pretty eyes. "Ay! Jeemy, you make me blush! I suppose you came for cash."

Jeemy handed her a withdrawal slip and she counted out forty-five thousand U.S. dollars. "*Gracias*, Mari, see you later." He stopped by Alameda's desk, stepped through the curtain of smoke and joined the group in coffee and conversation.

In just a little over two years into the operation, Jeemy was in Gordo City. That silly fortune-telling bird was right. He was close to being a millionaire. He had just over $800,000 in his account at Banco de Mexico. And nobody could touch it. Not the IRS, not his ex wife, not *nobody*. Jeemy also had a devoted wife and a horny mistress. Jeemy had it all. He was a frequent flier to the palm-fringed resorts of Baja for sun and sin. He and Elmira would usually take the morning flight, and they'd be on the beach by noon. Sarita flew in the next day for margaritas and cha-cha while Elmira took her siesta.

Early in September 1982, Jeemy was sitting alone on the beach at Cabo San Lucas counting his blessings one by one. He was watching the sun go down over two oceans, sipping a piña colada while assessing his new life. And he liked it. The sun, a red ball now, was just kissing the horizon. Everything held a pink glow, the sand, the surf, his soul. He could hear the mariachi music coming from the hotel terrace. Elmira was in their room at the Finistera getting dressed for dinner. Sarita was preparing dessert in a bubble bath at the Hyatt.

You've come a long way, baby, he confided to himself. Less than three years ago you were busting your ass to support the sharks. Look at yourself today. Nearly a million in cash, no debts, no worries. Shit, I'm living like fucking Donald Trump! It just doesn't get any better than this. I've found the land of milk and *nalgas*!

Jeemy's flight back from Cabo San Lucas was late getting into Tijuana. It took the taxi an hour to get them to Tecate. He and Elmira were exhausted when they got home and fell right into bed.

First thing the next morning Jeemy went straight to the bank to make his monthly withdrawal. "*Buenos días*, Mari, how was your weekend?"

Maria mumbled something in return, and Jeemy looked up to see that her big brown eyes were red and swollen. His heart went out to her. This was something more than a quarrel with her *novio*. "What is it, Mari, something bad?" His voice was soft.

"You haven't heard?"

God, who died? "Heard what, Mari, I just got back from Cabo San Lucas late last night."

"Oh, Jeemy, I don't know how to tell you. You better talk to Señor Alameda."

Jeemy looked over to Alameda's desk. He was surrounded as usual. There was a lot of action. Probably discussing a soccer game. These people could get so emotional over a soccer game. "Tell me what?"

"Jeemy, we don't have your money. The—" Her chin quivered and she burst into tears.

Jeemy bolted to Alameda's desk and broke through the

crowd. "What's all this shit about you don't have my money!"

Alameda looked ashen. "Jeemy, we have all been betrayed. Our wonderful president, José Lopez Portillo, announced that Mexico is bankrupt. He has nationalized the banks and eliminated the dollar. We are now a government agency by decree."

"What happens to my $800,000!"

"The dollar no longer exists in Mexican banks. It will be paid to you in pesos, sixty-nine to the dollar—about sixty million pesos."

"Give it to me right now, goddammit! I'll take it to the bank in the U.S. and convert it there."

"We are all ruined, Jeemy," Alameda sobbed, "no U.S. bank will accept our pesos!"

Jeemy went red. He grabbed Alameda by his shirtfront and pulled him out of his swivel chair. "Listen to what I'm going to tell you—"

An armed soldier appeared from out of nowhere and pushed Jeemy back with the muzzle of his machine gun.

"Get your filthy hands off my friend!" Alameda screamed. "You ignorant government *mierda*. He has every right!" He gave the soldier a violent shove. Alameda's face twisted and tears ran down his face uncontrollably. "Oh Jeemy, I'm so sorry, I'm so sorry, Jeemy . . ."

Jeemy didn't hear anything, didn't see anything. He went out into the streets of Tecate foaming and raving, blind with rage, like a rabid dog.

The nationalization of the banks was the worst manmade disaster in Mexico's history. The rich became the poor overnight. Houses and buildings that were under construction when the disaster struck died where they stood. Honest people couldn't pay their credit cards, department store charges, car payments, doctor bills, and bank loans. Local merchants closed for lack of dollars to pay suppliers. Merchants in San Diego and other border cities in the U.S. folded left and right, as eighty percent of their business came from Mexico. It requires over three thousand pesos to buy a dollar today.

"Tweeky tweeky kee-kee-kee!"

The warbling prophet had customers. The story had to be put on hold when a beautiful young girl who had discovered the sweet pain of contraband love arrived in the company of her mother. The girl, in early bloom of her fecundity, was no more than a teenager. The graffito of life was plainly legible on the mother's anxious face.

It was late in the afternoon. The plaza was still swarming. I noticed the human flamethrower held a crowd spellbound. The bug eater was nowhere to be seen. Probably on his lunch break. A diaper-clad toddler transporting toxic waste, who had only recently mastered the skill of walking, was now experiencing the power he held over the pigeons. Off in the distance where mist rising from the fountain overprinted a rainbow across the footpath, I could see the man in the wheelchair was still making his rounds. The dissonant bells of Our Lady began to clang, and my attention was diverted by someone waving to me from a distance. I recognized Father Ruben approaching the church and waved back. His gait in that direction suggested tardiness.

When I looked back, mother and daughter were gone and I was now able to gratify my curiosity. I asked Alvaro the burning question. "So whatever became of the poor wretch?"

"Poor Jeemy. He lost everything, his money, his mistress. His wife went back to her family in Guadalajara. *Pobrecito*, he is no longer the same man."

We were interrupted at that moment. Someone was speaking to me in English. The voice was distorted, like a warped phonograph record. "Want to earn some nonreportable income?"

In front of me was the man in the wheelchair, and I had to assume the query came from him. At close range I could see he was old, probably sixty or more. His clothes looked like they came out of the rag bag. He was staring right through me with eyes of penetrating blue. He was an American! The hair was white and sparse; I looked into a face the color of death. The eyes, the nose, and mouth were pulled away to one side. I was looking at his face through a viewfinder before you turn the knob and line up the image. I thought he was smiling at me, and maybe he was, but then I realized I was looking at the result of a paralytic stroke.

From a cigar box he carried in his lap he withdrew a deck of wilted cards resembling a stack of old rags. "How about a hand of twenty-one? Nonreportable, nontaxable!" I'm almost sure the chilling cackle that followed was intended to be a laugh.

It took less than thirty seconds. He dealt, I went over, and paid him three thousand pesos. I took the painful twist in his face to be a smile. He did not suggest another hand. The wilted cards, the money, were all stuffed back into the cigar box.

"I'll give you a piece of good advice." He jerked his head in the direction of the fortune-tellers. "Don't trust that goddamn bird, he fucking ruined me!" And he rolled away in the direction of the fountain and disappeared inside the rainbow.

The Miracle

f you were to drive south of Tecate on Highway 3 about ten kilometers or so, and if by virtue of vigilance you didn't drop into one of the cavernous potholes, you would then drop into the fertile valley of Tanama. The road of ill-fame, a treachery of deceitful curves and buckled asphalt, twists and turns through endless rows of shiny green zucchini, regiments of tassled corn, a macramé of tomatoes woven through stakes and twine. Grapevines poised like native folklorico dancers link arm in arm with their leafy partners. Gently sloping pasturelands are flecked with colored cattle with whom you are often obliged to share the road.

At Kilometer 12 the little one-room Café Los Alamos reposes in the shade of a clump of dusty poplars from which it gets its name. It is run by Tito and his wife Chola, both amiable early risers. They light their wood fires in darkness, well before the sun withdraws the stars. By five in the morning the seductive fragrance of wood smoke reaches the farmers and fills them with desire, and they arrive at Los

Alamos lusting for a plate of chorizo and eggs. The cocoa-brown building is about the size of a modern bathroom. In the early morning an assortment of pickups of various breeds and coloring encircles the adobe like piglets around a sow, a reliable indicator of who's inside with a plate of refried beans in front of him. The plump red and white chickens that cluck and scratch in the dirt out front are simply an indication that some of the best grubs of the region are to be found here if you know where to dig.

Inside, the café seems to get smaller. Three wooden tables (two with a serious limp) cramp the little room all the way to the walls. Each is covered in shiny white oilcloth blooming with red poinsettias. A small television set usually babbles from a shelf high against one wall. The moment you step inside, you're caught in a vortex of good smells—hot iron, fresh coffee, eggs and potatoes frying, beans hissing in simmering bacon fat. Cigarette smoke hangs above the tables like mares' tails.

Although it's been some time, the farmers and ranchers still talk about the Miracle with undisguised fear in their voices. Could it ever happen again? Of course it could. They are powerless to prevent it, and the very thought fills them all with a black dread. The pious pray that the Miracle will never again reappear in the Valley of Tanama.

It all happened on a Saturday morning about four or five years ago. The usual group of farmers gathered in the diminutive café for breakfast. At first glance Carlos, Amador, and Francisco appeared to be as similar as kernels on an ear of field corn. They all had handsome adobe faces, dark eyes, and matching mustaches, black and roguish. They were lean as a yucca stalk. None was tall, but the ten gallon sombrero (which never came off) added about thirty centimeters of macho pride to each. The difference was in their diverse personalities.

The exception was Father Ruben, whose face, the color of toasted almonds, was smooth as a girl's. Always hatless, and dressed in cotton blouse and pants when not discharging his office. He could no longer be considered lean, as the geometric angularity of his youth was beginning to yield to a gentle convexity owed to sedulous devotion to the rites of the palate. He also had a penchant for mischief.

Under cover of the front page of *El Mexicano*, Father Ruben kidnapped a tender sausage from Carlos, who was himself hidden behind the pages of the *San Diego Union*. "Tsk," Father Ruben clucked, putting down his paper. "I see there is an epidemic of cholera in the coffee plantations down in Chiapas."

No one at the table seemed overly alarmed at this news. Francisco's dark voice came from somewhere behind the sports page. "It looks like the Padres are going to blow another season." No one seemed alarmed at this piece of news either.

"How I hate Saturdays," Carlos grumbled. He put down the paper and turned his attention to the breakfast in front of him. The purloined sausage went unnoticed.

"We all hate payday, but what can we do about it? We have to pay the men." Francisco was a confirmed Gloomy Gustavo since the day of his first communion, and accepted the events of life just as they fell from Fate's fickle *cazuela*.

"It's the same thing every Saturday. Pay the men at noon so they can get a bottle of *mezcal* on the way home, and they can't show up for work on Monday." Amador contributed to the dismal topic of conversation without taking his eyes off "Cartoon Express."

Carlos always had a solution at the ready. "If there was some way we could pay them by the year. You know, after the last harvest. Then they could stay drunk for the rest of the year!" Carlos was a compulsive problem solver. He even had solutions for problems that didn't yet exist.

Father Ruben, who supervised the vineyard, scooped up the last trace of refried beans on his plate with a wedge of tortilla and laughed. "Now, if we made the wine, we would probably have a hundred percent attendance. But alas, we ship all our grapes." He rooted through the tortilla basket, and finding it empty, coveted the one remaining on Amador's plate.

Francisco pushed his empty plate away and lit a cigarette. "I refuse to even think about it." Francisco preferred to avoid trouble if he could.

"The only thing working on our crops next Monday will be ground squirrels," Amador replied prophetically, and rescued his tortilla from unauthorized fingers.

The requiem ended there. The four men rose, put money on the table, and ambled out the door. The big red rooster clucked an indecent proposal to a plump leghorn of easy virtue, and accepted the ultimate favor with the privilege of the species. The four men dodged the chickens, got into their vehicles, and headed for their respective ranches to make the payroll.

Back at his ranch, Carlos called his men out of the fields and handed each his week's wages. Each man thanked him, made the same stock comment about beans on the table for another week, and started for home.

"Try to make it to work on Monday," Carlos called after them. "We have much to do!"

"*Sí*, señor, see you Monday, God willing," they called back.

I wonder why it is God is never willing on Monday, Carlos mused. I'll have to ask Father Ruben.

A similar scene was played out on all the other ranches and industries of Tanama, as though they were all reading from the same script.

Early Monday morning the four friends gathered around their table for breakfast. They ate vigorously but silently. Occasionally they'd steal a glance at "Good Morning America." "What's new?" Francisco finally asked.

"My men didn't show up," Carlos responded.

"I asked you what's new." They all exhibited the symptoms of clinical Monday Morning Syndrome.

"*Inevitable*. I've come to accept it," Francisco said. "I don't even worry about it anymore."

But on Tuesday morning the four men were no longer complacent about it and they were in a thorny mood. Carlos opened. "Has anybody had a worker show up?"

"Not me."

"Not me."

"I haven't seen any of them—yours or mine."

"Maybe there is illness in the canyon where they live."

"There's illness, all right, hangovers and the dry heaves."

"No, I mean real illness."

"Like what?"

"I don't know, flu, black plague—cholera maybe."

"That would certainly explain it."

"There is no other explanation, they can't all be drunk for four days."

"Maybe we should give them one more day—mañana." A perfectly logical suggestion in a land where you can comfortably slip a millennium between thought and deed.

The scene on Wednesday was by and large a rerun of

Tuesday. By Thursday they were near panic. No one could afford to lose his crops. "What do you suppose we should do?" Amador asked anyone.

"We could go to the canyon and look for them," Carlos suggested. A plan was already taking form.

"I thought of that, but what good would it do? We'll either find them drunk or hung over," Francisco put in. "I don't want to listen to their excuses and watch them throwing up."

Father Ruben spoke. "You're probably right, and what's the point? Tomorrow is Friday already. No matter what we do, nobody is going to show up till Monday."

Monday came, and Monday went. Somehow one week melted into two. Not unusual in Tecate, where the fire engine pulls up with siren screaming the day after the fire; where gas deliveries are delayed a week because the driver was home with a cold; where the roads are flooded for days because the aqueduct blew a valve and it took the emergency crew a week to respond to the call.

The pickups were gathered around the café, and the men, with the conspicuous exception of Carlos, were gathered around the table ruminating with their hats on, as usual. You could now feel the high-voltage tension crackling at all three tables. The only sounds came from the kitchen, where things sizzled and dishes clattered.

Finally Amador spoke. "Has it occurred to anybody here that maybe they got a job somewhere else?"

"That's right," Francisco said around a mouthful, "these peasants are too shy to come up and tell you they're going to leave you for another job with more money. They would just disappear."

"Just like they've done—that's got to be it!"

"Let's assume it is—what do we do about it?" Father Ruben said, stabbing the last potato on Francisco's plate.

"Abandon your theory," a deep voice called from another table. "They didn't show up at the furniture factory either."

"Or at the brickyard," another voice echoed.

"And where would they go? Everybody pays the same wage rate set by the government."

"Then maybe there's real illness in the canyon."

"Did you see them in church yesterday, Father?"

Father Ruben concealed a devilish smile. "Not at any of my masses. But then I didn't see any of you either, and you're not ill." Father Ruben seized the moment to plunder a dollop of beans from Amador's plate without drawing attention.

"The mystery just gets deeper," Francisco said.

"Maybe we should go into the canyon and have a look for ourselves. Maybe if you went with us, Father," Amador suggested.

"You know it's against the law for me to appear in public in my habit. And without my costume, they wouldn't even know who I was."

"I completely forgot. That old law still on the books?"

"Since 1859. And we're not allowed to vote either."

Carlos walked in at that moment and squeezed into the empty chair against the wall. Chola came out of the kitchen and arrived at the table at the same time. She brought him hot coffee and a warm smile. "Chola, you are the first nice thing I've seen today. Bring me a big plate of bones. I think I could pulverize them!" Chola only giggled and returned to the kitchen. Tito began to fry eggs and beans. His friends were quick to see Carlos was not wearing a happy face.

"What is it?" Amador asked, not really wanting to hear the answer.

"What time is it?" Carlos asked through tight, angry lips.

Father Ruben consulted his watch. "Seven-thirty, why?"

"It's seven-thirty on a Monday morning and do you know what I just saw? I saw Cuco coming out of Pedro's Mini-Mercado. He was wearing a brand new nylon jacket, better than mine, and brand new boots, and he had a full jug of *mezcal* under his arm!"

The sudden gasp at all three tables was smothered by the crash of an iron skillet that hit the kitchen floor at the same instant. "Then my theory is valid," Francisco said. "They all got jobs for more money someplace else and they were just too shy to say anything."

"All the men?"

"Well, at least Cuco," Carlos answered.

"What other possible explanation is there? The money for the new clothes and the bottle had to come from somewhere!"

"We're out of options. We have to go into the canyon and see what we can find out." Carlos's voice was urgent.

"I think he's right."

"We might as well find out what's going on."

"Yes, if I'm ruined, I'd like to know."

Carlos was adamant. "I suspect there's a cat in a basket someplace, and I want to have a look."

Tuesday morning all four men gathered for breakfast. The meeting continued where they had left off the day before. It was almost as though all the events of the past two weeks had taken place during one very long dismal day.

"Did you get to the canyon already?" Amador asked.

"No, and didn't have to. Halfway up the road I ran into my Cuco and your Diego."

"And?"

"They were smashed."

"We can assume that much, but what did you learn?"

"You won't believe it. First they tried to pretend they didn't see me. But I walked right over to them and said, '¡*Buenos días!*' Diego had on a new pair of pants, a new shirt, and so did Cuco."

"And, of course, a bottle of *mezcal*."

"A full gallon. And can you believe it? They offered me a drink! Then I admired their new clothes. Cuco said he was also wearing new underwear. So I thought I might as well confront them. I told them how we all missed them at the ranch but that they must be happy earning so much money somewhere else."

"What did they say to that?" they all burst out at once.

"They looked at each other curiously. They seemed to exchange a secret signal, then suddenly begged my pardon and said they had to be going. Then as they left, Cuco gave me that toothless grin and said, 'There's been a miracle, a miracle!' "

"He must have been drunk. What miracle? The money didn't just drop in from Heaven. Can that happen, Padre?"

Father Ruben didn't get a chance to reply. Carlos's fist hit the table causing a tremor of 5.2 on the Richter scale. "Señor Jesucristo! I have it!" he exploded.

"What?"

"Think about it. Where do they all live?"

"In the canyon, of course."

"Think! What's the name of the canyon?"

"The Cañón de la Cueva," Francisco answered. "The Canyon of the Cave. So what?"

"Remember the stories we used to hear when we played there?"

"You mean about the cave?" Francisco was beginning to get the picture.

"That, and the story about El Tigre, the old hermit who sold goat-meat tacos in the plaza. They said he buried all his money in the cave. Remember?"

"Yes, yes! I remember!" They were all warming up to the idea. "I can still remember El Tigre. What a spook!"

"We were all afraid of him when we were kids. He lived in a tiny shack that he shared with about a hundred goats."

"He didn't die all that long ago. He must have put away a fortune if the story is true."

"I remember they used to say El Tigre would put all his earnings in a paint can at the end of each day and hide it somewhere."

"In a cave?" Suddenly the four of them began to shoot ideas back and forth across the table like Ping-Pong players rallying for serve.

"It's a good bet."

"And somebody found it!"

"Wait, before we all get carried away. We heard those stories all our lives. I don't know of anyone who actually ever saw the proverbial cave."

"But still, old legends take root in truth."

"Is it possible that somebody accidentally found the cave?"

"And El Tigre's money!"

"If you're right, we'll never see our workers again."

"Give me a better explanation, and I'll accept it."

Carlos got the serve and rose to the challenge. "We've lost too much time already. I'm going into the canyon right now!"

"What's the use?" Francisco asked. "You're looking for *chichis* on a snake—sorry, Father."

Amador came to his feet, bursting with purpose. "And I'll be at your side!" Amador was the quintessential aide-de-camp, and equal to those eminent seconds of legend including Friday, Little John, and the illustrious Sancho Panza.

Cañón de la Cueva has been supporting life since time began. It offers water. All year long the voluptuous creek tumbles noisily over rocks, and dams, and fallen trees, and finally comes to silent rest in a shallow lagoon. It offers food. Small game is plentiful. The canyon is abundantly forested with oak trees that generously deposit bushels of acorns on the ground for easy gathering. It even provides the rocks on which to grind the acorns into gruel. Several centuries ago the previous tenants patiently cut deep bowls into the huge slabs of living granite at the water's edge for grinding and milling. Their only purpose today is to hold the amber bars of laundry soap when the women do the family wash in the widest part of the creek. The canyon has been the labor pool for all the industries of Tanama for as long as anyone can remember. For generations it has been home to fifty or sixty families perpetuated by an unbroken dynasty of poor, ignorant, and illiterate peasants. They're born in the canyon, live out their lives there, and die in the canyon within ten meters of where they were born.

Carlos's pickup entered the canyon about eight in the morning, bouncing and lurching over rocks and gullies like a 727 caught in wind shears over East Texas. Amador suggested in a queasy voice, "We should probably park and do our work on foot."

"You think we'll attract too much attention in the pickup?"

"That, and I wouldn't want to throw up all over your nice interior."

Carlos obliged immediately. He pulled into the dense shade of a giant oak, waited for Amador to make foam behind a tree, and the two men began their trek. Soon they could hear women's voices chirping and gabbling. They sounded like birds. As they came 'round the bend they found five or six women kneeling at the water's edge, vigorously scrubbing clothes against the rocks. Each had a wicker basket of wet clothes at her side. A few little boys and girls frolicked naked in the pool.

"*Buenos días,*" Carlos called out with sunshine in his voice to mitigate the shock of the sudden intrusion.

Their chattering stopped abruptly. "*Buenos días,*" came the cautious but courteous reply. The children froze in place.

"If I give you my things, could you wash them for me?" Amador pretended to unbutton his shirt, and that broke the ice.

A dark woman wrung out a pair of blue denims with strong dark hands and slapped them into her basket. "Of course, *sí*, just take off your clothes. You can wait behind the bushes." Everyone laughed and the children resumed their play.

"I'm Carlos Espinoza and this is Amador Sanchez. Many of the men here work on our farms."

There was instant recognition of the names. "Oh, *sí*, Don Carlos and Don Amador, of course, it's nice to know you."

"*Gracias.*"

"We haven't seen the men at work, and just came by to see if everyone is all right."

"Those lazy good-for-nothing men. Why don't you hire

84

us and we'll put the men to washing the clothes," a dark woman scoffed, and they all shared in her laughter.

"Maybe you could tell me how to find Cuco's house."

"Of course. Keep going straight the way you're going and you'll see a white camper shell on the left. That's his house."

"*Gracias.*" The two men began to walk.

"But you won't find him at home," the woman said, pushing away a curtain of black hair with the back of a sudsy hand.

"No?"

"No, he won't be there. I'm his señora. He left with the others early this morning." She continued to pound a pair of soggy jeans against the rocks.

Here comes the very answer we've been looking for, Carlos thought to himself. Now I'll know where they go. "To work?"

"Work, those lazy men?" She cupped her hand in the air as though hefting a heavy invisible weight, a gesture understood throughout Mexico to mean "heavy in the balls," and all the women burst out laughing. "They are all like children," she continued. "All the men went up the canyon this morning. 'We'll bring you a nice rabbit.' That's all they would say, but we know better."

Amador thought he would venture something more. "Maybe you could tell us where Diego lives."

"Diego? That's easy. Go past the camper shell about six houses. Diego's is on the right. The whole front yard is covered with cactus. You can't miss it. Just don't lean on it!"

"*Gracias,* señora." The two men thanked the women and touched their hats. "*Con permiso,* then," and they moved away. The women returned to their task and continued to prattle. They sounded like birds again. Back on the road, Carlos and Amador continued to travel toward Cuco's house. The village was a mishmash of humble dwellings made of whatever material the builder had at hand when he broke ground: old packing crates, canvas, sheet metal, corrugated plastic.

"Not a rock or a leaf has changed in this place since I was here last," Carlos said, "and that was thirty-five years ago."

"Isn't that Cuco's camper shell over there?" Other than the dent in the roof, the camper shell looked adequate. It was surrounded by the festive plumage of red and orange and pink geraniums thriving in rusty coffee cans. A row of old automobile tires painted in vivid red, and green, and yellow and lashed together with bailing wire formed the garden fence. It looked like a row of giant LifeSavers. They stopped to look around.

"Look at that."

"What?"

"That tricycle. It looks almost new."

A young boy about eight or nine stepped out of the camper. He was wearing a new shirt and Hawaiian print shorts. He cuddled a portable radio in his arm. Madonna was moaning and groaning sensuously, but neither Carlos or Armando knew that.

"My papá isn't home." The youth was the color of bronze, with a thick black forelock of uncombed hair.

"And your mamá?"

"She's washing." He twisted a shoulder toward the creek.

"That your tricycle?"

"My sister's. I'm getting a two-wheeler next week."

"Regards to your papá."

"*Gracias.*" The boy and the nearly breathless Madonna disappeared back into the camper.

"How can anyone listen to that awful music? She sounds like she's in sexual ecstasy."

"Did you see how that boy was dressed?"

"Yes, and the radio."

"*Mucho dinero* is coming from somewhere."

"Or they're stealing all this. But I really don't think these simple peasants have the initiative required for stealing."

"That must be Diego's house behind all that cactus over there," Carlos suggested. Had it been necessary to knock, he would have been hard pressed. The house was made of canvas remnants and tarpaper sheets, and neither provided a solid surface. But it wasn't necessary. Diego's wife was outside stirring a clay pot of beans over a wood fire. She wore a turquoise velour pantsuit that screamed "new." An old woman swaddled in a black rebozo sat on a pitted chrome dinette chair. She was mending underwear. She wore navy-blue tennis shoes and green socks ribbed to the knees.

"*Buenos días*, señoras."

"*Buenos días*, Don Carlos."

"Oh, you remember me."

"Yes, and I remember Don Amador too, although it's been ages since I've seen either of you."

An old dresser without drawers, the veneer bleached and warped by age and weather, stood in the yard. It was stacked with canned goods. A two-slice Sunbeam toaster sat ostentatiously on top. Amador knew this family would never suffer burned toast at the breakfast table, as Señor Edison's miracle of electricity was still unknown in the canyon. A little girl played nearby. She was pulling her new doll in a red wagon. Her little tea set decorated with El

Snoopy cartoons was laid out and ready for company on a small table.

"It seems we haven't seen Diego at work for some time now. Is he all right? Nobody is sick, are they?" Carlos asked.

"He isn't here."

Carlos was well aware she hadn't answered the question. "Where can I find him?"

"I just don't know." Then she added, "They're supposed to be up the canyon gathering firewood."

"All the men?"

"That's what they said."

"Probably getting drunk!" The old woman wrapped in black came to life.

"Please, Mamá!"

"Well, all the better! Better he should be up there getting drunk than down here making trouble. Or giving my daughter another baby!"

"That's enough, Mamá!"

Carlos recognized a valuable source that could be mined for information, and directed himself to the old woman. "We just came by to make sure you were all right and didn't need anything." His voice was warm as balsam.

"It's just that we haven't seen Diego or the other men on the job for a couple of weeks," Amador added.

"And you won't!" The old woman cackled, revealing a few remaining yellow teeth. "These men will never have to work again!" Diego's wife shot the old woman a wordless threat with eyes alone.

Nothing was lost on the two investigators. Both men knew something very significant passed unsaid between the women. At that moment Carlos concluded that if there was any chance of eliciting the answer to the mystery, it was gone with that serrated look daughter gave mother. Accepting defeat, Carlos and Amador said *buenos días* and started back down the canyon toward the pickup.

"All men are the same," they heard the old woman rant when they were around the corner, "God just gave them different faces so we could tell them apart!"

The following morning, Francisco and Father Ruben were the first ones at the breakfast table. They couldn't wait to hear the firsthand report from the canyon. Dark men with solemn faces crowded around the other two tables. They wanted to hear it too. Every farmer in Tanama was going to lose his crops if they didn't solve the problem— and soon. Carlos and Amador walked in and took their places at the table. Nobody spoke, nobody picked up a newspaper. A chair scraped as someone got up and turned the sound off the CBS morning news.

"Well, señores," Carlos began, "Amador and I spent the better part of a day in the canyon, and we didn't see a single man. They were all supposed to be up the canyon hunting or gathering wood, or whatever you want, but it was obvious that they were simply hiding out with a bottle."

"But how can they survive?" someone from another table called out incredulously. "How do the women put up with it?"

"The women don't like it. They know what's going on but they're not telling."

"But here's the strange thing. There's plenty of food, and I don't mean just a sack of beans and a sack of flour. They have their cupboards loaded with canned goods. That's expensive!"

"And they all had plenty of clothes. Some even looked new."

"And you should have seen the toys and appliances, and radios. I'm telling you, it looked like Christmas!"

"I'd like to know how they do it."

"It is beyond explanation. They're better off than ever—and nobody works!"

Chola brought out plates of spicy sausages, and eggs and fried potatoes, and refried beans, and an extra basket of fluffy tortillas for Father Ruben. There were a few minutes of quiet while hungry men contained the initial flames of appetite.

Francisco took a long swallow of coffee and spoke. "There's only one explanation. They found the cave and El Tigre's paint cans are full of money. We're ruined, face it."

"I'm afraid Francisco is right," Father Ruben agreed. "No other explanation fits."

"If what you say is true, we're all finished, you know."

"I don't know what else to think."

"It just dawned on me! There is one person who would have the answer, and we didn't see her yesterday," Carlos said.

"Who?"

"The old *curandera,*" Carlos suggested with caution.

"The sorceress? I'd forgotten all about her."

"Doña Lala may not even be alive anymore. She must have been a hundred years old when I was a little boy."

"I remember her well. She lived in a kind of a hut with skulls and dead snakes. Do you think she really ever cured anybody?"

"She certainly must have. People have been going to her for as long as anyone can remember."

"Yes, I can remember when my mamá took one of her sisters to Doña Lala. I don't know what her ailment was, but apparently the treatment was successful."

A voice came from another table. "With your forgiveness, Father, I know a lot of people who will trust their lives to the magic potions of the *curandera*."

"So do I," Father Ruben replied equably. "And I can't blame them. When you lose faith you will kneel before a maguey."

"I think it's worth a return trip. If anybody has the answer to the mystery, she has," Carlos submitted.

"But will she reveal anything?"

"There's only one way to find out. What do you say, Amador?"

"I'm with you. I have absolutely nothing to do. And let's face it, señores, if we don't solve this thing in a few days, we're ruined for the year."

Once again Carlos and Amador entered the canyon, and Carlos burrowed the vehicle deep in a clump of shrub oaks nearly as tall as trees. It was Amador who identified the first problem. "You know something? We don't even know if Doña Lala still exists, and if she does, how do we begin to find her?"

"You read my mind, but I think I see our answer."

Coming toward them was a young boy, sent by providence no doubt, to answer their question. He was walking a bicycle.

"A handsome steed, but the savage must not be broke to ride." Amador chuckled.

The little brown face tilted upward and a smile burst into bloom like a migrant sunflower. The boy laughed spontaneously at the metaphor. His enormous black eyes sparkled with amusement, and entering into the idea, he improvised a voice of despair. "He's gone lame!" He slapped his hand to his side for emphasis.

"And where can you get it shod?" Carlos asked, observing the flat front tire.

"All the way to the Pedro's Mini-Mercado. But then I'll gallop the beast all the way home."

Carlos noticed a pair of roller skates strapped to the handlebars. "And if you get tired you can always skate the rest of the way."

The obviously impossible suggestion amused the boy. "You can't skate on dirt! I'm going to trade them to Don Pedro for a candy bar."

"How do you know Don Pedro will make the trade?"

"Only this morning my uncle traded a jacket for a bottle of wine."

"Would you know where I can find Doña Lala?"

The boy's intelligent eyes flickered. "Doña Lala?" He repeated the name for verification.

"*Sí*, do you know where her house is?"

"You mean Doña Lala, the sorceress?" The young voice cracked with pubescence and incredulity.

"*Sí*, the *curandera*," Amador confirmed.

"See that house with the stove pipe?"

"*Sí.*"

"Before you get to it you'll see an abandoned well. Turn left and keep going. Her house is the last one. It stands alone with a tall fence around it. There's no way you can get lost."

They thanked the boy, and he continued walking his bicycle. The two men headed for the landmark. "What a bright and charming little fellow, poor little thing."

"Yes, it's a tragedy. So much potential, and in a few years he'll just be one of the drunks in the canyon."

"We now know how they get their liquor, but where is all the merchandise coming from?"

"I tell you there's a cat in a basket somewhere."

"At least we know Doña Lala is still alive."

"God, she's got to be at least a hundred. You know the last time I saw her? I was about that boy's age, and that's nearly thirty years ago!"

"I remember well. She used to terrify us. Our parents promised us a good beating if we went near her place."

"What do we do when we find her?" Amador asked.

"I've asked myself the same question. I don't know, we'll have to think of whatever the moment demands."

They climbed for another twenty minutes, and there wasn't the slightest room for doubt whose house they were standing in front of. It was ingeniously fenced with old rusted bedsprings standing on edge and held together with bailing wire and tetanus bacilli. The gate was simply a gap between two twin bedsprings with a rope across. They approached as cautiously as two boys sneaking up on a snake.

Carlos and Amador stood in front of the gate, surrounded by silence and the pungence of wild arnica. With a glance and a toss of the chin, Amador directed Carlos's attention to the dead chicken hanging by its cold yellow feet just inside the gate, lifeless wings splayed in final statement of demise. Drops of blood oozed from its beak and formed a dark ring on the ground. They exchanged the same signal that thirty years ago would have sent the two running for their lives. But now adult pride posing as courage held them fast.

Carlos found the doorbell. He picked up the three-inch carriage bolt tied to a string and struck the metal dishpan lashed to the bedspring for that purpose. The three tinny dings melted in the sinister air surrounding the hanging chicken. They waited. There was no movement, no perceptible response to the summons. A few flies hummed. They could hear the frantic squawks and screams of a chicken obviously running for her life, which she felt was precious. A few cats lay lolling about in the shade of tables and cupboards out in the yard. Carlos was about to ring again when he felt something wet and cold touch his hand. His heart stopped and he nearly expired at the gate. When his heart resumed its normal rhythm, he looked down to see a friendly puppy at his side.

Doña Lala suddenly materialized before them without sound. Amador could have sworn that Carlos actually grabbed for his hand. Nerves twitched, reflexes were tense and prepared for instant flight. Had a twig snapped at that moment, both men would have abandoned pride and fled. They were looking into a face that resembled a huge walnut, brown and gnarled with deep wrinkles, creases, and dark grooves. The walnut stared back at them through yellowed eyes hidden in a pouch of puckered skin. Hair, white as gypsum, covered her back like a cape. Broomstick arms and legs poked out through a frayed rag sack of faded black.

"*Buenos días*, Doña Lala," the two men said in unison. Something made them want to whisper.

"*Buenos días,*" Doña Lala answered in a strong voice through one of the creases. A loose flap of wrinkled skin hung from her thin neck. The fleshy dewlap flapped when she talked.

Amador began in his friendliest voice. "You probably don't remember us, Doña Lala, but—"

"Don Amador, *sí*? And Don Carlos?"

How did she do that? The same thought flashed through each man's mind.

"You wish to see me?"

"*Sí*, if it is not a bother to you."

"No bother, no bother at all," the wrinkle pronounced, and dipping a bony hand into a pan of water on the table nearby, she splashed Carlos in the face and both shoulders.

She repeated the ritual for Amador and began to undo the rope that stood between them. "Enter your house, then."

"*Gracias.*" They stepped into the small yard. The dirt was swept clean, and still held brush marks from the broom. The dead chicken continued to drip blood on the ground, and the cats began to leap on the furniture in the yard. Mysterious charms and fetishes and various other instruments indispensable to Doña Lala's profession were neatly arranged on an old bureau in a corner of the surgery. There were vials of disgusting-looking things of unknown origin, and better left that way. A human skull grinned back at them. Were they in the house? No, the house was farther back and overgrown with sunflowers and honeysuckle and morning glory. Only a black rectangle of darkness implied an open door to a dwelling. Carlos was first to notice a young girl of twelve or so sitting silently on a couch covered in cracked maroon plastic that must have come out of a Denny's coffee shop many years ago. She was stroking a black cat.

"Have you been keeping well?" Amador began, and Carlos knew immediately that he was trying to kill time until one of them could think of some way to broach the subject of their mission.

"I'm indestructible."

Now it was Carlos's turn. "It's been such a long time." (Your turn, Amador.)

"You have seen many people come and go here in the canyon." (That's the best I can do, now you think of something.)

"Three generations. The girl is my great-great-granddaughter."

"Great-granddaughter!" Amador exclaimed.

"Great-great-granddaughter," the old woman corrected.

"Many of the men here work on our ranches, and we're

starting to see the second generation." Amador felt an oblique approach was called for. No reaction. The walnut face revealed nothing.

Carlos decided he might as well come to the point. "We heard there had been a miracle up here." Yellow eyes looked back at him uninformatively. (My God, what do we do now? We'd better come up with a reason for coming to her right now or it's all over!)

Ding, ding, ding! The tension of playing wits with a witch was broken. They all turned to see a man with a week's stubble on his face standing at the rope. "Doña Lala, *buenos días*, I have to see you." There was no attempt to disguise the urgency in his voice.

"I am presently occupied," she answered.

"No, no, Doña Lala," Carlos offered quickly. "Take care of his needs. We can wait."

Doña Lala dipped her hand in the magic water and anointed the man. She undid the rope, and he rushed into the emergency room like a man with a hemorrhage. As the visitor drew closer it was impossible for the olfactory senses to separate the layers of evil smells that followed the unfortunate man like his shadow. Wine, goat, sweat, tobacco?

"What ails you?"

"I need to be cleansed. I am tortured day and night. I haven't eaten, I haven't slept. Something is tearing out my very soul. Ever since the miracle came to the canyon, I have had no peace. I want you to purge me, release me from the demons I carry inside me."

"Ten thousand pesos." Doña Lala was all business now.

The old man reached in the pocket of his crumpled work pants, drew out five shiny coins and put them in the witch's stringy hand.

"This is only five thousand."

"It is all I have, Doña Lala, I implore you!"

Pay dirt! Carlos was quick to seize the opportunity. "Poor soul." He handed Doña Lala a bank note, which disappeared somewhere in her black dress. "Put away your coins, old man."

"*Gracias, gracias*, God bless you, God repay you!"

The look on Carlos's face told Amador they had just bought themselves some much-needed time and a ticket to watch the performance. They took a front row seat on the maroon remains of the restaurant booth to make themselves as inobtrusive as they could in that small yard. The little girl continued to stroke the cat.

"Sit over here." Doña Lala indicated a wooden kitchen chair under a ramada of dried palm fronds. The man sat down obediently. Then to the girl, "Bring me candles." The little girl ran to her errand and returned with three candles. Doña Lala then touched each candle to the man's lips, placed it in a holder on the table, and gave it life with a kitchen match. She took a small bouquet of aromatic leaves and berries and brushed his shoulders and chest. She began her diagnosis thus: "The candle in the middle is your brain, the one on the left is your heart, the one on the right is your soul. It's no wonder you're in this condition, look!"

All eyes turned to the candles. Amador gave Carlos a gentle nudge with his elbow as Doña Lala went on with her sorcery. "Look how the little flames tremble and wiggle. You are emotionally diseased. You have an infection of the soul." The flames shivered and twisted restlessly to confirm her diagnosis.

Carlos thought, You old fake, of course the flames flicker, we're outdoors.

"Take off your shirt," Doña Lala instructed.

The old man complied. The skin on his body was as

smoky as his face, the nipples almost black. Doña Lala plucked a feather from the deceased Rhode Island red that had been hanging patiently and passed it all around his head, around his body. She mumbled something, but neither Carlos or Amador could distinguish words. It was a mysterious litany of screechy incantations resembling the sound of a rusty hinge. The stranger sat motionless. Then his eyes closed as the chicken feather was passed near his face. Now his lips began to quiver uncontrollably.

"Bring some eggs," Doña Lala said to the little girl.

Carlos felt the nudge Amador gave him in the ribs. They could hear a gate open. Probably a chicken coop. The girl returned and put three eggs in Doña Lala's hands. Carlos and Amador couldn't help exchanging subtle jabs of the elbow. Doña Lala took the first egg, gently laid it on the patient's head, and began to chant with greater fervor and intensity. She put the egg down on the table and took another and held it against his heart. The chanting grew more animated as she brought out the third egg and held it against his diaphragm. Doña Lala left the chant now, dipped her hand in a bowl of water containing some reptile, and mumbling the same mysterious words, she splashed the patient in the face and he became alert.

"You are healed," she told her patient. "The infection has passed into these eggs. Notice how steady the flames burn now."

All eyes went to the candles, where indeed the flames held true and steady. This time Carlos and Amador made no attempt to hide their astonishment.

But Doña Lala wasn't through. One at a time she cracked the eggs into a bowl. "*¡Fuchi!*" she exclaimed with undisguised repulsion. "What an evil smell! Just look at that infection we withdrew." She placed the bowl of black rotting eggs in front of the man's face as proof that all the evil within him was found and removed. The stench was overwhelming. "Take them out of here," she instructed the girl, who obeyed quickly and silently. "You are healed. Put on your shirt and go in peace."

The stranger put on his shirt, thanked Doña Lala, then shook hands with Carlos and Amador. "A million *gracias*, may God repay your kindess. Your charity will never be forgotten." He departed and left only fragrant remnants of his visit.

When he was gone, he left Carlos and Amador realizing they must have been holding their breath. They sat numb in an aura of silence and reverence. Had they witnessed a miracle? Maybe they had. As though waiting for the last note of holy music to fade away, Carlos waited for a respectful minute before he could whisper, "What was wrong with him?"

"Poisoned, poisoned by the miracle."

"What miracle?"

"I warned them all that it was no miracle, but they paid no attention to me."

Here's my chance, Carlos thought. "Is that why the men don't come to work? Because of the miracle, I mean?" At last here comes my answer.

"The whole canyon is infected. Fools! I saved this man today. They will all have to come to me for cleansing. Nobody can fool Doña Lala." She did not elucidate.

Amador was frustrated now. They had gone full circle. They were covering the same ground, and the old sorceress would reveal nothing. The mystery only deepened, and was becoming inpenetrable. Now they needed a legitimate excuse to remain and hope to gain her confidence. Carlos must have been of the same mind because he took Amador by complete surprise. "Well, Doña Lala, now to the business that brought me here in the first place. I am here this morning because I have not felt well for some time."

"What is the matter with you?"

"I feel depressed all the time. I've lost my appetite. I can't sleep at night. Like there is something inside of me that wants to get out." He avoided making eye contact with Amador, who couldn't believe what he was witnessing.

"I see," Doña Lala croaked, and the dewlap flapped back and forth.

"Maybe you can do something for me too," and he placed a ten thousand peso note into the withered hand.

The candles from the previous patient were removed and fresh ones brought out. Carlos removed his shirt and took his place in the chair. Amador was afraid he would burst out laughing any minute.

Doña Lala brushed him with the nosegay of aromatic berries. She touched each candle to Carlos's lips, lit it, and studied the flame without word or comment implied by the yellow eyes. Amador could hardly believe what he saw. The flames burned without a tremor. And they were outdoors! Again the sorceress plucked a feather from the dead chicken and repeated the ritual. Amador saw Carlos's eyelids close. Were his lips really trembling? Doña Lala sent the girl for eggs. Amador listened. He heard the same sound of the chicken coop door. The chanting and croaking began as Doña Lala held an egg to Carlos's head, another over his heart, and the third on his diaphragm. The ritual complete, Doña Lala dipped her hand in the water with the lizard and splashed Carlos in the face.

Amador watched Carlos open his eyes and look alert. What a faker you are, he thought.

"Am I healed?" Carlos asked.

"You are healed."

"Is the infection in the eggs the same as before?"

"Sí, just as before. But you want to see, no?"

"Sí."

Amador held his breath. He could actually feel a constriction in his chest. Doña Lala then took an egg and deftly smashed it on Carlo's head. The bright yellow yolk and colorless white slime of a perfectly fresh egg slithered down his face and down the back of his neck. Doña Lala erupted into a cackling laughter any hyena could be proud of. "That is what you get for trying to fool me. Nobody fools Doña Lala."

A dozen or so chickens were busy gossiping and grubbing in front of Café Los Alamos. The big red rooster fluffed his glossy neck feathers and crowed into the stillness of Sunday morning in Tanama. It was early, but the pickups were already gathered under the yellow dapples of sunlight that filtered through the poplars like a Renoir scene. Inside, every rancher in Tanama crowded around the three tables. Some were already making progress against a plate heaped with sausages, and eggs, and refried beans covered with white cheese. All had a cup of steaming coffee. There were no signs against smoking. The little breathable air that remained in the tiny room was replaced with the wonderful smells of good things to eat. Sound on top of sound came from the kitchen, clattering, sizzling, running water. Tortillas puffed up like white balloons on a hot iron sheet. Big bursts of masculine laughter, detonated by Amador's account of the visit to Doña Lala's, exploded around the tables. The decibel reading in the café would have alarmed OSHA audiologists of even the most lenient disposition.

Chola came out of the kitchen to take their breakfast order. "I've seen enough eggs for a while," Carlos said, "just the potatoes and the beans today."

Father Ruben screwed his face into a mass of wrinkles, squinted his eyes and croaked, "Nobody fools Doña Lala!"

"How did you know?" gasped Carlos. "You mean you've actually seen her?"

"I was in her sanctum when I was a boy of ten."

"Should we ask why?"

"My older brother dared me to go in there and come back with that human skull she keeps. She came after me with a dead chicken." The little café rocked with laughter. "Well, you did everything you could to unravel the mystery, and it only got deeper," Father Ruben consoled Carlos. He didn't have a mass until noon today. "You suspected a cat in a basket somewhere, but now we'll never know."

"*Sí*, we might as well face the reality of it," Francisco put in, "we might as well accept it now. We're ruined!"

"Our crops will rot in the field."

"The whole year is a loss."

"I have no more ideas."

At the very moment when Father Ruben was removing a hot tortilla from the basket, a series of coincidences common to Mexican highways began to take place directly in front of the café. A man high on the wings of rapture sat behind the wheel of a blue Pontiac station wagon. An American. He was singing "Onward Christian Soldiers." The voice was deep and resonant and triumphant. His wife, who sat next to him, unfurled her voice like a banner of courage proclaiming victory on the battlefield of souls. Just as the impassioned voices got to "with the cross of Jaysus going on before," a half-ton Hereford decided to exercise its rights, and headed for what seemed to be greener grass across the road. The driver's defensive tactics were commendable. He cut the inspirational hymn short, slammed his foot on the brake and pulled the wheel sharply right to prevent what appeared to be an imminent collision. He did manage to avoid impact with the hindquarters of the careless bovine, but there was no possible way he could avoid a long squealing skid and a rough landing in a shallow gully where, by all that's reasonable, there should have been a shoulder.

The scream of the tires making every effort to stop caused the men in the café to pick up their heads and look out the window. They were in time to see the station wagon thudding and thunking into the ditch, scattering hysterical chickens in a flurry of feathers and cackles.

"Did you see that? I hope that stupid cow wasn't one of mine!"

"Come on, we better get out there and give the poor hombre a hand."

Carlos and Amador burst out first, followed by Francisco and Father Ruben. As usual, Carlos was already one thought ahead, and grabbed a coil of rope from his pickup on the way. They reached the listing station wagon just as the driver was crawling out, shaken but otherwise undamaged. He helped his wife out and looked up for the first time, to see himself surrounded by several rugged men in tall hats carrying a length of rope.

"Oh my God, bandidos!" he gasped. As soon as breathing resumed, he said to his pale wife, "I'll handle this, Ruth. We're Americans, I wasn't going fast, I didn't hit the cow and—"

"No problem, my friend, no problem," Carlos soothed the wide-eyed stranger. "We will help you."

The stranger calmed down visibly and his eyes retreated

into their sockets. His wife clutched her bosom. The American was a big man, taller than any of them, and contoured like a bowling pin with an ample, round bottom. A golden halo of light blond hair encircled a face of creamy pink skin and heavenly blue eyes. Rose-colored lips of tufted velvet shaped the unctuous mouth where the Holy Scriptures were stored. He seemed to float over the ground when he walked on sweet tiny feet. His wife was his identical twin, with several chubby chins and dimpled arms.

Amador backed his pickup to the edge of the ditch while Carlos put the station wagon in neutral and released the brake. Carlos rolled under the car, tied the rope to the frame, and tossed the free end to Francisco, who stood ready.

Francisco secured his end to the trailer hitch of the pickup. "Ready here," he called out.

Amador stepped on the gas, the rope strained, and with little effort the station wagon was resting comfortably on level ground.

"Everything looks okay," Carlos said to the American.

"Oh, yes, I'm quite sure," the American said, opening the back hatch to inspect his load. Carlos saw that the wagon was packed tight from floor to headlining with cartons. "Thank the good Lord everything is fine. Thank you. Grashus!"

Carlos noticed a couple of bicycles strapped to the top. "I see you are going on vacation. Have a good trip."

"Oh no, we're not on vacation. We're out to spread the Word!"

"That's nice," Carlos answered with enthusiastic indifference.

"I'm the Reverend Peach." He offered a soft doughy hand. And, consistent with the cannons of Mexican courtesy, each man shook his hand in turn. "And this is my wife, Ruth." Another marshmallow hand was offered, and the same sequence of handshakes was repeated. "We're from the New Life Community Mission of Long Beach, California." He warbled when he talked.

"That's nice," Carlos repeated.

"Yes, every Sunday we bring badly needed donations of food and clothing and toys for the poor. You should see the smiles on the faces of those poor families living in abject poverty. It isn't the men's fault they can't find a job."

Carlos began to put thought and theory together. "My God, the gringos are now exporting welfare—our campesinos are on the dole!"

"They've come to expect us every week. As soon as they see us pull up, they come down the hills in droves."

"It's a beautiful sight—it's a miracle!" his wife added.

"Where?" Carlos inquired, enthusiasm restored.

"Up in the canyon."

Carlos could simply not accept this. "But that's impossible. The people in the canyon do not even understand English."

"No, they don't understand English, but they do understand friendship and goodwill."

Father Ruben moved in closer. He didn't say anything, but the tumblers in his head were sliding into place.

Carlos, Amador, and Francisco watched with some curiosity as Father Ruben pulled a handkerchief out of his pocket and began to wipe his eyes. There was no need to nudge each other. They all knew they were about to see improvisational theater at the side of the road.

Father Ruben staggered over to the Peaches like a man carrying a heavy burden. The weary Padre rubbed sleep from his haggard eyes as though he could also rub away the horror of the night before, an all-night marathon against death, abandoning the dying to save the few who had any hope to live. He looked exhausted and spoke softly with grave authority.

"I am Dr. Juvenal Urbino," plot and protagonist borrowed in the heat of the moment from Gabriel Garcia Marquez. "I jus' arrive from Mexico Ceety last night. I am afraid you cannot go into the canyon."

"Whyever not?"

"Quarantine."

"Quarantine!" There was a noticeable loss of blush on both Peaches.

"Yes, I am afraid. Cholera."

Once again the reverend's eyes sprang forward from their sockets. Without comment he waddled to his car with all the speed terror could make. Mrs. Peaches got in on her side .075 seconds before her husband.

Carlos, Amador, Francisco, and Father Ruben watched the blue station wagon burn rubber and head north toward the U.S. border in a jetstream of dirt and chicken feathers.

They all stood quietly for a moment. Somehow the air smelled sweeter this morning. The gentle sun felt warmer on their backs, and it laid its soft golden cheek against the crops in the fields that would soon be tended once again.

"It was the right deed in the wrong place," Father Ruben said gently. "There are all types in His vineyard." Father Ruben moved toward his pickup and slid behind the wheel. "God forgive me, I'd better go find Father Guerra now, and see if he can take my confession this morning."

Testimony of a Mango Popsicle

April comes to Tecate with flower and bee—and *mango* popsicles. The icy gales and snows of winter were now a melted memory. The men shed their heavy leather *chamarras*, and the early blossoms of colorful cotton frocks could now be seen unfurling in the plaza. I was in Tecate, USA, and about to reenter Tecate, Mexico. In front of me was the tall chain-link fence that separates one sovereign nation from another. The Stars and Stripes waved proudly over the home of McDonald's Golden Arches. The Mexican eagle flapped its wings over the land of enchiladas, rice, and beans.

I was without a care in the world, an old love song playing in my heart. While waiting my turn in line, I looked around at the border station and realized that in Tecate nothing is ever really what it appears to be. There were a few uniformed officers loitering around a guard-house, a faded stop sign, and an official-looking building in a double-breasted brown stucco suit with the Great Seal pinned on its lapel. It had all the appearances of a port of entry, but in reality it was a blackmailer's drive-through checkout counter.

When I was about four cars from the guardhouse, I looked ahead to see who was on duty. I was unpleased at the sight of Big Caca, the most detested of all border guards, all of whom are held in low esteem. I should hasten to inform the reader that Big Caca was not his real name, no mother could do that. His real name was Ismael Cacabelos.

He was built with a low center of gravity. Haberdashers refer to this conformation as a portly short. The fit of the uniform was a capital crime. Even twenty-four brass buttons failed to convey stature. But the .45 at his side made him eight feet tall. Under the stiff-visored military cap was a grim brown soccer-ball face with a mustache that would make an acceptable eyebrow. The dark nevus embossed on his left nostril did little to improve his appearance. He flaunted his official extortionist's license on his bulging breast. It glimmered with authority.

"*Buenos días,*" I sang in a bright C major triad.

"*Buenos días,* open your *cajuela,* if you please." It was by no means a song, but it wasn't hostile either, and I took this as a positive sign.

I pulled my key out of the ignition and went around to obey the order. I offered him a smile as warm as the morning itself, and opened my trunk. As soon as he saw the little garden sprayer still in the carton, I knew there was going to be trouble. He began to salivate profusely, and I knew then what was causing the activity of his salivary glands; money from my pocket would soon be in his.

"What is in the carton?"

"A three-gallon garden sprayer. It cost me thirty-nine dollars at Dixieline. The price sticker is still on the box."

"Absolutely against the law!"

Now, I knew, and he knew, and he knew that I knew, that Mexican border officials write legislation wherever they happen to be standing. I now recited my expected line. "I don't know what to do now. I suppose I could turn around here and return it."

"We are not here to make trouble for nice people. Give me ten dollars and be on your way, señor."

I knew how it was going to end, but prescience doesn't alter consequence—I was nettled. I paid the bribe, crossed into Mexico, and went directly to Cuchuma Feed and Granary on my final errand.

There are two reasons for patronizing Cuchuma Feed and Granary, both sound. First, it is the only feed store in town. Secondly, it is the main newsroom for the Tecate network news. Proprietor and senior anchorman, Zeferino Gonzalez, brings you all the news, all the time.

I was still bristling when I pushed the door open. The musky smell of mixed grains and meals and chicken mash, bunny rabbits, baby chicks, and harness leather, inhibited normal breathing for the first few minutes. You couldn't have smelled a skunk had one wandered in off the street simply because there was no room left for another fragrant molecule. My entrance interrupted the flow of conversation, but when Tito spoke, I could see a big story was breaking.

"One day I shall have to kill the man." Tito was a big, tough, macho ranchero with a rawhide disposition. His colorful language could singe the hide off range cattle, but deep in his heart lay rich deposits of pure gold. Still, I thought his voice was dangerously calm, knowing the direction of his grain.

I knew without making inquiry that if Tito had plans to

shorten the allotted life expectancy, known only to the Maker, of anyone in this town, it had to be Big Caca. Nonetheless, Zeferino felt obliged to announce the lead story. "Tito was coming in to Mexico just this morning with a used refrigerator and Big Caca demanded a hundred dollars."

"*¡Cabrón!* I only paid fifty for the *pinchi* refrigerator!"

"Is that why you're so mad, Tito?" I asked unnecessarily.

"No! I solved that problem by turning around and going back to the United States. I figured I would try again tonight. Different shift, different hyena. I don't mind paying ten or even twenty, but that's not the worst of it."

Everyone in the store leaned forward. Zeferino froze behind the counter with a grain scoop still in his hand.

Tito continued his narrative. "When I crossed back to the Other Side, the gringos had their *pinchi* drug-sniffing dogs out. And when they came to my pickup, the *pinchi* dogs went crazy! The leaped, they howled, they tried to jump into the bed of my *pinchi* truck!"

"*¡Válgame dios!*"

"Of course, they pulled me over immediately and made me get out of the truck. They put a guard on me and ordered me to empty my pockets. It was humiliating! That's all I need to make my day complete—a load of illegal drugs in my *pinchi* truck. I would spend the rest of my life in a *pinchi* gringo prison! Who would ever accept my story? Two uniforms climbed into the pickup and opened the refrigerator. I stopped breathing!"

"You must have been passing thistles!"

"Sideways! Then, one of the gringo officers said, 'Come over here,' and I walked over to the truck fully expecting to be put into handcuffs or fed to their *pinchi* dogs or— Then

I saw what they saw. Someone had left a bag of fried pork rinds in the refrigerator!"

The little store shook violently under the explosion of laughter, sending one of the men seated on a grain barrel to the floor on his *nalgas*. There was no point in juxtaposing my own recent experience with Big Caca. It paled next to Tito's. When the guffaws settled down to chortles, I asked Zeferino to put a hundred-pound sack of laying mash in the trunk of my car. Shards of laughter were still falling when I walked out of Cuchuma Feed and Granary.

As I pulled away I heard the peal of tiny silver bells, a merry tinkle of sweet seduction. Ting-a-ling, ting-a-ling ling! My immediate response was not too different from that of Old Bowser, that nice dog whose master rang a bell whenever he tossed him a pork chop. It may have been Pavarotti or maybe it was Paderewski. You know who I mean. Anyway, the stimulus produced by the chimes brought the same results. My tastebuds burst into full flower.

I followed the sound, and when I rounded the corner I heard the cry that was the source of my ecstasy. "*¡Popsicles! . . . mango . . . papaya . . . melón . . . limón . . . chocolate!*"

The young boy pushed his cart up to my open window. "*¿Sí, señor?*"

"*Mango, por favor.*"

The sweet, cool taste of a popsicle made from fresh *mango* gathered in the jungles of Nayarit dispelled the sour leavings of my recent incident with Big Caca. Thus soothed, I headed back for my rancho with a new song taking form within my breast. When I came to the railroad crossing at the edge of town, I had to laugh. It's clearly marked with a huge white X and a flashing red warning light. There are no trains in Tecate.

It couldn't have been more than a week later when the preposterous story first reached my ears. Gossip and rumors in Tecate travel at a speed just a shade under Mach 1. I got it from a waiter at La Fonda who nearly dropped his heavy tray under the strain of laughter. He got it, he said, directly from his mother-in-law, who he swears is more reliable than XETV. And she heard it *directamente* from Zeferino's wife, who is her *comadre*. Zeferino was a name I knew and a source I trusted to be unimpeachable. I headed for News Central.

There were three or four local ranchers gathered around the counter when I entered the granary. "Can it really be true?" I asked Zeferino as he scooped a kilo of meal onto the scales.

"*Sí*, I wish it weren't," someone answered. "Big Caca will be impossible for weeks!"

"You think Tito?" I asked Zeferino.

"I don't have to guess. I sold him the Rompun. Two cc's and a thousand-pound animal is malleable as a teddy bear."

"Who else would have the *cojones* to do a thing like that?" one of the ranchers observed.

"Still, it's just too incredible to be true. Does anybody here know what really happened?" I asked the crowd in general.

"What really happened is that when Big Caca went to his rancho yesterday morning, he found his big Hereford bull on top of the barn!" All of us yielded to laughter, it couldn't be helped. "The bull is perfectly happy up there with a good supply of hay and a tub of fresh water."

"Is?"

"Oh, *sí*, he is still up there. Big Caca has not yet solved the problem of how to get him down."

We were still laughing when the door opened and Andrés Segovia walked in the door. If you were to see this man walking down the street in his khaki uniform, his glittering badge, the six-shooter at his side, you would logically conclude that you were looking at a municipal policeman. You would be mistaken. The maestro was a classical guitarist of astounding virtuosity. Whatever his assignment of duty may have been, his priceless instrument was cradled in his arms, and he emptied his soul with music so passionate it seemed to express the human side of God. I don't know anyone in town who knows his real name. Even his wife calls him Segovia. Today he was not carrying his guitar.

"*Hola*, Segovia! You're out early, what can I get you?"

"I'm not here this morning as your friend and customer, Zeferino, I am here in an official capacity." The voice was official too, and the face sober and strained. "I am under orders from the comandante to conduct a thorough investigation into a recent incident of a Hereford bull belonging to a certain government official. You understand I am only doing my duty."

The temperature in the room dropped perceptibly. Zeverino played with some grain in a bin. The rest of us shuffled our feet. The officer brought out his notebook and a pen. "Does anyone here know who committed this act, or does anyone here have any information concerning said incident?"

"No."

"Not me."

"*Nada.*"

Without another word the policeman replaced his notebook and turned toward the door. "Segovia, where are you going?" Zeferino asked.

"I have to report my findings to the comandante," he called over his shoulder on the way out the door.

I left Zeferino's, took a left at the plaza, and heard my song.

Ting-a-ling, ting-a-ling ling. "*¡Paletas de mango . . . papaya . . . melón . . . limón . . . chocolate!*" Once again I experienced the same symptoms Old Bowser must have exhibited when the professor rang his bell. Was it Papanicolaou? No, no, his interest lay in another direction altogether. Every woman has heard of him. The name will come to me eventually. I came away with *mango*.

I had no desire to be seen anywhere in the vicinity of the crime scene, but I also knew I had to see the spectacle for myself. I headed east on Highway 2. I always pause at K-8 to marvel at our masterpiece of misrepresentation. Fourteen cream-colored towers rise up like skyscrapers. The turrets allow a 360-degree view from behind high-tensile-strength, bullet-proof glass. Each guard tower surveys a sprawling complex of modern cell blocks, bunkers, and administration buildings of pastel hues painted to harmonize with the watchtowers. The sign, now badly peeling, informs the passerby that he's looking at the new state penitentiary. No inmate has ever checked into these modern buildings for bed and breakfast; no guard has ever climbed the tower to enjoy the view. When the project was about eighty percent completed, it was decided that what Tecate really needed was a city dump. And this is what it has remained to this day.

Another few minutes and I turned off the main road. Big Caca's rancho was one of the many with their entrances along a rough, corrugated dirt track. Tito's ranch was farther up the same road.

I couldn't have been more astonished if I had witnessed the cow's celebrated leap over the moon, although I remember seeing pictures of that. Not far from the gate I could see the adobe barn with a flat roof. A two thousand-pound, rusty-red Hereford bull was pawing the asphalt shingles. A long ladder leaned against one side, and I could see the figure of a man I couldn't identify making his way up with an armload of hay.

But from my position on the road I could see they now had a new problem. One of the cows in the yard must have come into heat that morning, because Big Caca's bull was fully extended (a condition impossible to hide) and was bellowing his urgency. I didn't stop the car, but headed directly for my rancho.

When I pulled in I found Chemo shoeing El Alazán. Chemo was the best ranch hand any man could wish for. He was clean, sober, honest, and remarkable. He received his degree in animal science without cracking a book. The main reason for this was that Chemo couldn't read. He was graduated from the school of experience.

"*Buenas tardes*, Don."

"*Buenas tardes*," I returned.

"El Alazán goes through a set of shoes like a twelve-year-old *muchacho*." I watched fascinated as he skillfully leveled the sole of the hoof before placing the shoe and then drove the nails just outside the nerve line with the precision of a surgeon.

"Any disasters during my absence?" Last week we had broken water lines, cows loose in the corn, and a burned pump.

He answered with a big grin. His few remaining teeth

looked like the candy corn you see around Halloween. "No, Don, everything is well in hand." He slipped El Alazán a treat from his pocket and turned him loose. Chemo had to be in his early seventies, skinny as a hoe, agile as a vaquero's lariat. His muscles must have been made of drop-forged steel. He could work from dawn to dark without tiring. In fourteen years I have never seen Chemo without his beach umbrella sombrero.

I could see Chemo had something weighing on his mind and waited for him to free himself of his burden.

"I trained the new pup not to teethe on the chickens. She promised not to do it anymore." Chemo was the peacemaker on the ranch. He spoke on behalf of all the creatures in his charge and he was quick to come to their defense. I saw he still had more to unload.

"El Demonio told me he is sorry he kicked you this morning," Chemo said with the voice of a father, who, representing his son, had to admit to the latter's offense. El Demonio was our resident burro. He had a cute furry face, long adorable ears, and a depraved mind. This information brought me little comfort. As far as I was concerned, the illtempered burro was on probation until I could sit in the saddle without pain.

I avoided the subject by relating to him the story of Big Caca's bull. "How in the world could anyone get the animal up there? And a better question might be, how are they going to get him down?"

He couldn't contain a smile. "I'll bet the *muchachos* at Los Alamos would know how a thing like that could be accomplished."

Early next morning I threw a saddle on El Alazán and he took me to Los Alamos Café for breakfast at an uninspired dogtrot in low gear. I left him anchored in the shade of an *alamo* to contemplate Life, stepped carefully around the chickens and pushed the door open.

An all-male chorus of *buenos días* came from the three small tables that subjugated all the available space in that tiny cafe. "*Buenos días,*" I answered, and looked for my good friends and neighbors. The air was thick with the good smells of frying beans, and sausage, and golden potatoes.

I found Amador, Francisco, Carlos, and Father Ruben seated together at a small table near the only window. We exchanged greetings, and Amador pulled over a wooden chair with a crack in the seat that was known to bite. I sat down cautiously and joined them in a plate of *huevos rancheros*.

They may have been waiting for me to open the conversation. "It looks like a huge rusty locomotive with a white face," I said, and as soon as my words were airborne, I wished them back. They were all good neighbors in the café, but still, I didn't know how much they knew. But it was too late for repentance. I could see by the faces that my words were already vibrating against their eardrums, made the tricky turn into the cochlea, and were at this moment being processed by the brain.

"You've seen it?"

"I've seen it," I answered and caught sight of Father Ruben nipping a sausage from Carlos's plate. "How on earth did he do it?" I judiciously omitted the name of the prime suspect.

Carlos answered the question. "The *cabrón*—excuse me, Father, the *loco*—stole into the ranch at night and sedated the animal. He strapped him on the skip loader and delivered him on the roof!"

"But what about Fidel, his watchman?" I asked.

Amador answered. "That was the easy part. He wasn't alone."

"He wasn't?" I couldn't imagine Tito risking the use of an accomplice.

"No, José was an accessory to the crime."

The only José I knew of was José Tapia, the city treasurer, and he wouldn't know a tamale pie from a cow pie. They saw the perplexity on my face, and as they began to laugh, I realized they were talking about Cuervo.

Carlos explained. "It was José's job to distract Fidel. And soon he too was sedated." There was another ripple of laughter.

"How do you know all this?" Francisco asked.

"It was close to midnight when the *loco* came by my place. He confessed everything."

Father Ruben raised his bushy eyebrows. "I am comforted to learn he confessed to someone."

"You don't offer tequila and lime at your place, Father."

You probably noticed that throughout this entire exchange you-know-who was never mentioned.

Father Ruben turned to me. "Are you going to leave that tortilla?"

"I was saving it for you, Father." The tortilla vanished. "By the way, any recent outbreaks of cholera?"

Father Ruben knocked on the table, but his eyes rolled toward heaven. *"Gracias a Dios, no."*

We had more coffee, and more laughs, and I went out to find El Alazán dozing with his head buried in the swishing tail of a big bay mare.

I have never claimed to know what goes on in a horse's mind. But I have to believe that El Alazán was fantasizing about the Horse Fairy, who in his absence visited his feed box and left him a carrot. He picked up his feet and flew homeward on the wings of blind faith. I didn't have the heart to destroy his illusions and tell him his benefactor was really Chemo.

I wasn't back at the rancho long enough to unsaddle when I saw Chemo walking in my direction across a melón field. He walked in his own shadow, as the sun was now at its zenith. His solemn gait was enough to tell me that the nadir of my day was near at hand.

"You better come and look at La Monita. She does not look too good, Don."

We found La Monita, my prize Holstein cow, standing in the shade of a ramada. She was munching her hay without gusto. Her breathing was heavy and she displayed the most obvious symptom—she wasn't eager for society. All subtle symptoms to be sure, but enough to cause concern to the keen observer.

It's now time to tell you—because you're going to find out anyway—Chemo not only talked to the animals, he attributed anthropomorphic competence to every animal on the ranch. I watched him approach La Monita.

"What is it, Monita, where does it hurt? Tell Chemo." I watched him try to comfort the animal. His long oval face was the color of an old penny flecked with silver bristles. With no mustache to break the monotony of his topography, he looked as desolate as the Vizcaino Desert. "Tell Chemo what ails you, *chiquita*."

"I'll get Dr. Cruz right away," I said, and went into the house with my fingers crossed against the cosmic forces that hold majority interest in Teléfonos de Mexico.

It wasn't long before Dr. Cruz made his appearance and the three of us stood looking at La Monita. Dr. Cruz studied her eyes, checked her pulse, and took her temperature. I knew she was less than herself when she didn't offer to kick his hat off when he slipped a thermometer as thick as my index finger into her rectum. The doctor spoke. "You know, these things are common with cows. She obviously doesn't feel good, but she has a very low-grade temperature. I'm not concerned."

"What do you suggest?"

"I'll definitely give her an antibiotic. We should see quick improvement, but I'll be by first thing mañana to be on the safe side." With that, he left and the ceaseless chores of the ranch occupied us for the remainder of the day.

Next morning Chemo and I were observing La Monita when Dr. Cruz arrived. "There is no obvious improvement," I said.

Dr. Cruz had to agree. He took her temperature without exciting so much as a flick of her tail. "Still low grade," he announced. "It must be a very stubborn infection," he admitted. "I'll give her a double dose this time. You should see remarkable improvement in two days. If not, you call me."

The next day the patient looked no better, but no worse. I told Chemo we would wait out the two days and see which way she went. After all, her temperature was low grade and Dr. Cruz wasn't too concerned.

Next morning my heart sank. La Monita stood slightly swaying where she stood. Her eyes were dull and lifeless. Her breathing was labored, and worst of all, she wouldn't even look up at me.

"It doesn't look good, Don," Chemo said darkly. "I have never seen anything like this, but I don't believe it is germ bugs. She told me something hurts inside. It is a very serious thing."

I didn't believe she told him anything of the sort, but I had to agree she didn't look good. I ran to the phone. "Dr. Cruz, *por favor*."

"I'm sorry, he is not in. Who calls?" I recognized his mother's voice, gave my name, and told her the nature of the problem.

"It is the beginning of Holy Week, and he has gone to the seashore at San Felipe with his family." My heart fell on the floor. I had completely forgotten. Everything closes down in Tecate during Holy Week. Everyone from the governor of Baja, California, to the *mozo* who empties the wastebaskets was on holiday.

"I'd better call Dr. Medina."

"You won't find him. He went with him. Everyone is at San Felipe." She laughed nervously. "The only reason I'm not there too is that I'll get more rest here than chasing children on the beach." She laughed again. There were only two veterinarians in Tecate, and at this moment they were both sipping icy piña coladas under a ramada, or pulling big beautiful halibut out of the water. I rang off.

Desperation triggered a thought, and I dialed Zeferino at the feed store. If anyone knew of a veterinarian in town, he would know how to find him. "Zeferino, listen, I need a favor." I shouted into the phone to overcome the sound of frying eggs on the line. "I have a very sick cow and—"

"And Cruz and Medina are wiggling their toes in the surf at San Felipe, *sí*?"

"How did you know?"

"Holy Week. It's going to be very difficult. We don't have anybody else. Even if we called one from Tijuana forty miles away, I doubt he would make the trip. But let me dig around. I'll find someone—even if it's some unfortunate doctor who came to Tecate for lunch, and I'll send him over *inmediatamente*!"

I thanked him and put the phone down with no great optimism. I took another look at La Monita. She looked pitiful, but I decided that if we had to wait, time would go faster if we were busy.

Chemo and I were up on the water tower when we looked up to see a spiral of yellow dust and the glare of the sun on a windshield. A pickup truck that looked like it was good for another fourteen miles pulled up to the barn. Zeferino had found a veterinarian. My spirits soared!

"You are the doctor?" I inquired when he stepped out and we shook hands. I noticed the engine continued running in fits and spasms after he turned the key.

"*Sí*, I am the *veterinario*. Zeferino tells me you have a very sick animal." The pickup went into convulsions, the engine coughed, then expired.

He arrived dressed in tan chinos and a white guayabera blouse. He wore a wilted sombrero. His face was the color of dark cavendish, the hair straight and black as licorice. Something about the face was familiar. I knew I'd seen that face before. But where?

"What seems to be the problem?"

He spoke from beneath a black thicket of wild ragweed hanging from his upper lip. Now it came to me. I knew that face—Pancho Villa!—the notorious revolutionary of Mexican song and legend. The resemblance was so remarkable I knew I was guilty of staring.

"Follow me and I'll show you the patient." I led Pancho Villa into the barn where La Monita was deteriorating rapidly. I explained the events of the last few days. Pancho Villa said nothing. He looked at the animal, cupped his chin in his hand and cocked one leg in thought. He raked his fingers through his thick hair.

"This cow is dying."

I felt sick. "What is wrong with her?"

"She has obviously swallowed nails or wires, and all the

churning in the rumen has lodged the foreign body into the opening of the reticulum."

"That is what she has been trying to tell me!" Chemo blurted.

This remark startled Pancho Villa. He turned to me with a question on his face, but I made no attempt at an explanation. He placed his hand on the cow's back and applied pressure. She grunted painfully and nearly sank to her knees. "The symptoms are unmistakable. If we operate immediately, we might save her."

"Do it!"

Pancho Villa went to his pickup and returned with his medical bag. He made no attempt at conversation. He loaded two syringes with anesthetic and injected them subcutaneously in the lumbar region. He waited silently for the anesthetic to do its work. La Monita remained standing. Presently he poked the point of the scissors in several places and elicited no response. "*Bueno,*" was his only comment.

On his second trip to his truck he came back without his hat and with a length of garden hose. He cupped his chin again and contemplated the left side of the animal. With a wad of cotton he cleansed a site on the cow's flank. He held a scalpel in his right hand. Now he spoke, and he sounded like the voice-over narration on a medical film. "The rumen is a huge elastic bag that holds, in liquid form, everything the cow has eaten. The rumen can hold the contents of that fifty-five-gallon drum you have over there. Now, we don't want gallons of muck running into the incision, then we would kill her for sure. So, I will make a small incision above the water line, and we'll drain her. Hold your nose."

In a quick, accurate move the scalpel made the incision. I handed him the hose and he slipped it into the wound. He fed several feet of hose into the rumen like a plumber would drain a laundry sink.

Immediately, green muck spewed out the end of the hose. A huge puddle of slime began to form on the ground. It was vile. The evil fumes made our eyes burn, and while I cannot reliably say what his stomach was doing, mine was doing cartwheels.

The smell was intolerable, but apparently not for all. Every fly with an acquired taste for fermented cud came to the orgy. They arrived by the thousands in huge buzzing waves. They must have come from as far away as Texas because in a few minutes you couldn't see the wet stain on the ground. It was lost to sight by layers of humming flies. They sounded like a Mahler symphony for large orchestra, organ, and mixed choir.

When the size of the swamp satisfied Pancho Villa, he removed the hose and threw it to one side. This disturbed the flies but only for an instant. He now took the scalpel and lengthened the incision another ten inches. Clamps and retractors held back the flesh.

I had no idea what was to follow, and the narration track had stopped. When Pancho Villa removed his blouse, I assumed he was getting too warm or he didn't want to get it soiled. I couldn't believe what I saw him do. He poked his hand through the gaping wound, and soon his entire arm disappeared into the animal up to his armpit!

The surgeon's facial expressions were sufficient narration. I could see the obvious strain in his face as he groped in the wet darkness of the enormous bovine rumen. He pressed farther into the animal, and had to push his cheek against the wound to lengthen his reach. He was unaware or unconcerned that the side of his face and hair were covered with rumen slime and blood. Now the eyes squeezed tight to heighten the acuity of the fingertips. He bit down on his lip. The tension suspended breathing. Long minutes passed. I was holding my breath too. Suddenly, the eyes opened to announce triumph.

Slowly, a brown arm coated with green slime came sliding out of the wound. In the dripping hand he held a ten-inch skein of barbed wire, a rusty nail, and a three-inch carriage bolt.

I was seized by a sudden paroxysm of giddiness and I began to laugh involuntarily. I wanted to shout, I wanted to applaud. "How did you know? Have we saved her?"

He may not have heard me. He placed the trophies in a pail of water, swished his hand, and prepared to thread a needle. He sutured the enormous wound with two rows of tiny stitches any seamstress would be proud to claim as her own.

Chemo brought him two buckets of clean water, a bar of Lava soap, and a towel. If it were my arm and my hand, I probably would never use it again. The doctor added a glug of strong disinfectant to the water. When he was thoroughly washed and dried, Pancho Villa slipped into his blouse and replaced his sombrero.

"I think we caught her just in time."

"But how did all that get in her?"

"Well, cows aren't like horses. Horses, you notice, have very agile lips. They can maneuver their flexible muzzle deep into a pile of hay and sort all the choice bits just like a ten-year-old *muchacho* can sort out all the vegetables he doesn't like out of a *picadillo*. But a cow, with no upper teeth and a stiff muzzle, bolts down everything in the feed bin like a vacuum cleaner. What always amazes me is that it goes right through the esophagus without harm."

"Can it happen again, Doctor?"

"Not to this animal. I left a small but powerful magnet lying in the rumen. She will eat more hardware, to be sure, but it will cling harmlessly to the magnet that, for its weight, will lie at the bottom of the rumen."

"I can't thank you enough, Pancho, err, Doctor. What do I owe you?"

"That can wait. I will be by tomorrow morning and look in on her."

"How long for recovery?"

"We may have been too late with the surgery. But cows heal quickly. If she doesn't die tonight, you can be sure she is restored as good as new."

I can tell you I didn't sleep much that night. Long before the morning light came to take away the stars, I crept toward the barn. I might as well know if I should put fresh hay in the feed box or have Chemo start digging a deep hole. The aroma of coffee reached me from somewhere. As I slipped into the barn, I found Chemo watching La Monita with mist in his eyes and a cup of fresh coffee in his hand. The coffeepot stood on a little fire he prepared in the corner of the adobes.

His voice was so gentle he could have been speaking to a child. "See, *chiquita*, I told you everything would be all right." He became aware of my presence. "Isn't she beautiful? She says she is feeling much better."

I tilted the coffeepot over a tin cup and took a swallow. La Monita was eating ravenously. Her tail switched in all directions. Once she pulled her head out of the feed bin to look at me with bright eyes, but hunger overcame social refinements and she returned to the business at hand.

"I didn't expect to see anyone so early."

We both turned in the direction of the voice. Pancho Villa walked into the barn. "She was on my mind all night."

He went over to La Monita, ran his hand affectionately over her back, examined the incision. "We're out of danger—*¡qué bárbaro!*—the coffee smells good!"

Chemo put a cup in his hand, I poured. "You performed a miracle, you know."

"Hardly a miracle, but *sí*, I am satisfied."

When we had finished coffee, speculations, and praises, Pancho Villa administered a heavy dose of antibiotics. "Just to be on the good side of safety."

"Well, Doctor, I couldn't be more pleased. What do I owe you?" I was fully expecting the fee to be excessive under the circumstances, but I no longer cared. La Monita was saved.

"Medications came to a hundred thousand pesos and my fee is the same."

Two hundred thousand pesos was slightly more than sixty-five U.S. dollars! I was incredulous. I paid him, we shook hands all around. Pancho Villa slipped behind the wheel of his spastic vehicle and rumbled down the dirt road against the pink of a newborn sun. The incident of the cow took its place among the many crises and disasters common on a ranch that frighten before they fade into obscurity. Life returned to normal.

A few days later I was entering Mexico with a car full of groceries. "*Buenos días,*" I said to Big Caca with a melodious chirp that in my view compared favorably with that of the Mexican golden-breasted pewee listed in Harper & Row's *Wildlife Guide* as a melodious warbler, *chi-chi tee-wee, kee*!

Big Caca did not chirp in return. Nor did he warble *buenos días*. His demeanor was more like that of a turkey vulture, which, according to the same authority, eats dead flesh.

By now Big Caca stood alone in the limelight of mockery, and all Tecate was laughing at him. More than anything in the world Big Caca wanted to be feared. He feasted on fear, he hungered for respect, and he was now obliged to eat the bitter broth of ridicule. This was more than he could endure, and he defrayed his losses with hostility.

"Open your *cajuela*!" he snarled. The words curdled on his fat lips. It was a command from a man sadly lacking a sense of humor. He followed me to the back of the car, and I threw open the trunk. He stared into an empty compartment with a freshly vacuumed blue carpet. He pulled the carpet away with a malevolent gesture, and saw only a spare tire of undisputed virginity.

"*¡Adelante!*" he growled, and I drove into Mexico with my brand new Sony VCR tucked away under the grocery bags.

As I got to the main street I had the misfortune of getting stuck behind a huge vehicle impersonating a municipal sanitation truck. It looked almost real. It flaunted the red, white, and green seal of public works and crept behind two men who were throwing trash into the front loading bucket. But the impostor was uncovered, and a blizzard of trash was flying out the back, leaving the street behind it as littered as before.

But I was still tingling with elation. I simply couldn't wait to get to the news desk and tell the boys of my triumph. Maybe it was a slow news day. My story would give Zeferino a chuckle and Tito comfort.

Parking in Tecate is becoming pie-in-the-face of reason. I would have to park on the other side of the plaza and walk back to the feed store. The sun was celebrating the merry month of May, and when I stepped out of the car, I was caught in a veritable downpour of solar rays that were beginning to melt the pavement. I made for the square and took refuge in the shade of a huge yucateco. It was here that I was overpowered by a popsicle pusher who lay waiting in ambush behind the fountain.

Ting-a-ling, ting-a-ling ling! "¡Popsicles! . . . mango . . . papaya . . . melón . . . limón . . . chocolate!"

Here, I thought, was the only thing in Tecate that didn't misrepresent itself, the ubiquitous popsicle fleet. The little unassuming pushcarts were painted an honest white, a bright red popsicle on the side panel plainly disclosed its purpose. And when the purveyor opened the small door, he withdrew nothing less than a popsicle as promised. Here was Beauty, Truth, and Love in one!

I felt my glands prepare for the expected treat consistent with that elusive scientist's famous paper, "Demonstration of the Conditioned Reflex" (1902). Now I remember his name—Pavlov—of course! I had him confused with Papanicolaou, the medical scientist who is known to every woman by his abbreviated name. He was awarded the Nobel Prize. Not the one who saved the lives of a million women, but the one who discovered that a dog will drool when anticipating a chop.

"Mango, por favor."

"¡Sí, señor!" The dark face looked up at me from under the shade of a floppy sombrero of yellow straw and beamed a smile.

I had a sudden momentary shock. I was looking into a face I knew—Pancho Villa! "Doctor! What are you doing here?"

"Earning my daily tortilla."

"But I don't understand. You are a veterinarian—you saved my cow, remember?"

"An imposter, a fraud, saved your cow." He saw confusion on my face. "It is the usual tragedy here in my beloved Mexico. I was only a year away from graduating with my MVZ credential when the devaluation came. We all lost our jobs, and I was forced to quit school. Now we do whatever work is available. I came north to the border, my papá stayed in Michoacan. He is an accountant, but today he waits tables. My mamá does ironing."

I was overcome with embarrassment. "But you will go back, sí, and get your degree?" I said optimistically.

"It is no longer possible. I am married now. We are expecting our first in three months. No, no, that dream is for another to realize. Practicing medicine on your cow was illegal. I could be sent to jail."

"But you did it."

"*Sí*, but that was an *emergencia*." He opened the lid to his cart, and for a moment his face disappeared behind a puff of white vapor. He withdrew a popsicle of deep luminous orange lightly dusted with frost. "*Mango*, wasn't it?"

The Man
in White

It is probably safe to say that every town in the world has a restaurant that one day becomes all the rage and remains so for years for no reason that's immediately apparent. Why La Fonda should become center stage for the society of Tecate is an undisclosed mystery. *Inexplicable!* La Fonda's eminence in mediocre fare stands unchallenged to this day. Nor is the service efficient, as the staff is not acquainted with this agreeable state and the citizens of Tecate wouldn't recognize it. But the sincerity and cordiality of the waiters flows unrestrained from the depths of their hearts. When your waiter says, "How are things?" (and he will), he really wants to know. Is Tía Maria over the *gripa*, did you get your car running? It matters. When your waiter is obliged to bring you the news that they are out of mushrooms, he nearly weeps. But the *ambiente* is all that could be desired. The mariachis come in here every night and bring with them that unique musical form, violins that cry and wring your heart, and a little fat man on trumpet that can melt bone marrow. There is a subtle tinkling of tableware,

131

a golden light glimmering on familiar faces, warm laughter, a mixed chorus of voices conversing above and below the vivid melodic colors of the mariachis. The scene touches all the human emotions.

But La Fonda is more than a restaurant to me. I've come to regard it as my private cable TV channel. The dramatic *novela* that unfolds here in the large dining room night after night is a tangled web of romance, intrigue, trysts and triangles, and power struggles. It's a long-run show, and I try not to miss a single episode.

I call your attention to that young couple holding hands across the table, lost in the abyss of each other's eyes, alone in the crowd. She looks so sweet and feminine in her crisp pink sundress. But she also looks fragile and vulnerable. Look, he presses his forehead to hers, and empties his soul. Isn't that adorable? You don't need a sound track to know he is pledging his ever-abiding love, a love that will continue to burn until the sun itself expires. A gorgeous girl, soft face, soft lips, softer breast, eyes misty with the dew of a virgin's dreams. What sweet deception! He's known here as the Prince. It's a quarter to nine, they're leaving now. Notice how he kisses her fingertips as they get up. Please make some effort to contain your prurient thoughts as that lovely creature passes our table. There they go— look—the poor thing can't feel the ground under her feet. In an hour the Prince of Lies will be back with a fresh new flower.

When the waiter steps aside, you'll see a portly gentleman with his family. He's wearing an expensive gray suit and his radiant scalp rivals a sunrise in the desert. What well-behaved children. Look, he's helping his wife with her shawl. How attentive! If he's not careful, his lolling red tongue will fall straight into the gazpacho the way he's gurgling and gushing and fawning all over his in-laws. Isn't he charming? No one would ever doubt the sincerity of that buttery mouth that misrepresents the man. He was here last night with that chunky little Tina Martínez from the bank. You know the one I mean, dark, curly hair, looks like she's hiding *mangos* in her dress. They didn't leave until two-thirty this morning, and even the mariachis were beginning to fade.

Ah! Look who just walked in the door, and they're headed for the corner table. I thought it was a meteor! That tall military officer with the silver mustache, all starched and pressed into the cardboard uniform with all the sparklers, is Comandante Pedroza, chief of the Mexican border station. In broad daylight he can blind you. See the two men with him? They have a pickup truck standing by on the U.S. side with a refrigerator waiting to cross into Mexico. When they have sated his lust for food and drink, the comandante will quote the amount of his bribe. After coffee and brandy they'll leave. Payment will be made in the darkness of the parking lot, and the refrigerator will be humming in someone's kitchen tomorrow. Can Pedroza really believe that no one here knows what he's doing? It couldn't be more obvious if the comandante marched in here wearing glossy eyeliner and black net panty hose.

See what I mean about a long-run soap? When you can look without being too obvious, I would like to direct your attention to the table on the far wall. See the American with the reddish hair and the zippy rugby shirt? At the moment he seems enraptured with that dark-haired chili pepper with the dangly earrings. He's a U.S. customs inspector. You'll see him tomorrow standing tall under Old Glory in his blue uniform, searching vehicles for illegal drugs. When he gets off duty at six o'clock, he goes straight home to the little wife and kiddies. But he has another life on this side of the border. By nine o'clock he's here with *numero dos*. The mariachis love him. He spends more on music than anyone here. Recognize the song they're playing for her? "Tú Solo Tú"! Can you believe it? You know why they call him Cenicienta—Cinderella? He must certainly be aware of the appellation. Because he must flee before the clock strikes twelve. No, his car won't turn into a *calabaza*, the border closes at midnight!

I honestly don't understand how this little town holds in all these explosives. I mean, why doesn't it just blow up? Probably because all these events haven't been compressed into high-density secrets waiting for a spark of emotion to set them off. Everything we see here is accepted as normal and as unremarkable as the water in the aquarium is to the occupants.

But these little vignettes of human folly, entertaining as they can be, are not all that interesting to me. See the large table at the center of the dining room? There is the mayor, I see, his male secretary, the judge who's already smashed. The one with his back to us is the district attorney. The other two men I don't recognize. But now observe that formidable gentleman at the head of the table, the man in white, who looks like he's dressed for his first communion. He's wearing a white guayabera and white pants. Notice the white shoes and socks, and we must assume he's wearing white underwear. Now, his is truly an extraordinary story, a story of true love, of life and death, and noble deeds. I made his acquaintance only recently when we met quite by chance in the ladies' room.

Notice how the liquor is flowing. See how the man in white stays with them drink for drink. But I can tell you he's drinking pure tamarind water on the rocks. Alcohol has not passed his lips in nearly twenty-five years. He's the richest man in Tecate. When the governor comes here to dinner, the man in white is at his table. He carries a great deal of weight in local politics. He owns Bancatec, the bank across the street, several blocks of downtown real estate, a large factory that assembles electronic components for Motorola, a radio station . . . there's no end.

The man in white is known as *hombre de palabra*. His word is his contract, and it's wrought in gold. He'll make a million-dollar deal on his word alone. If you need a favor and he says he'll do it, it's done. When the school desperately needed a gymnasium, they came to the man in white for a donation. He said he would build them one, and six months later the students were practicing slam dunks.

It happened that the day we met, the men's room was out of order, a not infrequent occurrence at La Fonda. When this happens, the restaurant owner's wife, that attractive woman in the clingy lavender pantsuit, stands at the door to the ladies' room, and if it is all clear, shakes a little silver bell, the cue for those gentlemen in need of relief.

I learned his name is Rodolfo Fernandez. At first I expected to find him a little cold and distant, especially toward a stranger. But no, the acquaintance was made easily. He's extremely pleasant and affable. He even revealed a keen sense of humor. As he walked into a stall he said, "I suppose we are expected to sit down." He was hospitable enough to invite me to his house the following week. And from his own lips came the story I'm about to tell you.

He lives on the outer edges of Tecate. I arrived at eleven o'clock as requested. The house itself is an enormous colonial structure built around a central courtyard ablaze with roses, enormous red hibiscus, and purple clematis. I felt like I was riding a float in the Pasadena Rose Parade. Baskets overflowing with giant orange begonias illuminated the niches in the shaded archways. A pretty peasant girl with a Mona Lisa smile made of pink stone poured water into a large fountain faced with brilliant blue and yellow tiles.

He received me in his *estancia*, easily fifty feet in length. I have never seen anything as white as his clothes. The chalk-white blouse vibrated against a magnificent face modeled of red clay. I got the impression I was looking at a life-size terra-cotta bust mounted on an alabaster pedestal. He looked like Anthony Quinn. He had the eyes of a man who had allowed life to teach without destroying him. His teeth were large, whiter than the blouse. But when he smiled, you got the feeling someone had just put their arms around you. It occurred to me this man had to be close to sixty years old, and other than a faded scar on his forehead, his skin was flawless. Black hair, straight and glossy as a raven's wings covered his head. I didn't see a single gray strand. His upper lip was innocent of hair.

"Enter your poor and humble house."

I nearly laughed, but caught myself. One look into those soft and gentle eyes and you knew he was unaware of the irony in his greeting. Those were the same words that greeted a guest when his house *was* humble. "*Gracias*," I answered.

"Will you have *almuerzo?*"

"*Gracias*." The "no" was built into the inflection, and he understood I'd either had my breakfast or I was too polite to accept his kindness.

"Will you accept some coffee?"

"*Gracias*." Same word, different inflection, and he instantly understood the affirmative. We sank into big comfortable leather chairs looking out on the courtyard through the French panes. The room was filled with the pleasant fragrance of cedar. An Indian maid in a full red skirt floated in and served coffee with a plate of little dome-shaped *pan dulce* and floated out again.

His story really begins when he was five years old. He was entered into kindergarten as Rodolfo, but his mother called him by the more affectionate Rodolfito, and the diminutive immediately became Fito to all who knew him, including his teacher, who adored him. She welcomed him in a singsong falsetto, an affectation common to all Mexican elementary teachers and intended to put little children at their ease. "Would you like to play with pretty blocks? Or would you rather color? We have a lot of crayons and lots of pretty colored paper."

Fito was too shy to reply directly. He looked down at his feet and whispered, "Color."

His teacher sat him on a rug with two other little boys. One boy was busy coloring, the other lost in a fantasy with a little plastic car. "This is Fito," she sang to the two boys. "And this is Concepción and Carlitos." She left the three boys and crossed the classroom to organize another group.

Fito shyly selected a crayon and began to scrawl on a large sheet of bright yellow paper. The three boys amused themselves independently for a while. Presently the boy called Carlitos turned to the boy named Concepción and snatched the car out of his hands. Concepción looked like he was going to cry and yet he didn't. Instead he took a crayon and began to color. The little bully then put down the car and snatched the crayon away. "¡*Mío!*" he cried. Concepción then timidly went back to the car. But the bully was quick to grab it back. "¡*Mío!*" He held the car firmly in his grip and the crayons with the other hand in triumph. Concepción now had nothing at all and looked crushed. His lower lip began to tremble. The big dark eyes grew even larger and they filled with salty tears.

Fito looked uncomfortable. He put down his drawing and drew closer to the two boys. Fito didn't utter a word. He simply repeated what his big brothers did to him on occasion. He gave the bully a quick *coscorrón*, one word freighted with meaning, a sharp rap across the head with the knuckles. The bully fled without making a sound. Fito picked up the toy car and put it in the little hand. Concepción gave Fito a smile a mile wide and received one in return. Concepción was overcome with an emotion he couldn't yet understand, and gave Fito his new lunch box with Walt Disney's Ratoncito Mickey cartoons. Then and there the golden ingot of friendship that was to last a lifetime was poured and cast into the chalice of each heart.

From that day forward they became *inseparables*. No one ever saw one when he was not in the company of the other. They ate at each other's house, and so often spent the night that each became like a sibling. When either mother was looking for her son, she would ask, "Has anyone see *los gemelos*." The twins. It didn't matter which one was found. Finding one found them both.

All through school Concepción was the class clown. He enjoyed the attention it brought him, and though sometimes it came with penalties, it rewarded him with a delicious moment of infamy. In the early *primaria* years he'd hide a toy car in his desk, only to get caught playing with it and have it taken away. He would talk to Fito and entertain anyone around him without the slightest petition. The teacher finally put Fito on the other side of the room, but that didn't prevent Concepción from being sociable.

One afternoon Fito noticed that no one was paying attention to the teacher. The teacher noticed it too. There seemed to be something interesting going on around Concepción's desk. Realizing she had lost her audience, the teacher spoke. "Concepción, there seems to be an inordinate amount of activity in the vicinity of your desk."

Suddenly all the students scrambled back to their seats like startled squirrels. Concepción shot upright, geography book snapped open, eyes intense, ears pricked up intelligently. The teacher now stood above him, and there on the top of his desk was the cause of all the commotion. Little crinkled wads of colored red and green tissue paper were crawling across the top of his desk. There must have been at least four or five zipping in every direction without apparent means of propulsion. The teacher thought she would sweep them off onto the floor, but as she went after them, the little creatures would suddenly zigzag in the opposite direction as though equipped with some highly classified sensing device.

"You're much too old to be making *toritos*, Concepción. You may now come up and sit next to me for the remainder of the class." She brought out a headband with the enormous ears of a jackass and placed it on his head.

The entire class giggled. Concepción was burning with embarrassment. Fito could only feel sorry for him. When the teacher had said *toritos*, he knew at once that Concepción had caught a number of flies and wrapped them in tissue paper. The flies couldn't develop enough lift to become airborne, but they could scurry across a school desk at amazing speeds.

The boys earned pocket money by gambling behind the outbuilding that housed the rest rooms. Each boy would put down ten centavos and pee. The one producing the most abundant foam picked up all the stakes. Both boys developed remarkable skills for this contest. They were always sure of their candy money when they were lucky enough to enter the foam tournaments. But as often happens when the students have a good thing going, the faculty got wind of it and put a stop to it.

One afternoon after school, Fito brought Concepción some electrifying news. He was nearly breathless and trembled with excitement. "Guess what? I know a girl who will show us her *chocha* for fifty centavos. Let's go right now!"

"Where will I ever get fifty centavos? The foam game is over."

And that's how it was that Fito and Concepción went into their first business venture. They shined shoes on weekends, and nearly all the proceeds went to Anamaría, Fito's new discovery. Anamaría was an exceptionally pretty girl with the sad misfortune of having been born with a club foot. The humiliating limp excommunicated her from the society of her peers.

Together the two boys shared all the adventures and misadventures of growing up. For a while they played in the junkyards, where they would get into various cars, and Concepción would pretend to drive them. His passion for cars had not diminished. "I'm going to be a taxi driver when I'm older," he would say. Occasionally one or two tough types would threaten them, and Fito would have to fight them off so Concepción could get a head start for safety. Concepción always needed looking after.

One Sunday morning the friendship nearly came to an end. It was saved only by an act of divine intervention. In those days what is now the public park was an enormous *cienega*. The swamp teemed with fish and turtles and all sorts of crawly things to delight young boys. The water fowl, ducks, egrets, and herons that fed, bred, and played there were unaware they would soon become an endangered species. The tules grew so tall and thick in some places you couldn't see the water they grew in, and parts of the *cienega* looked like a vast green meadow.

There is no doubt that every boy who grew up in Tecate has had his *nalgas* blistered by one or both parents for going near the *cienega*. Fito and Concepción were no exception. But the chastening failed to dampen that childhood insouciance that is so impervious to reality.

They walked around the edge of the marsh that quiet Sunday morning, poking sticks into the wet mud or throwing them like boomerangs at startled birds. Fito found a rusted wheel from a child's wagon. "Here's the great Olympian discus thrower!" and he hurled it across the swamp. It came down with a spectacular splash that would please any boy.

Concepción was first to spot a rotting plank half submerged in the sticky mud. It was a waterlogged two-by-six about six feet in length. Concepción pulled it free, balanced himself carefully, and pushed off. He was surprised to see how effortlessly he glided into deeper water.

"Hey, look at this! Here's the great Balboa off to discover new lands in the name of Spain!" At that point the board split down the middle and the intrepid explorer was in swamp water over his head and screaming for his life.

Fito looked up to see his friend of a lifetime drowning in front of his very eyes. Ten thousand volts of fear jolted through his body and left him paralyzed. A bloodred scream took form in his throat but never came out. He was blinded by a flood of tears, and in his panic forgot that he too didn't know how to swim. Fear remained on the shore while the boy with a man's heart dog-paddled out to his friend and threw his arms around him. To help him or to die with him? No one will ever know.

"It's all right, it's all right," he soothed, "calm down, stop flailing. I'll get you out."

It was a lie, but the noblest of lies, well-intended and filled with love as much as with his own hopes. Concepción always listened to Fito. He stopped churning for a short minute, allowing Fito to take possession of him. Fito himself wasn't sure of anything. In desperation he grabbed the one remaining splinter of the plank and drove it into the soft mud bottom. Immediately both boys realized they could hang on the pole and keep their heads above the water. They couldn't go anywhere, but for the moment, at least, they could breathe. Fito wasn't even aware that a nail in the board had gashed his forehead and that he would carry the scar the rest of his life.

As it has been suggested, an agency of a higher order assumed command at this point. A man and his young son who were on their way across town decided at that moment to take the shortcut by way of the *cienega*. The driver assessed the scene immediately. He ordered his son out of the truck, put the pedal to the floor, and drove his pickup directly into the swamp until it was mired to the fenders in wet clay. It was close enough to allow the boys to dog-paddle the short distance and climb in.

The boy on shore knew exactly what to do. He ran out on the main road and flagged down another pickup. Now it only became a matter of rope and muscle, spinning wheels, and a little profanity before they were all on dry land.

"Stay in the pickup, I'll take you boys home," the rescuer said, and they drove away. The boys were pale and cold, and the reality of how close they had come to dying hadn't reached them yet. They rattled along in silence. When the cistern on the corner of their street came into view, they knew they were nearly there, and each boy pondered the same dilemma. There was no place to go but home. But whose? Where would the punishment that was sure to follow be the least severe? But as often happens in crucial decisions, the choice was made for them. Their benefactor dropped them in front of Fito's house. Immediately Concepción began to feel a little more secure. Fito's mother might burn her son's *nalgas*, but certainly not his. It would have been the reverse at his house, of course. They were wet, muddy, cold, and beginning to shake.

Fito's mother removed their soggy clothes, cleaned them up, and put them on the sofa with plenty of warm blankets and a steaming cup of chocolate. When Concepción's mother arrived, he took one look at her face and panicked. They would now both get it. But he was wrong. He was too young to understand. Relief sublimated anger and both women wept copiously.

The Siamese twins joined at the heart went on to *secundaria* and they completed the required three years of *preparatoria*. At this juncture in their lives they discovered there was more to *chocha* than just looking at it. They went to all the dances, they dated and double-dated. Together they conquered new territory. Soon after they learned about the pleasures of the body, they were seduced by the courtesans of alcohol, and communion with the spirits became a passion.

When drink took possession of Fito, and it didn't require much, a dark and dangerous surrogate stood in his place. With ego leavened by eighty-proof cactus juice, Fito became hostile, belligerent, and worse, unpredictable. The same beverage amended Concepción's character in a totally different way. Concepción became sweeter, more peace-loving, and then he could get very silly. And whenever the two of them went in search of a good time, they exchanged places and Concepción became his best friend's guardian.

The bustling Port of Liverpool is an important trade center and refueling facility that has enjoyed continuous growth and dominance since World War II. The port throbs with activity seven days a week. It lies at the end of a busy estuary off Highway 3. The extensive docking facilities are crowded day and night with horses and pickup trucks moored along its extensive perimeter. It is the oldest cantina in Tecate, yet no one can remember how it came to be christened Puerto de Liverpool. Tecate is forty miles from the nearest body of water.

It was late on a Saturday night when Fito and Concepción decided to put into port for refueling before embarking on the final leg of their journey home. The smoke was dense as November fog in its namesake across the Atlantic. The heavy smells were insufferable for only the first few minutes and were hard to classify. Smoke, beer, tequila, urine, and horse sweat competed for recognition.

Fito and Concepción pushed through the swinging doors, ducked their heads to avoid a flying boot with spur attached, and groped their way to a table. A shapely waitress pulled up to their side and they ordered the house red turpentine. She returned shortly, put two glasses in front of them and turned to talk to another table.

"*Salud.*"

"*Provecho.* This will have to be the stirrup cup."

"Why, you drunk?"

"And we're out of money."

A dark man who had a remarkable resemblance to a shrunken head, and drunk beyond redemption, was seated at the next table. He slobbered his drink and turned to admire the rear end of the waitress who was still chatting. He blinked his eyes and noticed that her skirt had adhered to the contours of her *nalgas* and left a deep groove between the two hemispheres. He gently pulled the fabric away and smoothed the surface with the palm of his hand. The waitress turned her head instantly. She did not give voice, but the glare could have left him blind.

The stranger then quickly ran the edge of his hand down the full length of her *nalgas* and replaced the groove. "All right, all right—I put it back the way it was!"

The waitress whipped around and was about to settle up when Fito interceded. "Keep your dirty hands to yourself!"

"Ah, look at this, the stallion is rearing up on his hind legs." The shrunken head croaked, "Your *madre*!"

"I am going to have to put you in your place."

"If you think you're hombre enough—you got the *cojones*?"

"I've got the *cojones* and the biggest *pito* here!" Fito shouted loud enough to get everyone's attention.

"Correction," the shrunken head hissed, "I have the biggest *pito* here—seven inches of machismo!"

"You must be a señorita, I carry a ten!" Fito yelled back and grabbed the edge of the table and threw it against the stranger.

The drunkard was now on his feet. "You have committed *un grave error*, señor." He was waving a gun.

Concepción could see the fuse sizzling toward the powder, and shouted to every man in the cantina. "All of you in here are liars, fakes, and *cabrónes*! I have the biggest *pito* here!"

The entire cantina was stunned into silence. You could hear a pin drop. Everyone froze in place for an instant. Fito couldn't believe what he'd just witnessed.

"You!" the shrunken head shouted.

"Me!"

"How big, *cabrón?*"

"Nearly four inches!" Then Concepción added, "From the floor, *cabrón!*"

The laughter came in huge waves, and Concepción knew he had disarmed the unexploded bomb. Those few moments of delay in the proceedings provided enough time for the *judicial federal* to make their appearance and haul them all off to the *hotel municipal* for bed and breakfast.

Fito charged through life like a knight errant of the Third Crusade. Concepción, on the other hand, remained shy. He cried when Fito cried, laughed when he laughed. Fito was his universe, and Concepción followed in his assigned orbit.

It was the custom then, and still is today, to take your intended to the Romeria, an annual ball given in June at the local gymnasium. Fito and Concepción arrived with two gorgeous dark-eyed señoritas on their arms and high hopes in their hearts. The only fly in the flan was the presence of their girls' older brothers, traditional guardians of virtue in Mexican society.

"Tonight I ask Leti to marry me," Fito confided at the urinals during intermission. "And maybe her big brute of a brother will stop threatening to tear my head off and throw it in the Tecate River."

"And this very night, if I can give her brother Gregorio the slip, I propose marriage to Adela. I hope she doesn't say no."

Fito laid out the plan. "During the first dance after intermission, we'll arrange with Leti and Adela to slip away together and meet us out back of the equipment room. There, we will pledge our troth."

Immediately following the Chickenhawk Polka, Fito and Concepción casually strolled outside and waited behind the equipment room as arranged. In a few minutes Leti arrived in a frothy pink dress and her eyes full of stars.

"Where's Adela?" Concepción asked.

"We got separated. I thought she was already here," Leti answered.

"I don't want to go back in there," Concepción said. "Adela's brother Gregorio will see me."

"I better go back and find her," Fito said, and disappeared.

Concepción and Leti waited silently, each wrapped in their own dreams. The balmy night smelled of jasmine, the sky sparkled with stars, flying insects fluttered happily, enjoying the summer evening. Among those fluttering was a giant Mexican princess moth with a defective navigational system. The princess became tangled in Leti's abundant hair.

"Help me get the thing out of my hair!" she screamed.

Concepción was doing the best he could to comply. They both assumed the footsteps they heard to be those of Fito returning. They were in error. When Leti's behemoth brother Bruno came around the corner of the building, he saw his sister with her head buried in Concepción's chest while he groped in her hair with both hands. Concepción recognized him at once and remembered that Bruno had a perverted passion for separating heads from bodies and throwing them in the Tecate River.

"Get inside, Leticia," Bruno growled to his sister. She obeyed immediately.

"It isn't at all what you think, Bruno. Very often things present a totally different appearance."

"I'll tear you apart! Part of you is going swimming!"

"Now, Bruno. We knew each other in school. Your family knows my family. I buy all my shoes at your papá's store."

Bruno lunged toward him while Concepción continued his effort to open dialogue. "See these shoes? I got them at your papá's store only last week. How do you like the stitching? They pinch a little here at the big toe, but your papá—and he is an expert—said they would stretch out."

"I intend to put you in the hospital tonight!"

"I love your shoes—is that real leather?"

Bruno grabbed him and turned him upside down. Concepción could hear the contents of his pockets spilling on the blacktop. He had little doubt that his head would soon be shooting the rapids of the Tecate River. He squirmed away and began running at high speed around the dark environs of the gymnasium. He could hear the orchestra playing "Guantanamera," and felt he would much rather be inside dancing with his sweetheart than out here fleeing for his life. He ran into the darkened parking lot and rolled under a low-riding Chevy. He'd seen cats do this when avoiding the punk schnauzers who terrorized the neighborhood, and he was glad the maneuver worked for him.

An eternity later, when Concepción was convinced he was safe, he crawled out, found his own car, and jumped in with his heart pounding. He would have locked the doors if the locks worked. Before his díastolic and systolic readings could return to normal, the door on the other side opened and a dark man slid in beside him. Concepción's heart froze and he quickly turned to stone. Then and there he commended his soul to God.

"Fito!"

"Concepción! You scared me into the next life! What are you doing here?"

"I just barely managed to keep my head from going for a swim without me. God! What happened to you? You have no pants on!"

"I just had a very narrow escape. I ran into Bruno and Adela's brother Gregorio. This place is infested with brothers." Fito pulled his bottle of macho fuel from under the seat and lowered the level significantly prior to replying. He spoke in breathless gasps. "I'm lucky to be alive. The *cabrónes* stole my pants and threw them in the cistern!"

"What do we do now?"

"You don't have to do anything, but I intend to settle the score." Fito reached under the seat and withdrew a heavy tire iron. He returned the bottle to his lips. Concepción saw that Fito was standing on the slippery edge of an ugly mood.

"Calm yourself, Fito, don't go off like a horse unbridled."

"Nobody offends Fito without paying the price."

Concepción saw the bottle go up again and knew what Fito would be like in only a few minutes, crazy mad and uncontrollable. "Listen! They're playing 'Vals de Amor.'" Then the mouse roared. "Quick! Put on my pants and get in there and propose to Leti now!"

"What about you and Adela?"

"Don't worry about me. If you happen to see Adela, propose to her on my behalf. You'll probably do it better anyway." Concepción jumped out of the pants and Fito jumped in. "But I'll need my keys—where are my keys?"

"Time is running out!"

"I'll worry about the keys later. Just go!"

Fito obliged. Concepción heaved a sigh of relief and be-crossed himself.

Concepción now turned his attention to his keys. They could be anywhere, but the most likely place to start look-ing was behind the equipment room where he scuffled with that Neanderthal Bruno. In the relative safety of darkness he could take a quick look at the scene of the confronta-tion. He headed in that direction.

The summer air felt cool and unfamiliar on Concepción's bare legs as he groped the blacktop behind the equipment room. The angels were on his side tonight. The keys, along with all his small change, lay where they fell. He scooped them up. Normally, he would have put the keys in his pocket, but this was not practicable under the circumstances, and he dropped them into his Jockey shorts. They felt icy cold.

The sound of footsteps dangerously close caused his left ventricle to snap shut like a mousetrap and he found it dif-ficult to breathe. If it was Bruno . . . he was about to have his body rearranged. If it was Fito and the girls, he felt un-derdressed for the occasion. Once more he took the exam-ple set by cats who survive by virtue of an agile mind, and leaped into a large metal trash barrel. He went into a steep dive and settled at the bottom like a submarine. Whoever it was that came on the scene was standing near him, but he didn't dare surface for a peek.

What Concepción couldn't see was that the new arrival was Adela, all alone in her party dress of blue eyelet. "Leti," she whispered, "are you there?" She didn't understand it. She was sure this was where Leti said to meet her. She looked up into the magical night covered with grated sap-phires and a gold crescent moon that promised her every-thing. "I do hope you're listening, Señor Dios. Please bring

Concepción to me tonight. Give him courage to speak his heart. I love him with all my heart, Señor Dios, and promise to be a good wife to him."

It hardly needs to be said. Concepción was so electrified by this bit of good news that he came straight out of the barrel to speak his heart as suggested and seal the proposal with a kiss in the warm summer evening. It also hardly needs to be said that Adela was not expecting anyone to come popping out of a trash barrel. Her scream could be heard all the way to Mexico City.

At almost the same instant, her brother Gregorio presented himself, assessed the scene and attacked. Concepción went into another steep dive, submerged, and shut off all breathing apparatus. It was of little use. Gregorio threw the barrel on its side, and with one good push, sent it rolling down the steep embankment.

Adela screamed again, but Concepción couldn't hear her, as he was gaining speed and the rumbling in the barrel was ear-shattering.

As it turned out, Concepción never did rendezvous with Adela that fun-packed evening of Romeria. Fito too was having problems making connections, and told Concepción to go home without him. Late Sunday morning the two friends met for fish tacos at El Taco Contento, a local taco emporium. "Well?" Concepción inquired while he anointed his fish with salsa, guacamole, shredded cabbage, onion, tomato, cilantro, then baptized it with a squirt of fresh lime.

"Leti said yes," Fito announced in triumph. "And Bruno and I are friends again."

"Congratulations! Oh, happy day!"

"*Gracias*, but now I congratulate you warmly."

"For what?"

"I saw Adela this morning on her way to early mass while you were still making love to your pillow. I asked her for you, and she said yes."

Two happy men in a warm macho embrace after an evening of dining, dancing, and barrel riding is not an unusual sight in Mexico.

A year later Fito and Concepción were married to Leti and Adela respectively in a double wedding ceremony at the Church of Our Lady of Guadalupe. They were barely twenty years old. Their children were born only days apart. The running joke in Tecate was that Fito and Concepción synchronized their lovemaking. Fito's firstborn was a girl, and he asked Concepción and Adela to be the godparents, and thus they became *compadres*. Concepción's firstborn was a son. He asked Fito and Leti to be godparents, and now they were double *compadres*.

As they continued to have children and raise their families, Fito went to work at Banco de Mexico. He began as a teller and worked his way up to senior accountant. Concepción realized his lifelong dream—he became a cab driver. Nothing could have made him happier. They were thirty years old by now, but still every Saturday night belonged to them. They went out on the town, got very drunk, and often greeted Sunday morning in jail—together. Always together.

It was one of those mellow afternoons where life's problems seem to melt away in the warmth of summer's sweet embrace. Fito and Concepción were on their way to their friend Clementino's ranch for a typical all-macho evening of *carne asada*, tequila, and ribald stories. Fito didn't drive and had flatly refused to learn to operate "the devil's evil and traitorous contrivance." Concepción drove them in his taxi, and this gave Concepción one of his rare moments of glory. They arrived in a cloud of red dust. Everybody was already there, Clementino, the host, El Topo, and El Gordo.

"Here comes the guest of honor!" Clementino shouted as the *inseparables* came out of the taxi.

"No, no, the guest of honor is here," Fito cried triumphantly as he produced a bottle of tequila from a paper bag. "I take great pleasure in presenting you to my good friend, José Cuervo!"

"Delighted to make your acquaintance!" Clementino accepted the bottle, uncapped it and gulped before he handed it to El Topo.

El Topo, the gopher, tilted the bottle to thin rodent lips. He got his nickname owing to a remarkable physiognomic resemblance to that species. "Aah, that burns so good!"

"What about me, am I on a milk diet?" El Gordo, the fat one, called out from the campfire.

All the men gathered around El Gordo, who was browning strips of beef over a hot manzanita fire. El Topo handed him the bottle. A stack of corn tortillas and a stone crock of hot salsa were sitting on a broken chair. They ate tacos and drank, and then drank some more. They talked about barley, and tires, and carburetors, and of course women. Bottles of José Cuervo appeared from somewhere, and soon they were all drunk enough to toss the empty bottles up in the air and watch them explode on the rocks like grenades and think it very funny.

The sun was low now, making long shadows. A thousand crickets chirped in a soothing dissonance. Quail rustled in the chaparral as they got ready for bed and the rabbits prepared to go out for the evening. Coyotes bayed from somewhere behind the hill.

Soon their stories became more lurid and more pointless. But the laughter they produced was the genuine laughter of impaired minds. Gradually alcohol began to make changes in their personalities.

Their slurred conversation was interrupted when a startled rabbit scampered across the field at that moment, followed by another, and yet another. "Why did we bother to buy meat? Look at all the rabbits you have here," Fito observed.

"You should see what they do to my crops. Shoot all you want, and I'll put them on the fire," Clementino answered.

"Have you ever tried to shoot one of those demons?" El Topo asked. "It's not as easy as you think. It calls for a sharp eye and a steady hand, like this." He bulged his eyes, exposing the whites, and held out a palsied hand.

"Bring me the rifle," El Gordo said to his host. "I'll get you all the rabbits you want."

The bottle went around again as Clementino went inside the house to get the rifle. "Hey, don't pass up my turn while I'm gone. I know how much was in that bottle!"

"Don't worry, we'll wait for you," El Topo assured him, and they quickly passed José Cuervo around once more. Clementino returned with an old beat-up .22 with a cracked stock and an unaligned sight. A rabbit came out from behind the brush. Clementino aimed, fired, and the animal ran for cover, certainly frightened, but otherwise unscathed.

"You're not supposed to frighten them to death, you're supposed to hit them!" El Gordo teased.

At that moment another rabbit came out running, stopped a moment and stared directly at the men as though confused. BANG! Clementino fired again. But the rabbit didn't move a hair. He remained frozen in place, staring at the crowd of drunks. Everybody doubled up with laughter. "Forget about shooting them, why don't you just take prisoners?" someone cracked, and they all broke into guffaws. They could hardly stand up by now.

"Put another stick on the fire, I'll get your rabbit," Concepción said, and took the rifle.

"You! Concepción, you couldn't possibly know how to shoot," they all jeered at once. But the men just swayed where they stood and watched Concepción raise the rifle to one eye.

A small cottontail nibbled at a tender slip of grass. BANG! The rabbit flipped over and fell dead instantly. "That's how it's done, señores," Concepción crowed with drunken bravado. Concepción was as surprised by his marksmanship as the late rabbit. All the men cheered him, slapped him on the back and handed him the bottle. The approval of his friends made him glow.

"All right, here comes the next victim!" Fito slurred, and took the rifle from Concepción.

"Be careful, *compadre*, it's loaded," Concepción said in a hush. He didn't want the others to hear.

Fito's roaring reply negated the precaution. "I know what I'm doing. I was shooting rabbits before any of you were born!" Roars of laughter followed. They were all about the same age. "Now we just wait patiently for an unfortunate rabbit to come into my view."

And so they waited in a hush. Nothing. They waited some more. Still nothing. The men contained themselves as much as five drunk men can. They weren't too successful in maintaining quiet. "I have to make foam," El Topo shouted.

"Then go make foam, but keep quiet!" Fito growled. He stood as soldierly as he could manage with the rifle up in firing position, the end of the barrel bobbing and swaying a figure eight in the air. Nothing came into view. Fito finally put the rifle down with open disgust. It was getting heavy in his arms. "See what you've done with all your dumb commotion. You've frightened all the rabbits. We won't see another one all night, and I won't have a chance to shoot my rabbit." There was true anger in his tone.

"Don't be mad, Fito," soothed his host. "Here, you get the first shot out of the bottle, come on."

"I could have got him, you know." Fito took the bottle, but without grace, and went off to drink alone slouched against the fender of Concepción's taxi.

"Don't be mad at us," the others called out. "Don't be like that, Fito." Fito ignored them and continued to sulk.

"You come back here, *cabrón*, and be civil!" El Gordo yelled.

"Your *madre*!" Fito spat in return.

Now, Fito and El Gordo, when in full possession of their faculties, were the best of friends, but subtle changes in their character were gradually beginning to surface. The surrogate personalities were the progeny of José Cuervo and thus afflicted with deranged minds.

"I'll straighten out the *cabrón*!" El Gordo threatened. This would be a good time to mention that El Gordo was not only chunky, as his byname implied, but he was built like a locomotive. If he ever were to tangle with a bull, the latter would be sure to get the worst of it.

"Come over here and try, if you think you're man enough!"

A spasm of fear seized Concepción. He could see a fight with El Gordo taking form. Concepción would have preferred to die before allowing his *compadre* to be humiliated like this in front of his friends. "Don't laugh, muchachos," Concepción called out to them, "Fito is a marksman *formi-*

dable. I've seen Fito shoot a squirrel on the run between the eyes at twenty meters!"

The extravagant lie gave Fito his moment of glory. There was a sudden respectful silence among the men while Fito swelled visibly.

"Hey *compadre*, look, here's your rabbit!" All the men turned their attention toward Concepción, who had suddenly evolved into a twitchy-nosed rabbit. Knees bent, rump out, his long fingers flipping on either side of his head, and the metamorphosis was complete. He wiggled his nose at the men and hippity-hopped a few yards off and into the chaparral. Instantly, drunken tempers surrendered to drunken laughter. Concepción's spontaneous prank pulled Fito out from the path of the locomotive and restored his dignity.

"Come on, Fito," the men called, "there's your rabbit."

"Now show us what a great shot you are, come on, hombre!"

Fito swaggered out among the men, handed the bottle to a waiting hand, and raised the rifle. He'd show these *cabrónes* a thing or two, he thought. "All right, *conejito*, where are you?"

Concepción, now drunk beyond reason and disconnected from reality, came bouncing out of the thicket with a hop, skip, and a jump. In the fanciful logic known only to drunks, he *was* a rabbit. He bounced and frolicked like a cottontail under contract to Walt Disney. He stared at Fito with deadpan and goofy eyes, wiggled his long fingers at the side of his head and puckered his nose. Hop, hop, hop. "Bunny, bunny, bunny!"

BANG—twaang!

The rifleshot echoed across the canyon. Concepción hippity-hopped a short distance and flicked his long fingers.

The men went into wild laughter. Hop, hop, hop. "Bunny, bunny, bunny!"

BANG—twaaang!

But the rabbit deceived the rifleman again, bringing down an avalanche of laughter. It might even have been funny had they all been sober, Concepción hopping, wiggling his "tail" and flicking his "ears," and Fito too drunk to even hold the rifle. He looked very much like Elmer Fudd looking for that "mean ol' wabbit."

Hippity hop, hippity hop. "Bunny, bunny, bunny!"

BANG—twaang!

"Give it up, Fito," the men called out, "you'll never get him." But it is a dangerous thing to challenge a drunk.

"You think that, do you, *cabrónes?*"

Hippity hippity hop. "Bunny, bunny, bunny!"

BANG—twaaang!

The bunny dropped.

Fito was struggling to run out of a dark nightmare. Visions. Voices. The visions were all his friends, but they were grotesquely distorted, like a television picture that tears the image on the screen. The voices disconnected, disembodied. He tried to open his eyes. Pain. He had to climb out of that nightmare or die. He tried to get to his feet. More pain. He went down again.

He drifted in and out of a highly disturbed sleep. At long last he forced open his heavy eyes in an effort to escape. The pain was excruciating, but at least familiar now. He looked around him carefully, ever so carefully. Even his eyeballs hurt. He made an effort to rise, to see if he could identify his present whereabouts. Of course, it was familiar. It was his home away from home. He was in jail, so it must be Sunday.

But something was very wrong. He was alone. Alone! If

he was in jail, where was his *compadre*? Suddenly parental instincts took possession. Like a mother answering a sick child's cry, he was on his feet. The pain didn't matter anymore. Only one thing mattered right now. "Where is my *compadre*!" he screamed, rattling the bars of his cell. "What's happened to my *compadre*? Why isn't he here? Answer me, *cabrónes*!"

A uniformed policeman appeared. He was bringing him a cup of coffee and a sweet roll from the bakery across the street. "Eat this."

Fito didn't like the look on his face. "If you did anything to my *compadre*, I'll kill you! You understand that?" There was no reply. The face remained expressionless. Then Fito hissed out his warning. "If my *compadre* has come to any harm, if anyone—and I mean anyone—has laid a hand on him, I'll kill the *cabrón*! Can you understand that?"

Without comment the policeman placed the coffee and bread into Fito's shaking hands. Fito slammed it to the floor with a fury. The uniform disappeared down the hall. Fito heard a door open then close.

Fito gripped the bars to keep himself from dropping to the floor. He'd known hangovers, but today he was sure he had only a few hours of life remaining. He strained his brain to try to remember. Even arranging his thoughts was painful. He rolled back the tape in his mind. It was blank.

Moments later he heard the same door open and close. Footsteps. The policeman reappeared. His keys jingled in the lock. "The comandante wants to see you."

Fito stepped into the comandante's private office, a splintered desk, cracked vinyl chairs, a dead ficus in the corner. The frayed carpet no longer had a color, and the rip ran nearly the length of the room. A metal filing cabinet regurgitated its contents. Fito saw a large man sitting at the desk littered with official papers. Comandante Enrique Carranza, though only a year or two older than Fito, had reached the point in his life where he must enter a plea of no contest to the charge of self-abuse. A corpulent man on the outside, clogged arteries and black lungs on the inside. He held a cup of coffee in his right hand, a cigarette gathered ash in the other. On the brown wall a large photograph of the President of the Republic looked over his shoulder. "Sit down."

"Where is my *compadre*!" It was not a question, it was a demand.

"Sit down, Fito." The voice was dark as a shadow.

"If I learn that any of your *cabrónes* have even so much as touched him, you will all pay the price. That is my oath!"

"Sit down, Fito," a darker echo of the first. Fito sat. The comandante raised his cup of coffee to his lips and scalded his mouth. "*¡Ay cabrón!*" It was the same every morning; sip, scald, slurp, swear. Fog formed on the lenses of his glasses. He put his coffee down and removed his glasses.

"You shot your *compadre* last night."

Fito didn't move from his chair. He had passed out.

In a few minutes or an hour, Fito wasn't sure, he was being given a cup of coffee. He recognized the policeman who stood over him. The comandante was still behind his desk, wet cigarette in yellow fingers. El Presidente continued to stare at him. Fito took several sips of coffee and spoke. "What did you say? I didn't hear you, Señor Comandante."

"I said, you shot your *compadre* last night."

This time Fito heard, and he fought hard to keep from losing consciousness. "I must go to him at once, to his house, I mean," he whispered. "I must go see Adela."

"You know I can't let you go, Fito. I've known all your family for a long time, but this has nothing to do with friendship. My orders are to hold you." The severity of the voice repudiated the pang he felt for the wretched man who sat in front of him.

"Quique." Fito hadn't used his nickname since school days. "Quique, you've known me all my life. You know you can trust me. Let me go, I beg you. You know I'll come back here."

The comandante had made up his mind. Nothing could move him. But it was Quique who made the decision. "Go get yourself cleaned up. You have one hour."

"God bless you!" Fito's voice began to break and tears coursed down his manly face.

"I want to see you back here in one hour."

Fito's physical condition as well as his self-respect was in shreds. Fortunately, it was early enough on Sunday morning that he would not be seen by anyone he knew as long as he avoided any street that led to the Church of Our Lady of Guadalupe. For this reason he walked along the riverbed as far as he could. He didn't see anyone close enough even to require a wave of recognition.

A few minutes more and he caught sight of the cistern on the corner, and suddenly he recalled that Sunday morning in the *cienega* a lifetime ago. And now Fito relived every minute of that incident; their boyish laughter, the black water, the cries for help, the moment he dove in and saved his little friend's life. And now he had taken that life. How could he have done such a despicable thing? He could remember twenty years ago, but he couldn't remember yesterday. He rolled the tape in his head again. Still blank. He wished he could remember. He wished that he were dead.

And now, should he go first to see his wife? Or go and face the unequivocal consequences that waited for him at the house of his best friend's wife, whom he had made a widow? *Viuda*. The ugly word twisted his heart. But of course, he knew there was no choice.

Just as he stepped around the corner, he caught sight of Father Ruben and Dr. Pugh. He wished the earth would open under his feet and swallow him. He took a quick step back. He would die right where he stood if they looked at him. The two men were just coming down the path. They were walking side by side. There was an unmistakable gesture of disgust in their body language. When they reached the street where their cars were parked, they exchanged one final look. They shook their heads resignedly, got into their cars and drove gravely away.

Tears welled up in Fito's eyes, but he refused to surrender to them. He had his duty to perform and he would not allow himself to fall apart.

Adela was still standing at the door where she had watched the solemn departure of Father Ruben and Dr. Pugh, when she saw Fito coming up the path toward her. He was almost running. When he got to the door he didn't know where to hide his shame, he couldn't bring himself to show his face, and he looked away. On sudden impulse he threw his arms around her and wept bitterly. He began to speak.

"I cannot ask you to forgive me—" Painful sobs choked his words and he had to stop and take a deep breath before he could go on. "Even God will not forgive what I have done. God, I loved him—" and again he began to retch and cry uncontrollably. He bit down on his lip until he regained control. "I cannot bring him back to us, but let me make this sworn statement." He left Adela's arms and, dropping to his knees, gently took both her hands in his. "I swear, before you and before God, that from this day forward alcohol will never enter my body again. I swear, before you and before God, that I will continue to support this family until the day that I myself die. House, food, clothing, the children's education is now my responsibility and mine alone!"

I watched Fito Fernandez take a sip of tamarind. I couldn't help but see that those big warm eyes were glistening with unshed tears. My voice abandoned me. I was unable to make a comment. The room was breathless, and silent as the shadows in the courtyard. Somewhere a clock ticked. I could hear the peasant girl weeping at the fountain. Fito, always the gentleman, must have perceived my discomfort and seized the opportunity to suggest lunch.

I immediately rose as a sign of my acceptance, and instead of showing me to the dining room, he picked up a phone and spoke briefly. "It's lunchtime."

We crossed the courtyard and made our exit through a heavy iron gate. There stood a black Buick Riviera with a *chofer* behind the wheel. We got in, and in a few minutes were in the center of Tecate. We stopped for a light in front of the Church of Our Lady. I noticed I had lost my host's attention. His gaze went past me and continued on to some activity near the church entrance. My eyes followed his to a diminutive nun patiently assembling her class, a platoon of little girls in navy-blue pinafores and white knee stockings. When she had them all lined up in two neat columns, she stepped aside and they all marched into the sanctuary. As the last girl went inside, I watched the little nun following with a steep limp.

My host's eyes returned to me now, but he said nothing. He didn't have to. I knew we were both thinking the same thought: how fortunate for all of us that all those little indiscretions of childhood seem to dissolve and disappear in the floodwaters of human events.

In a few minutes all three of us were standing on the

corner of Juarez and Madero eating calf-head tacos from a pushcart. The proprietor fell into a highly animated conversation with the *chofer*, while Fito and I ate and said little. The gracious proprietor declined payment. From the skit that followed I concluded that this same scene had played here only yesterday. Fito crumpled a bank note into the man's apron, causing them both to laugh.

A short time later we were back in the soft leather chairs in his *estancia*. Countless shadows gathered in the courtyard. The peasant girl at the fountain was now in full shade. She looked subdued. My host poured me an exquisite sherry and himself a tall tamarind on the rocks.

"*Salud.*"

"*Provecho.*"

Then, as though he knew the question I was dying to ask but etiquette would not permit, he said, "I eat on the street every day. Do you know why?" He didn't wait for an answer. "I never want to forget who I am."

He took a long draught of his icy tamarind water and said, as though to bring to conclusion his long narrative, "Well, you can imagine the burden, what with two families to support. I held down three jobs. I had three girls, he three boys. You should see them now. They're absolutely wonderful. I am very proud of them. They love each other like brothers and sisters."

"All grown up by now, I suppose."

"*Sí, sí,* of course, my oldest is a *licenciada*. His oldest is a physician practicing in Guadalajara. All the rest are still in their studies."

"But you did it, señor, you did it! You kept your promise and in the process became a rich and powerful man."

"*Sí,* but with many sacrifices. To become rich was never

my intention. Wealth was a fortuitous result of hard work. And power is simply a by-product of wealth."

We were interrupted by the *chofer*. "The car is washed and waxed. Will we be going out again today?"

"No, no, we're all through for the day. Put the car away, *compadre*, and come pour yourself a drink. I was just telling this young man about the old days."

I nearly dropped my sherry. I looked at my host incredulously. Maybe I misunderstood. But then uncertainty turned to undisguised shock. I didn't say anything until the *chofer* was well out of the room, and even then I kept my voice within a low whisper.

"You mean he didn't—didn't die?"

"No, no, he recovered completely. I shot the rabbit in the ear. My *compadre* lost a finger."

"I can't believe it."

"After I had made my convenant with God and recovered from my weeping, I asked Adela if I couldn't go in and see my friend for the last time. She led me into their bedroom, and there he was, my beautiful friend, sound asleep—like an angel—with a huge bandage on his hand. The doctor had given him something for the pain."

"And you kept your pledge."

"He made me what I am today."

"But if he didn't actually die, you were *eximido*, off the hook, as it were. No one would have thought any less of you."

The magnificent terra-cotta face dimmed for a moment. "It is not how I appear to others that concerns me. No, señor! How do I appear to God? My word was *irrevocable*." Then the man in white put down his glass of tamarind and looked at me with gentle piety. "I made a vow to my *comadre*—and to God."

The Other Woman

*C*laudia put a plate of tenderloin strips with thin slices of fried tomatoes, and onion rings lightly browned in butter, in front of her husband. She could feel her hands trembling. She was terrified to think she might drop the plate, and wondered if he could see it too. A dark rage smoldered dangerously somewhere in the deepest corners of her soul. She stole a glance at José as he picked up his fork. He probably looked the same today as he did yesterday. But Claudia could already see subtle changes in his skin, his eyes, the set of his mouth. All confirmed her conjecture. A woman knows.

Back in the kitchen, Claudia put slices of French bread and butter on a plate, fighting back hot tears that burned her eyes as though she were slicing an onion. How could he do such a thing? Maybe, just maybe, it wasn't true. Don't be a child, Claudia, she told herself; the stories came to you from enough sources to know it's true. You don't want to believe it? That's fine, but don't put your head in the sand. She carried the bread and butter into the dining room.

"Is everything all right? You're rather quiet today." Her voice was gentle.

"Soup was cold."

"I'm sorry, let me heat it up for you."

"No time, let it go."

"Coffee?"

José answered with an affirmative silence. Claudia poured a cup of coffee, put the customary half teaspoon of sugar in it, stirred, and placed it in front of him. José took it to his reading chair and began to study the briefs he would soon present at court. He preferred the discomfort of reading at arm's length to hanging disfiguring appliances on his face. That was for old people, he thought. I'm not old. Thirty-nine is *not* old. I won't be forty until next year. Well, five months.

"What's wrong, *mi amor?*" It was in the form of a plea.

"Nothing."

"You seem so quiet." She laid a hand gently on his shoulder.

"Women! If you're not chattering like a kettle on the stove, they immediately think something is wrong."

Claudia pulled back as though she had put her hand in a flame. She retreated to the dining room and began to clear the table. She saw him in his chair, poking the eraser end of a pencil in his ear, then tapping his teeth with it. Claudia recognized her husband's signs of anxiety better than he did.

Claudia busied herself in the kitchen, hurt and close to tears. All the ugly, sordid rumors had to be true. Nothing else explained José's strange behavior. But still, they mustn't be true, for if they were, she would simply *die*. She felt that someone had yanked the earth out from under her feet. She was numb with grief, and didn't realize she had been standing at the sink with a plate in her hand like a pillar of salt until José stuck his head in the door.

"I'm going back to the office now. By the way, I have a court date Friday in Mexicali, so I'll stay over rather than try to drive the highway at night. Ismael has business in the capital, so we'll all go in one car."

"Yes, of course, I don't want you on that road at night either." If her brother was going with him, it must be legitimate.

"What did you do to your hair?"

"I had it cut."

"It looks terrible." The statutory kiss conveyed all the warmth and affection of an oyster.

José walked out the door, and Claudia went into the girls' room to check on them. Four-year-old Tina and two-year-old Mari were still fast asleep. They had played hard at the park all morning and they came home exhausted. It would be a long nap today. They slept so peacefully with their little pink faces scrunched into the sheet, Mari's tiny fist pressed into her cheek. Poor little things, was this their future too?

How did it happen? Married only six years and already the things she knew happened to other couples were now happening to her. She was a devoted wife, a good mother, a good homemaker. In six years of marriage she never once refused José anything. Then why? Why, why, why!

Tears wended down her face. Claudia needed to talk to someone, she *must* talk to someone. She went to the telephone, began to dial, and put it down again. I can't talk to my mother, she realized. God no! Her mother would immediately consider herself deputized to lead the investigation. And besides, it's just too intimate a problem. It would embarrass both of us.

There was one person she could talk to, someone she'd known all her life. Her aunt Rosa in Los Angeles. The thought of her almost made Claudia smile. Tía Rosa was a nonstop talker, but she would move heaven and earth for her. They could talk about *anything*. Claudia went to the desk and leafed through her address book. She had the phone in her hand when it rang. She nearly dropped it.

"Tía Rosa! God must have heard me and told you to call me."

"Actually, I was looking for your mother, but there's no answer. I thought she might be with you."

"Oh, Tía Rosa!" Claudia began to cry.

Tía Rosa was now expecting the worst. "Claudia, *cálmate*, tell me what's wrong. Is somebody sick?"

Claudia answered between sobs. "José—José—is involved with another woman!"

"Ay Claudia! Is that all?" Tía Rosa was heir to the Figueroa larynx, and as a pitiful consequence, the dear woman was awarded the shrieky voice of a parrot. Claudia pulled the phone away from her ear. "You scared me half to death. I thought someone died. José has been *involved* since I've known him. He's no different than any other Mexican husband. Why do you think I chose to live in Los Angeles?"

"Oh, I suppose I've always known some men are like that," Claudia had to admit. "But I thought José was different. I didn't think it could happen to *me*. He's a good father to his children, a good husband—"

"And he may have a heart of pure gold, but his *pito* is all flesh. José was playing at *nalgas* while you were writing out your wedding invitations."

"Then I've been playing his fool for six years." Claudia

169

knew a conversation with Rosa was going to be as long as Handel's Messiah, and pulled a chair over.

"Mexican men always choose a timid little sparrow. You were barely eighteen when you got married, and he was an experienced man of thirty-three. Can you be unaware of what your mother had to endure? I love my brother-in-law dearly, but in Mexico all men are the same."

Claudia winced. Tía Rosa may have been talking about her brother-in-law, but she was also talking about *her* father.

"I saw it all as a young girl—and you know me—I've always been very outspoken. That's why the family sent me here to finish high school. I was raised by my Tía Lupe, God rest her. I'm glad I decided to make my life here. I have American values I could never give up."

"Tía, are you going to tell me there is no infidelity on the Other Side?"

"Of course! The difference is that over here both parties know it's against the rules. A man running for public office accused of infidelity is politically ruined over here. In Mexico men think it's their birthright."

"I just can't believe it."

"I'm married twenty-four years, and my *viejo* knows that if he ever decided to go looking for *nalgas*, he would be out on the street. It's against the rules, Claudia!" Claudia released a long sigh. "I know what you're thinking, Claudia. I'm as American as Oscar Mayer—and you're right. Oh, we still have piñatas for the grandchildren, and we still do *las posadas* for nine nights before Christmas. But on the Fourth of July, it's hot dogs and potato salad. My *viejo* even puts out a flag! But the rest of our customs, the inferior station of the Mexican woman, I want no part of it."

"But Tía—" There was no interrupting Tía Rosa when she was on a roll.

170

"I've seen your mother always watching, spying, searching his clothes and his face for signs of another woman. I couldn't live like that. By the way, have you told your mother?"

"No."

"A wise decision. She would make a commotion worse than Watergate."

"Than what?"

"Never mind. When we were children we used to call your mother La FBI."

"I just don't know what to do."

"There are only two soups, Claudia. You divorce him or you do like most Mexican women, you pretend you don't see it—you shade the sun with one finger, as we say."

"No! If I divorce him, I break up the home, my family—everything. And I'm certainly not going to pretend I don't see it!" Claudia slapped the top of the desk to underscore her rancor.

"There are only two soups, Claudia."

"*¿Qué pasó, qué pasó?*" It was Dora, coming through the back door without benefit of a knock, as Dora held the rank of Best Friend and this brought with it certain privileges. "Claudia, where are you?" she yodeled.

"I have to run, Tía, thank you for talking to me, I'll call you later." Claudia was no nearer a solution when she put down the phone, but it did calm her down. She understood everything Tía Rosa said, but couldn't accept it. She felt she was different. I will do everything I can to work it out with José, she resolved. I'll win him back.

Claudia met Dora in the kitchen with a finger over her lips. "They're still asleep?" Dora poured herself a cup of coffee and sat at the kitchen table. She saw an unclaimed cream horn on a plate and popped it in her mouth.

171

Claudia slid into a chair and buried her face in her hands. She felt the need to urinate, but she knew it was only nerves, and she ignored the annoying pressure on her bladder.

Dora pushed more cream horn into her mouth and mumbled, "Well, I'm here, you'd better go now."

"Maybe the stories aren't true. I would look ridiculous."

"Of course they're true, how much proof do you need? Liliana has seen them together in Tijuana, the whole town knows it. I know where she works. Her name is Sonya Moreno Avila. She's a legal assistant at city hall. I found out where she lives, an apartment over in Colonia Juarez. They've been *seen* together, Claudia!" The words were as delicious in her mouth as the cream horn.

"I just don't understand José, is she—"

"Not even young, she's a cheap, vicious tramp."

"I can't do it, Dora."

"You have no choice, you have to do it. You're not going to sit here and let her destroy your marriage, your whole life." Dora had exactly the same problem with her own husband for the past seven years. But within the safety of third party immunity, she enjoyed encouraging Claudia to do what she herself lacked the courage to do.

"I would die."

"Don't be silly. You simply call on her and inform her that you are aware of what is going on, and advise her it would be wise to stop seeing your husband. When she finds out you're the daughter of the judge, that the mayor is your brother, she'll vanish, believe me. You won't be there five minutes." Dora couldn't enjoy her savory role in her best friend's tragedy any more than if she had been turned loose in a pastry shop.

"The humiliation!" Claudia wasn't the type that confronted anyone. She would rather wash a neglected skillet herself than have to confront the servant girl. She went directly from sweet obedient daughter to sweet obedient wife. She was never really aware of all the family secrets Tía Rosa revealed so bluntly.

"Humiliation or a broken marriage, take your choice. I'll stay with the girls like I told you yesterday, now you go before you lose your nerve. It will take you ten minutes, and you'll feel better just knowing you saved your happy marriage. You can tell me *everything* when you get back. I just don't understand men!"

Claudia went into the bathroom. Maybe there *aren't* only two soups. Maybe she could salvage her marriage. This could be the third alternative. The eyes that looked back from the mirror were humid and red, but she no longer cared. A courage she never knew she possessed came to her from somewhere. She hurried to her arsenal and withdrew her weapons. The presumptuous little clerk would soon know who she was dealing with. She pulled out a white silk suit that José complained cost more than his car. The tunic was trimmed with a wide black belt and big bold square buttons. A formidable pair of black stilettos, an awesome matching bag, and she was ready. When she was dressed, she was the image of one of Manet's ladies with the luminous face, the frothy wreath of raven hair, and the large inquisitive eyes under graceful arches.

Claudia took the address from Dora, got in her car and drove off. She knew she was upset, and like someone who knows she's had too much to drink, drove with exaggerated caution. It was the perfect time to call. At four o'clock all the men were still busy at work; the secretaries, who got off at three, would be home.

She hit a pothole that shook the car, and heard her

husband's voice. He might have been sitting next to her. "Women are the worst drivers! How many times do I have to tell you, keep your eyes alert for potholes. You'll break something!" She found Calle Madero Numero 17 and drove past. She couldn't do it. Then, seized with a sudden sense of righteousness, went around the block, returned to Numero 17 and parked. She sat still for a moment with the engine idling while two minds fell into conflict. Indignation and pride won the argument. She gave the key a violent twist, the engine died, and Claudia marched toward Apartment 8. She was in the proper mood now, equal parts of rage, pride, and rancor.

The apartments were set back from the street. Claudia started up the walkway nervously rehearsing her lines. My God, what do I call her? I refuse to call her Sonya. She is certainly no señorita, my husband has seen to that. I can't call her señora . . .

She tortured herself with all the social procedures until she woke suddenly to find herself with a finger on the bell of Apartment 8. The sound of approaching footsteps behind the door caused her stomach to leap. It was like coming down an elevator in a sudden drop.

The door opened and she froze. In front of her stood an attractive woman about her own age who simply did not square with Dora's description. No claws, no fangs, no horns. Claudia printed her image with all the speed of a Polaroid camera. The woman in front of her was still in her office clothes, a light blue batiste blouse and navy skirt. She had removed her shoes. The figure was perfect, the abundant contours of her breasts did not escape the observer. She took in the fresh, clean cover-girl complexion framed in radiant auburn hair with luxurious waves and feathery wisps teased into all the right places. Velvety lips, inno-

cent of paint, formed a tentative smile, and large hazel
eyes looked inquiringly while she waited for her visitor to
speak.

Here, Claudia's courage abandoned her like an orphan
on a doorstep and left her to work it out by herself. She
could feel her heart pounding. With her enormous purse
pressed to her chest like an aegis against a mortal wound,
she forced herself to speak. Her voice cut the air like a
blade. "Sonya Moreno Avila?" She sounded like a process
server. She was pleased with herself.

"Your *servidora*."

"I am Claudia Méndez Figueroa." She fired off her
names like an AK-47 assault rifle.

"Please come in." Sonya stepped back cordially, pushing
the door open wider.

Claudia marched in livid. She was fighting for self-
control and momentarily unable to say more.

"Please sit down." Sonya indicated a chair. "I was just
putting up a pot when you rang. Will you have a cup?"

Claudia remained standing, but the cue helped her find
speech. "This is not a social call." She dipped her words in
acid in a failed attempt to conceal the wavering tremors in
her voice.

Sonya pressed the button on the television and Oprah
vanished from the room in mid-sentence. She seated herself
on the sofa and tucked her legs under her. "What can I do
for you?"

Claudia knew she had failed to intimidate. She didn't
really know where to go from here. She could feel her
cheeks burning, they were on fire, and she could hear her
own voice breaking as she began. "It has come to my attention that you—that my husband—that you and my
husband—" Claudia collapsed into the chair she had de-

clined a moment earlier and gave herself to a flood of tears. "I'm here to humiliate myself before you, no, to beg you. I will go down on my knees to you—please, *please*, don't take my husband from me. We've been so happy, and now—" She held her breath to fight back the sobs pressing painfully against her chest.

"Dear señora, please be assured that I have absolutely no intentions of taking your husband from you." The voice was firm, almost authoritative, and yet, ever so gentle, the color of innocence.

Ashamed of her exhibition, Claudia stoked the fires of her anger and quickly reclaimed her wrath. She now spoke in an icy third person intended to brandish her social distance and contempt. Her sentence could only have been parsed with a chisel. "You deny that you have been seeing my husband?" She used *usted* like a knife. "You have made a grave error."

"Yes, I know. The mayor is your brother, no?"

"He is."

"Would you like to know who he's sleeping with?"

"That's filthy!"

"Nevertheless true."

Claudia pulled auxiliary courage from somewhere and immediately seized the offensive. "I will destroy you in this town, and you know I can do it."

"Please, señora, please! How did Temistocles put it? Strike, but *listen*."

The ancient Greek quotation was not lost on Claudia. But as often happens when words issue in advance of thought, she began to wonder if she hadn't made a terrible mistake by coming here in the first place. "I listen."

"I would be a fool to deny in your face what everyone

knows. But believe me when I tell you with the utmost sincerity, I have no intention of taking him from you." Her voice could have been that of an intimate friend, sweet, calm, reassuring. "I don't want your husband—I don't want any husband."

The unpretentious candor in the pleasant voice disarmed Claudia. "I don't understand."

"I enjoy going out to dinner, dancing, I like to go places, but I want nothing else from any man."

"This is incredible."

"Not at all. I had a husband once, I must have married about the same time you did, we're probably the same age. After about four years of married bliss, I discovered that I was in the same position you find yourself in today."

Claudia felt the ice in her voice was showing signs of melting and turned her thermostat down. "This is of no concern to me."

"Oh, but it is. It serves to show that your marriage is not in any jeopardy—at least as far as I'm concerned. Will you let me plug in the coffeepot?"

Claudia accepted by not saying anything, and Sonya went to the kitchen. Claudia looked around the apartment. Simple but tasteful, she thought. I wonder if José is paying for it?

Sonya resumed her place on the sofa and in her narrative. "I was devastated, of course. But I'm not the stupid little sparrow my husband thought he married." She didn't say "like you," but it was hardly necessary. "We had no children, so I did what few Mexican women have the courage to do. I divorced him immediately. But I didn't matriculate into the convent of Santa Brígida. I enjoy the company of men, certainly, but I have no use whatever for a husband, their moods, their criticisms, their rudeness, and on top of all that, their womanizing. It's always some business in Mexicali."

How impertinent! Claudia had no intentions of allowing the interview to deteriorate into the familiar. She stiffened in her chair, cold, silent, fury undiminished.

"Would you agree that a marriage is by its very nature *una unión sexual?*"

Claudia refused to participate. She fought back a blush unsuccessfully and remained silent.

"But the Mexican wife was never the sex object to begin with. The mistress is in place before the honeymoon. The wife is nothing more than the broom and the skillet. What chance does the marriage then have under these conditions?"

As much as Claudia tried to hate this woman, she didn't, for some strange reason she couldn't understand. She was aware that she went through life with her hands over her eyes. But now she found herself peeking between her fingers to see what every Mexican woman knows is there and tries to ignore. She felt as if she had walked into the Devil's chambers and sat listening to a witness for the defense.

"I have to admire the American woman. She's an *equal*. She's free to be everything, wife, mother, friend, partner, lover. It's a cultural thing and has nothing to do with intelligence. We're as intelligent as the gringos. Look at this article." Sonya took an issue of *Cosmopolitan* from the end table and handed it to Claudia.

Claudia made no attempt to reach for it, and Sonya took this to mean she couldn't read English. "I'll translate for you. 'Better Sex: What He Doesn't Know About You and How to Tell Him.' Would you share this article with your husband?"

"I wouldn't dare!" Claudia squirmed in her chair. The pressure on her bladder was almost unbearable, but she refused to demean herself by asking for the bathroom.

"Exactly! The good wife can never suggest *anything*. The Mexican husband will simply not have his wife thinking like a libertine. Why does our society insist on placing impediments on this aspect of the relationship? That is what drives our men to seek counterfeit love. But that is the prison they have us in. As a wife I was always wrong, my skirt was too short, my pants too tight, I didn't know how to drive a car, and the soup was cold."

Claudia felt the sting of a dart.

"As a mistress everything I do is wonderful, everything I say is witty, and I'm so charming, my lover falls over backwards to be pleasant. He can't take me for granted, so he venerates the ground I walk on. I am his princess. He wouldn't dare be rude to me at breakfast for fear I would walk out on him at any given moment. He can only hold me through love. Isn't that what a marriage should be?"

Claudia couldn't stand it another minute. She was sure she was going to wet right through to the chair. "Would you permit me your bathroom?" She spoke in the brittle third person, as dignified as the nature of the request permitted.

Sonya showed her the way, though it was hardly necessary in the small apartment. Claudia now felt that any psychological edge she may have gained when she stalked in, she forfeited sitting on the other woman's toilet.

When Claudia returned, Sonya was still in the kitchen. She noticed a photograph in a gold frame on the end table for the first time. The young woman in the picture was unmistakably Sonya. She was cuddling a happy baby in her arms in a pink knitted dress with an adorable toothless grin. Claudia had to bite her lip to suppress a smile.

Sonya saw her looking at it when she returned with the coffee. "Not mine," she said. "My sister's. I may never know what it is to hold my very own baby. Cream or sugar?"

Claudia couldn't bring herself to refuse. They sipped in silence for a few minutes, Sonya talked out, Claudia emotionally drained. Claudia put her cup on the coffee table. Her voice was no longer tight with fury, just gray and tired. "I came here to hate you, to scream at you."

"I'm afraid your ire would be misdirected. We are not enemies, señora, we are in bondage to our culture, our customs, our religion. You are one chapter behind in your husband's escapades. We stopped seeing each other over a month ago. He has another. You know what I think?" Sonya didn't get a reply and didn't wait for one. "I think men are emotional parasites who nourish their egos by sucking the life out of women."

Claudia rose from her chair even before Sonya finished her sentence. She had come to her decision. Tía Rosa and the whore were both right—there really were only two soups. And Claudia made her choice. *I know exactly what I'm going to do.*

Sonya walked her to the door. "No one will ever know you were here, señora."

Somehow Claudia couldn't hate her anymore. "*Gracias.*" It was a whisper.

On the way home the tempest struck Claudia with all its fury. Her chest was so tight it hurt to breathe; she could feel her pulse throbbing in her temples. She was driving too fast and she knew it. She made a right turn in front of an old man struggling behind his pushcart piled high with yellow corn, and missed him by a whisper. The sudden fright squeezed her insides and she slowed to a crawl. By the time Claudia got in the house, she was seething, roiling like *agua para chocolate*. She threw down her purse and fought back tears and nausea. I have every right to be furious, she affirmed. I've chosen my soup!

Next day, while the servant girl took the children to the park and she was home alone, Claudia placed a red votive glass on the mantel in the living room. She lit the candle, forced back her tears, and spoke to God. "*Dios mío*, I come to you to beg your guidance, though undeserving and a sinner. *Dios mío*, I implore you listen to my plea. I carry the burden and *desgracia* of a man who has broken his vows to me and to God. Please give me the strength to annul this union I entered into chaste and with faith. I beseech you, don't let me weaken at the moment I announce my decision. I ask all this in the name of your son, Jesucristo. Amen." Claudia recited two *padres nuestros* and one Ave Maria.

Claudia replaced the candle every day and kept the flame of her pain alive. She continued to discharge her duties. She prepared José's early morning coffee, as always, and fixed breakfast for the girls, who were up before Venus went home to bed. She had his dinner ready for him every day at one-thirty when he walked in the door. She went to bed before he got home and affected deep inviolable slumber, or retired well after José was snoring if he got home early.

Today José sat eating his dinner. Claudia served him a thick pork chop, fried potatoes, and sliced cucumbers. She watched him scald his tongue on the *consomé* without even the slightest complaint. Claudia remained courteous but distant. When he'd finished dinner, she brought him his coffee with a half teaspoon of sugar. José took it to his chair and Claudia repaired to the kitchen.

It required no great perception for José to realize he was out of favor. And he knew why. But Claudia's withdrawal really didn't bother him. José felt no guilt, only inconvenience. She'll get over it, he thought. They all get over it. I meet my obligations as husband and father—beyond that, anything I do is nobody's business. I will never live to understand women! What's the big deal? And she used to be so mild, so easy to manage. How my docile little sparrow has changed! I hope Claudia hasn't talked to her mother. That woman would start such a scandal. She would interrogate Claudia's brother, she would even call that parrot-face Rosa, everybody. There would be scenes. My father-in-law would blame me. Nasty, nasty, nasty. Can't let that happen.

José strolled into the kitchen with what appeared to be words poised on his lips. Claudia stopped him cold with a question. "What time will you be getting home tonight? I have something to say to you. Something important to both of us."

"I shouldn't be too late, *corazón*, and I better be getting back to the law offices. You know what I was just thinking, *mi amor?*" The voice was buttercream in a pastry bag equipped with a number 5 star tip.

Like any wife, Claudia could read his every mannerism. José was stroking his tie. He was on the defensive. "I haven't yet learned to read minds."

José caught a chill, but continued. "I was just thinking, it's been a long time since we've had a few days together—just the two of us. Why not make it a long weekend? Call The Ritz-Carlton in Laguna Beach—you've always like Laguna."

Claudia gave no indication that she'd heard. If he says, "I love your hair," she thought, I'll throw something.

"Just imagine! Three days of lying around the pool, dining, dancing, late champagne brunch. Maybe we can even take in a show or—Disneylandia!" José finished piping the frosting with a warm kiss on her lips. He kissed cold marble. He picked up his briefcase and went out the door.

Claudia knew José understood completely the implications of her cold announcement. And she was ready for him. She knew exactly what she was going to say. She'd been rehearsing her speech every day since her visit to the Devil's chambers.

Claudia walked into the living room and stood before the mantelpiece. The candle continued to burn in silent prayer. Once more she ran through her prepared speech. The squeals of the children brought her back into the present moment. She could hear Tina and Mari playing house in their bedroom.

"I'm the Papi, you can be Mamá."

"*Hola*, I'm home, *mi amor*. What's for dinner?"

"Eggs, and chicken, and meat, and apples . . ."

Claudia closed her eyes to assist thought. It was easier to think in the dark. Choose a soup, Claudia! Discard your pride or destroy your family. Presently she opened them. Her decision was made. Yes, I know in my heart I'm doing the right thing. With a single puff the faithful votive flame, loyal to the latter end, shivered and died.

Claudia went to the telephone and dialed the area code for Laguna Beach.

Q. E. D.

*T*he gods of March were angry. From their secret vaults where the weapons of winter are stored came vicious winds, flood, ice, snow. Here in the high hills of Tanama we had been under siege for eleven straight days.

Every light was on in the library, in addition to the oil lamps and candles in anticipation of the predictable power failure. The wind moaned like a wounded animal, rain blasted the windowpanes like bird shot, then came hail the size of marbles. I drew the heavy drapes tight across the balcony and returned to my guests. Jim and Sharon Langford were seated near the hearth in the warm embrace of a blazing oak fire. We were making gains on a bottle of Sangre de Cristo.

I'd never set eyes on the Langfords before today. As so often happens, mutual friends had suggested to them that they come by the villa for a day on their way to Hawaii in order to "see" Mexico. They had arrived only this morning from their home in Jefferson City, Missouri. Like most of my American visitors, they were eager to hear some local anecdotes. I had just finished telling them about Don Pedro Gonzalez Rosencranz, precipitating a breathless silence. Jim Langford's undiplomatic remark really came as no surprise.

"You don't really expect me to believe that, do you?" His wife shot him a look charged with censure. Her glare came together with a sudden crash of thunder implying divine authority. Mr. Langford quickly amended his remark. "What I mean is, it's hard to believe, you know. Like Ripley's *Believe It or Not*."

The lights went out at that moment, and we now sat in the frail light of sputtering oil lamps. Candles fidgeted nervously in their sconces. Everything in the room flickered like an old-time movie.

"Oh, I quite agree with you," I said, more for his wife's comfort than his. "If I hadn't been witness to the events, I wouldn't believe it either. Magic potions and witch's spells are a part of everyday life in Tecate."

The next morning the Langfords had coffee and cakes with me. I walked them to their car and into the aftermath of the rampage of the night before. Olive trees in silver mail lay sprawled like fallen soldiers in new snow. Once proud and stately *álamos* stood stripped naked of leaf and dignity. A half-dozen black and white cows grumbled sullenly around their frozen water tank. A mud slide rendered the driveway impassable, and my guests now had to use the lower service road to reach the main gate. But the sun was out in full power and we had to squint our eyes against the dazzling brilliance. Above us, a millpond sky, cloudless, cold, and blue, pleaded innocent to the charge.

As soon as they were out of sight I returned to the library, resurrected the fire, and began at once to commit the curious story of Don Pedro Gonzalez Rosencranz to paper before time could fade the curious chain of events like a newspaper left in the sun. I now leave it to the reader to exercise his prerogative of doubt.

It was just this past November, late in the afternoon, I was sitting out on the front terrace with full cup and empty mind, gazing at the scalloped edges of blue sky against the chocolate hills. A crisp autumn day was making its final statement with big fiery brush strokes. Suddenly a large funnel of dust rose up from the road in front of me. In a few seconds I could discern the dark silhouette of a lone horseman taking form within the brown haze. Presently the ghost rider materialized. I recognized Florentino from Rancho El Condor.

I've known Florentino for some years, and yet whenever I visit with him, I get a case of the collywobbles. He looks like one of those Mayan idols you often see reposing in a glass case in the museum of natural history. You know the type, red clay face, mean eyes, flat nose, fat lip. And quick to toss a pretty virgin into the Sacred Pool when all they need is a little rain. This description calls for a brief footnote. It would be uncharitable of me, if not an injustice, to suggest that Florentino was mean. Why, he didn't have a mean thought in his pre-Colombian head. He *wasn't* mean—it was his face. One look into those glistening anthropoid eyes could paralyze speech. His smile was, I'm sure, intended to be friendly, but when he exposed two rows of razor-sharp needles more commonly seen on the South American fruit bat, it induced severe spine chills.

"*Buenas tardes,*" he called, coming out of his stirrup and swinging to the ground. He stood two hands shorter than the mare.

"*Buenas tardes.*" I poured another tequila and pushed it toward him. "This should cut through the dust in your throat."

Florentino tied his mare to a nearby olive tree and jingled toward me on bent legs. "Just one, Don, darkness will soon overtake me. I bring a message from Don Pedro. He told me to wait for a reply. *Salud!*" The pure rocket fuel went down like Kool-Aid.

I took the crumpled envelope from his horny hand and poured him another. The note read as follows:

Scoundrel!
    It's been donkey years since we have seen your face at coffee. If you are still among the living, send word if you can come up this weekend.

                                —PGR

I couldn't remember the last time I joined the local coffee klatch. I looked up to see the messenger advancing on the fiery beverage. "Tell your *patrón* to expect me tomorrow before noon. Another one?"

"Just one, Don. Darkness, like evil, comes without invitation."

"What have you to fear?" As soon as I gave the phrase life, I knew it was a mistake, because one of his many first-person ghost stories would follow.

"La Llorona."

"Surely, you don't believe—"

"I have *seen* her, Don."

It is necessary to briefly interrupt this narrative to apprise the reader of this notorious phantom woman who dates back to my grandmother's time and maybe hers too. La Llorona, literally, the Weeper, is a frightful hag with a face pale as death and hideous lidless eyes. Long white hair pours off her shoulders and reaches to her waist. She rises out of the mists when day finally takes its last breath, and dies under the shroud of night. Anyone bold enough to walk near the arroyos after dark can plainly hear her agonizing sobs, the terrifying screams that can coagulate blood. She's dressed in the latest cry of fashion for nether spirits, a lifeless white gown with matching flowing panels of ghostly chiffon. The story may or may not be true, but every village in Mexico that has even a small arroyo claims sightings of the ubiquitous witch.

"These parts are full of strange occurrences," Florentino went on. "One night—on this very trail—I encountered El Indio."

"El Indio Loco?" Another spook of renown.

"*Sí!* The very one!"

"No."

"*Sí!* You know that flat stretch with the big rocks as tall as a horse? Right there, Don, right there he came out to meet me."

"He spoke to you?"

"He wanted to show me where an olla filled with gold coins was buried."

"And did you go?"

"Are you serious, Don? His eyes turned red as embers. I know his game. He wanted my soul!"

"What did you do?"

"I buried my spurs into the poor animal and she flew home without touching the ground!"

At that moment the mare elevated her flaxen tail and made a generous nitrogen deposit in contempt of convention. "She's been saving it for you the whole way here." He laughed and sucked the life out of two limes. "With your permission, Don, I'll be getting back. *Gracias.*"

"Have a safe journey."

"I carry protection now, Don, but it is never wise to

tempt the spirits." He withdrew a tiny vial of magic liquid from his breast pocket and held it up for me to see. "Blood of the rooster," he claimed, as though that explained everything. I didn't ask him where he got it. Florentino swung himself up into the saddle and with a wave jogged down the road and disappeared into the gathering dusk, followed only by his own long shadow.

Friday morning the thermometer shivered around the low forties and an evil Santa Ana wind, rating at least an eight on the Beaufort scale, sliced through Tecate like a cane cutter with a machete. I went directly to La Fonda, where the hard-core caffeine addicts gathered for support every day. They're known locally as the Cafeteros, the self-appointed upper chamber that meets every morning to pass resolutions, draft legislation, and announce new decrees. They do not appear to be at a loss for an agenda. I've seen them go from the meaning of Life to the flirty little bank teller at Banamex in something under thirty seconds. They'll even argue with the weather. I've no doubt a chapter of the Cafeteros convenes at nine o'clock local time in every civilized country in the world. It was basically the same crowd every morning: the doctor, the dentist, the manager of Banco de Mexico, two or three local merchants, a lawyer, a couple of ranchers, and Pedro Gonzalez Rosencranz, the architect, known locally as El Teetu. He lived in town with his wife Perla and three young daughters in a blue tile missile silo three stories high of his own design. On weekends he took the vows of lethargy and retreated to Rancho El Condor, his private brain preserve.

As soon as I pushed through the door at La Fonda I walked into a chorus of masculine voices, each in a different key signature.

"That argument is invalid!"

"Logic decrees it!"

"Gentlemen!"

"Let me call your attention to—"

"*Buenos días*," I sang out. "What has this august body so impassioned? The water shortage, the deplorable condition of our roads, the lack of garbage pickup and removal?"

"*Buenos días*," the Cafeteros answered in an a cappella canon.

The *licenciado* immediately jumped to his feet and impaled me with his question. "Are your loyalties with Los Cowboys de Dallas? If your answer is affirmative, you sit on this side. If by some genetic defect you are backing Los Forty-niners, you are on that side."

"What if I'm rooting for Los Chargers?"

"Then you sit in the men's room!" The honorable body capitulated to laughter.

They made a place for me at the long table and poured me a cup. There was enough secondary caffeine in the air to assure even an abstainer a fun-packed night of sheep counting. The doctor slid a huge plate of sweet cakes in my direction. "Here, raise your blood sugar level."

I was watching Hector the bank manager struggling with the wrappings on a bundle of Cuban cigars. He finally gave up and pleaded, "Who's got a pocketknife?"

I held out my Swiss army knife. "Here, end your suffering."

"Put it down on the table," he said. I complied with the request. Hector picked it up and went to work on his package.

"I don't believe what I just saw!" the doctor exploded. "You, an educated man, the manager of a bank, believe in that old superstition that says if you take a knife from another hand, a fight will ensue."

"It isn't that I'm superstitious, just cautious."

"If I don't see it, I don't believe it," continued the doctor. "I wonder why Mexicans have a predisposition to mysticism?"

The dentist entered the conversation. "I have a patient that comes in wearing the rattles of a rattlesnake around her neck to ward off a toothache."

One of the merchants warmed to the theme. "When my mother-in-law accidentally drops a tortilla on the floor, it stays there until someone else can pick it up and bury it. I'm sure the doctor must see a lot of this sort of thing."

"Every day. I have patients that won't follow my advice. They will go to a *curandero* who tells them to bring him flowers from a grave. He turns them into a magic potion and dispenses it without a prescription!"

Hector finished with his package of Cubans, closed up the knife, and put it down in front of me with a self-conscious grin. "Doubt encourages prudence."

I thought of Florentino and remembered why I was here. "Has anyone seen Teetu this morning?" I asked the group at large.

"He was here earlier, but at the moment you'll find him directing traffic at the corner of Juarez and Hidalgo," the banker answered. "I'm surprised you didn't see him."

"I didn't come that way. Elucidate, please."

"Consistent with our time-honored tradition, the traffic light has expired and city hall doesn't have enough sense to send a policeman out to untangle the traffic."

"And you're going to tell me now that El Teetu became incensed and went to do it himself."

"You know El Teetu."

"He was mad. He went around the corner to the police station. The comandante was not in yet, and a half-dozen policemen were sitting around having coffee. He came back here and said if this town of eight square blocks couldn't solve the problem, he could. And he borrowed two red dinner napkins from Sergio and went out the door."

"Dinner napkins?"

"Semaphores. El Teetu is a man of action."

"I remember when he went before the mayor and warned him the new bridge wouldn't last a year," the merchant contributed.

"And he was right, the following winter it collapsed."

"Teetu always knows what he's talking about."

"He's a graduate of the University of Mexico. He did his advanced studies in Germany."

"It is whispered that he is a faithful husband," someone added incongruously. The Cafeteros are agile thinkers. We quickly adjusted our minds to deal with the new topic.

"That's unnatural."

"I don't believe it."

"A vicious rumor!"

"Maybe El Teetu will convince the *presidente* to fix the signal."

"Forget the traffic lights. I'd like to see them fix the streets."

"Please, don't get me started about our roads." It was Federico, who had the largest curio shop in town, catering almost exclusively to Americans. "The subject is the source of constant embarrassment for me. Americans come into my shop and say, 'When are you going to fix your roads?' What do I tell them? We are too stupid to fix our streets, we don't have the skills? Or maybe I should tell them we're too lazy. My face colors every time the gringos ask me the question."

"Wait until some gringo falls into that chasm in front of the post office. It's big enough to swallow a car."

"On the subject of hazards, has anyone here seen that tiny little skirt Carmelita at the telephone company was wearing yesterday?"

I knew the Cafeteros could go on like this all morning. I disposed of two coffees and the same number of sweet rolls and got to my feet. "Well, *caballeros*, I must leave you. I'm on my way to spend the weekend with Teetu at his ranch. If he shows up, tell him I came by, *sí?*"

When I got to the door, I heard the accusatory voice of the prosecutor. "You never said who you favored for the playoffs."

"My money is on Los Buffalo Beels." Another heated debate burst into flames behind me.

I drove by the intersection lately under discussion and saw no sign of Teetu. His frizzy helmet of auburn hair and the ginger mustache made him easy to isolate in a crowd. A policeman with a red nose, a formidable organ easily exceeding the candlepower of that reindeer made famous in song and legend, was directing traffic with a noticeable lack of élan. I headed for Rancho El Condor.

It was after twelve when I spotted the weather-eaten board reading RANCHO EL CONDOR. The lettering may have been a nice shade of blue at one time. The main gate was no less pretentious, four strands of barbed wire stapled to four willow poles and hooked to the gatepost with a hoop of bailing wire. No condors were in evidence when I drove in. Gnarled oaks, *álamos*, and towering *fresnos* dyed in autumn colors congregated around the entrance, their golden leaves scudding over the ground like giant cornflakes. The air was clear and sharp and laced with little fragrant wisps of wood smoke.

The main house was a long, old-fashioned one-story adobe dozing in the shade of ancient pepper trees. It had a long porch that ran the full length of the house. I heard the greeting before I got to the wooden stairs.

"*Buenas tardes*, señor." The voice was sweet as a love song, and I recognized Concha, the lumpy housekeeper, sitting out front on a wicker chair. She was shelling fresh shiny green peas into a bowl on her lap. She always called me señor.

"*Buenas tardes*, Concha," I answered, and before I could reach a chair, she put down her bowl of peas and went into the house. She was dressed in a spotless housedress that appeared to be stuffed with a number of feather pillows of assorted sizes. Her legs were sheathed in heavy maroon ribbed stockings. They may have been full-length tights. She walked in tennis shoes. She progressed toward the door pitching and rolling from side to side like a boat in heavy seas. In an instant she was back with a steaming cup of aromatic coffee which she brewed with a stick of cinnamon.

"*Gracias. ¡Muy rico!* I see I interrupted your work."

"Just shelling some peas, it's the only green vegetable El Teetu will eat. He won't be long, just over at the well. A problem with the pump I think he said."

I always thought it quaint that Concha should call her employer by his baby name. "How has Pedro been these days?"

"As always, he works much too hard. My tongue is permanently creased from so many years of telling him, but he doesn't listen to me."

"You've known him a long time, then."

"Since the day he was born."

Pedro was in his early forties, and Concha just didn't look that old to me. Her straight hair was raven. Her face was smooth and finished with a thin coat of dark varnish. Her teeth were large and white as chalk, a gleaming gold incisor the only exception.

"I should come here more often just for your coffee. *¡Qué bárbaro!*"

"I was just a girl when I went to work for his mother, God rest her. He was the last of four children—all girls."

"And you have been with him all those years?"

"Oh yes, I never married. What do I want with a man? He was my child. His children are like my grandchildren. I've had all the fruit without the thorns, *gracias a Dios.*"

I've known Concha for as many years as I've know Pedro, and this was the longest conversation we'd ever had. "Tell me, how did he get to be known as El Teetu?"

"He baptized himself."

"*¿Cómo?*"

"When he was very little, maybe two, he had a little fluffy duck. He couldn't be parted from the silly thing. They were *inseparables*! But he couldn't say little ducky, *patito*. The best he could do was teetu, teetu, and he was never known by any other name."

This was a rich vein, and I was going to mine it for additional nuggets, but at that moment a black Ford Bronco pulled up and the subject of our discussion came running up the porch and threw his arms around me in a typical Mexican macho embrace that I was sure would result in a set of X rays to determine the full extent of the damage. He stood a head taller than myself. He had a peaches-and-cream complexion that any woman would sell her body to possess.

"*¿Qué pasó, viejo?*"

"*¡Viejo!* Listen to that, I'm younger than you, little ducky."

His smoky eyes brightened, his laugh was big and spacious as the ranch itself. "Oh, I see you've been talking to Concha. And I also see she's given you refreshment suitable for old ladies with no teeth! Let me get you something a little more substantial."

"Listen to the big macho!" Concha snorted. "We thought his mother would have to take him the breast when he started kinder!"

"See what I have to put up with? Concha was my first intimate experience with a woman." He made to nip her neck.

"Ay! I used to wipe his *nalgas*!" Having played her trump, Concha took her bowl of peas and pitched and rolled toward the door. "I should give these to the chickens and serve you something green and ugly!"

We were soon sitting on the porch with a Presidente brandy and soda. "How is everything at the villa?" my host asked.

"The orchard produced a bumper crop this year."

"*¡Magnífico!*"

"The ground squirrels loved it. But they never got any of my corn."

"Well, that's something, at least."

"The rabbits mowed that down before it matured. And your family? I expected to see Perla and your children."

"Her sister is up from Mexico City, so guess where they are today."

"Disneylandia."

"*Exacto.*"

"And that reminds me, I want to show you something." I followed him to a garage as old as the house. It could have easily held three cars—by Mattel. He opened the double doors and revealed a brand new Geo Prizm, glossy red as a waxed tomato.

"You've been stealing cars."

"My wife's birthday present. I sneaked it in here yester-day."

"When will you give it to her?"

"Next Saturday, and that's where you come in."

"What are you talking about?"

"I need you to deliver it to the house late Saturday night. When she goes out in the morning—surprise! Can you do it?"

"Of course, but what if she hears me?"

"Unlikely. I will be giving her another birthday present at about that hour."

"Done!"

"I'll leave the keys in the ignition. Can you manage it?"

"No problem. I leave Monday morning for a three-day shoot. I'll be back early Friday morning. I'll come directly here, pick up the car, and deliver it that night. I'll get one of the Cafeteros to drive me back."

"¡Magnífico!"

We walked back to the porch and he freshened our drinks.

"By the way, I was in for coffee this morning, but the Cafeteros told me you were out directing traffic. Then the subject changed to the condition of our roads."

"Don't even remind me. It's a disgrace!"

"Teetu, why can't we do anything right, why are we so resistant to change?"

"It's our culture."

"You can't be serious. We have plenty of well-trained engineers."

"That is the tragedy. We have the competence. What we lack is the will to put the competent on the project. It's the result of nepotism and favoritism. We build highways and bridges with painstaking carelessness. They barely hold up for a year, then we build them again."

"You're telling me we are to be victims of our culture forever."

"Of course. We don't control our culture, it controls us. Man would like to think he is in charge of his destiny. It's an illusion. Even if we design bold new buildings or raise the hemline of women's skirts, *we* don't do it. We are operating within the latitudes of our culture. Does a raindrop have influence on the rainstorm? No, it is only a *part* of the storm."

"That's kind of defeatist, isn't it?"

"Not at all. Man once thought he could control the weather. Now that he knows he can't, he's better prepared for it."

"And here comes a man who still thinks he can."

Florentino shuffled up on his mare at that moment. "*Buenas tardes*, Don," he said to me, his black eyes scanning the two of us like motion detectors. He didn't dismount, but now directed himself to his *patrón*. "We better go bring that cattle first thing Monday before we lose some, no?"

"An excellent idea. I won't be here, so who will you take with you?"

"El Prieto."

"That's all? Why not take Miguel? He's a good man for that sort of thing."

"He fears the black dog, Don." A smile formed on Florentino's clay face and I felt an icy zipper run up my spine.

"Nonsense!"

"Remember last year, Don."

"Go ahead then, do it any way you want."

Florentino did not speak. He touched his sombrero respectfully and trotted off.

"What was that all about?"

"The same *chingaderas* as always. My men are driving me crazy with their superstitions."

"But all campesinos are superstitious."

"But they seem to be getting worse—especially Florentino."

"Get rid of him."

"I can't. He's been with me a long time, and the truth is, he's the best vaquero I've ever met. It's just that his obsession with all the spooks and evil signs drives me crazy."

"What was all that cryptic *pasapasa* about the black dog?"

"Last year five of us went to the outback to bring back about a hundred head of last year's calves. Miguel and Regino and El Prieto were riding up front three abreast. Florentino and I were in back. From somewhere, a black mongrel wandered out on the road and just lay there watching the men come toward him. As they drew closer I noticed the dog didn't move. He just stared up at them with glassy eyes. Just before Regino got on top of him, the dog got up slowly. His glazed eyes seemed to be looking directly into Regino's face. The mongrel then walked a circle around him, slinked into the chaparral and disappeared. Well, Florentino opened his mouth and said, 'That was La Muerte.' I threw him a fierce look and told him to stop talking nonsense, but he repeated it. 'La Muerte always finds its mark.' "

I had to laugh. "It's incredible in this day and age what these poor campesinos believe with all their heart. I hear the same kind of thing but I pay no attention to them."

"On the way back with the cattle next day, Regino gets killed."

"What!"

"We had eighty, ninety head in front of us, and one *cabrón* broke away and ran off into a ravine and into the dense brush. You know how they do."

I knew.

"Regino was on him in an instant. The beast scrambled behind a tree. Regino's horse smacked into the tree with full force. There was nothing Regino—or anyone—could have done."

I felt a sudden chill and my shoulders shivered involuntarily. Neither of us spoke for a few minutes. Then Pedro put down his Presidente. "Come on, keep me company. I want to see how they're doing at the well." We got in the Bronco and bumped our way over.

When we got to the well, I saw two men I'd never seen before. They were dressed in felt hats and ill-fitting three-piece suits probably discarded by hardline corporate bottom liners, and eventually migrated south in the old clothes bag under the auspices of some club or church. One had a rather extensive circumference, the other was as skinny as a rake. They reminded me of Laurel and Hardy. Each leaned on a shovel, contemplating a hole in progress about six feet away from the well.

"We found the problem, Don," the fat one said, hitching up his pants as we stepped out of the Bronco.

Pedro looked at an excavation about three feet square and two feet in depth. A pyramid of dark moist earth rose at one side. "You can see by the dampness the leak is here," Oliver continued with authority.

"When you left the pump running, the water surfaced," the skinny one explained further.

Pedro stepped over to the pump and turned it off. "All right, muchachos, go at it. It is a four-inch line, so lengthen your ditch to at least ten feet so we have room to cut and splice."

Laurel and Hardy set to work immediately. The shovels moved rhythmically, one shovel digging in while the other tossed dirt to one side. The blades made a light shushing sound as they pierced the damp earth. They worked with admirable precision, like high-wire aerialists. "We'll be there soon," Oliver said to all present. "The dirt is quite soft."

Pedro and I stood watching the shovels digging, shushing, dumping, digging, shushing, dumping. Suddenly there was a metallic clang as the two shovels collided with each other. The two men stopped what they were doing and, still holding their shovels, looked at one another. Their smiles vanished like the sun hiding behind a cloud. For a moment I thought, this is where Oliver slaps Stanley over the head with his hat. Two tragic faces looked up at Pedro. No one said a word. At last Laurel and Hardy went to opposite ends of the excavation, drove their shovels into the earth and left them standing. I thought they were going to break for lunch, so I was surprised to hear the skinny one say, "We will finish tomorrow, Don."

"But it's only one o'clock, muchachos. Come, get the thing finished so I can make the repairs this afternoon."

"The shovels touched. You saw that yourself, Don." Oliver's voice was dark.

Stanley was wringing his hat. "You saw it yourself, Don," he echoed. I was sure he would now begin to weep.

"I have a bottle of fine tequila for each of you muchachos," Pedro said with high hopes.

"We'll get to work on it right after sunrise, Don." Oliver elbowed his partner in the ribs.

"Sí, it will be ready for you right after sunrise, Don."

"But the barn is without water."

"We will carry enough water for the day in buckets." Oliver hitched up his pants preparatory to the task. "We go right now and bring all the containers we can find."

I could see the exasperation on Pedro's face. He made no further appeal. We climbed back into the Bronco and started toward the house. "You're going to have to explain that one," I said.

"If it wasn't so frustrating, it would be funny. I've never seen such a superstitious lot. I'm sure you've heard the old fable—if two shovels collide, the sun must set and rise before they can be touched. Rubbish!"

"And they really believe that? Maybe they were just tired."

"They believe it. You saw them refuse the ultimate bribe." Pedro remained within his thoughts and turned into a narrow road. We stopped in front of the vaqueros' living quarters, a melancholy adobe cottage sheltered by a century-old oak the size of a California redwood. The little house had an abandoned look. I followed Pedro to the front door. "I want to show you something inside."

But as we reached the weathered door I saw it was secured with a lock and chain heavy enough to restrain King Kong in a snit. A faded print of the Blessed Virgin was tacked to the door, a bouquet of fresh carnations, red and pink and white, piously arranged in a plastic water tumbler on the stoop. It wasn't hard to guess who nailed the head of a late rattlesnake above the lintel as an additional invocation.

"What's this all about?"

"All my men moved out last summer."

"Where are they living."

"In the barn."

"But why?"

"They believe La Muerte is still in the house waiting to claim the first one who walks in."

"What are you talking about?"

"You're not going to believe it. Four of them were sitting around the table having their noon meal. Conrado, one of the men, picked up a kitchen knife to cut a wedge of cheese. The knife slipped from his hand and fell on the dirt floor. The blade broke off at the handle. Then Florentino announced, 'One of us is going to die.' Conrado bent down to retrieve the knife, and Florentino shouted, 'Don't pick it up! One of us is going to die. We don't know who, but the one who touches that knife will die too!' "

"You're right, I don't believe it."

"They didn't even finish their meal. Florentino herded them out of there like refugees fleeing an erupting volcano. They moved all their belongings, bedding, utensils—everything but the knife—and they've lived in the barn ever since."

"Why did you let it go so long?"

"Truthfully, I wanted to see if the prospects of wintering in the barn would induce them back on their own. But apparently they really believe the spirit of death waits to claim them. Ay, ay, ay!"

"Your problems are over," I said boldly. "Have you got the key? I'll go in there and get the knife out right now."

Pedro reached in his pocket and withdrew a ring of keys that jingled like a Gypsy's tambourine. "*Madre!* I have the wrong key ring. The one we want is up at the house."

"Can we look in the windows?"

We walked over to the side window and peered into the kitchen. I had to pull away a huge spiderweb sprinkled with dead flies. It was sticky and made a soft crackling sound.

Cupping my hands around my eyes, I looked through a thick curtain of dirt and heavy cobweb draperies on the other side of the pane. The room looked cold and silent as death. It was a room where fear slayed faith and black curses crouched behind every shadow. I could make out an old-fashioned wood stove, a crude table, and several splintered chairs. On the dirt floor near the table was the infamous kitchen knife, the blade separated from the handle forming an L. I was going to suggest gaining entrance through the window when I caught a whiff of something awfully good and we heard Concha's dinner bell. We returned to the main house, washed up and entered the kitchen.

"Tsk! Look at that shirt. I put a clean shirt on your bed." Concha's voice was sweet and melodic but must have contained overtones of past authority. Without a word Pedro obediently left the kitchen and returned tucking his shirttails.

Concha served us large oval plates filled with beef and potatoes swimming in *chile colorado*. A smaller dish held fluffy rice garnished with fresh green peas. Her tortillas were small, thick, and wonderful!

"It would be safe to say that you are the best cook in all the Republic," I said.

"And for that you get an extra wedge of flan!" She laughed.

"I've been showing our guest the haunted house," Pedro announced.

"It's plain you're not the superstitious type," I said to Concha.

"Concha is too intelligent. She's not one to abandon the kitchen because the milk spilled or because a blackbird flew in through the open window! Thank God you're not superstitious, Concha."

"I only believe what I see with my own eyes."

"See that?" Pedro crowed. "She is an enlightened woman!"

"And La Muerte has been here."

Pedro froze, fork in hand. "You too, Concha? I give up!" He ripped his tortilla in two.

"Pedro showed me the vaqueros' cottage and told me the whole story. It's pure hokum, Concha. Obviously no one died, right?"

"Well . . ."

"Well what?"

"'Tell him," Concha urged in a tone she must have employed when Pedro was six, cute, and recalcitrant. "Tell him."

"Well, yes, as a matter of fact, Conrado died."

"Jesus! You didn't tell me your whole rancho is under an evil spell! Even as you and I sit here and eat all this wonderful food, the prehensile hand of Death may find us. I think I better be going—I just remembered I have to feed the cat." I caught sight of Concha making a hasty sign of the cross.

"Stop it, both of you! You're as bad as the campesinos."

"But Pedro, you have to be willing to admit one thing," I said.

"What?"

"Regino died, Conrado died. You have to admit that if the prophecy came to pass, it's *not* superstition," I said.

"Enough from the two of you!"

"But," I pressed on, "with two predicted deaths, the campesinos have sufficient grounds for belief. The events support their prophecy. *Quod erat demonstrandum*—it has been proven!"

"But what you must understand is that Conrado was a

heavy drinker. His blood pressure was always at the bursting point. The doctor gave him some medicine to control it, but as soon as he felt a little better, he was sucking on a bottle again."

"Let's have the whole story."

"The day after the knife incident, Conrado was out throwing corn to the cows and he had some kind of seizure. He had been drinking, of course. He could have gone at any moment. The knife incident had nothing whatever to do with it."

"Maybe there really is a curse on El Condor," I suggested.

"I give up! No more Presidente brandy for this man!"

That evening Teetu became restless, and we decided to go in to town for dinner. La Fonda was packed to capacity—young lovers, old lovers, men in the uncomplicated company of other men. Americans of all ages were in the majority. We found a place at the *licenciado's* table. When the local mariachis came shimmering through the front door, every heart in La Fonda skipped a beat. Their black felt sombreros sparkled with more sequins than a New Year's Eve party dress from Saks. There were three violins, two guitars, and a mushroom with a *guitarrón* strapped to his belly thumped the bass line. A tall dark man brought a shiny trumpet to his lips and trimmed the festive melody with garlands of pure silver.

As soon as they began to play, all the vibrant tone colors of that unique musical form came showering down on us like a bursting *piñata*. New loves in crinkly red foil, old loves in pink ribbon, loves lost in bows of faded blue, and all the sweet and tender yesterdays came gently wrapped in sadness cloth. The Americans felt the beat. They were having the time of their lives cavorting off the walls in shorts and jeans. The Mexicans felt the pain. Violins stirred the ashes of their hearts and the big bad machos sang with tears in their eyes. Everyone was there. Even those who could now only live in memory came to be with us as soon as they heard the music.

At eleven-thirty there was a mass exodus as the Americans hurriedly paid their checks and ran for the border before it closed at midnight. The locals remained at their tables talking, drinking, singing. We ate too much, drank too much, and sang too much. We didn't get out of there until half past three.

"*Buenos días*," I whispered when I staggered into the kitchen at eight-thirty Sunday morning.

Concha's voice was sweet and lyrical as always, and this morning, rich with sympathy. "*Buenos días*, Don, I'll bring you a bowl of *menudo*. I made it yesterday knowing what this man is like when he goes out." She put a cup of cinnamon coffee in front of me ever so gently. There was a look of genuine pity in her dark eyes.

"*Gracias*," I slurped. I glanced up at my host at the table. He looked as fresh as though he had gone to bed at nine. His face was radiant and the bright light of his smile was annoying.

"Poor man, just look at you!"

"Concha, make him stop. How long have you been up?"

"Since dawn."

Concha confirmed his statement with a nod.

"It is a beautiful morning!" His exuberance was disgusting. "All the vaqueros are back in their house, the ranch is operating efficiently, the water pipe is fixed. God is definitely in his High Heaven and everything is right at El Condor!"

"What are you talking about?"

"I exorcised the cottage."

"You what?"

"*Sí*, while you were still sleeping with the *angelitos*, I called all the men together, walked into the cottage, and removed the damnable knife. The men are so happy, they were singing when I left them."

"I don't believe you."

Teetu reached into his jacket and put the broken knife on the table in front of me.

Concha stifled a gasp. "I wish you wouldn't bring that thing in here." She sounded like a mother talking to a child who had just walked in the house with a wriggling frog in his hand.

"I'm going to keep it on the mantel as a souvenir."

Shortly after breakfast I took my leave. Concha gave me a plastic bag containing a bundle of her wonderful tortillas and a container of flan. Teetu walked me to my car.

"I'll be back Friday to pick up Perla's birthday present—that is, if I survive."

"To tell you the truth, I don't feel so great myself." Teetu gripped his chest.

"What is it?"

"Just a little heartburn. I'm getting too old to stay out all night." There was pain in his voice.

I didn't like the looks of that at all. I put the things in the trunk of the car. I felt a sudden drop in temperature and looked up to see Florentino had just trotted up on his mare.

"Good news, Don. Both Miguel and Paco agreed to help me drive the cattle in tomorrow."

"¡*Magnífico!* What changed their mind?"

"When they saw you remove the evil from the cottage."

"I knew they weren't superstitious men."

"I buried the head of the rooster for each of them."

A tight grimace twisted Teetu's face. I thought it was frustration, but then realized he was in real pain.

"What is it, Don?" Florentino noticed it too.

"Too much nightlife." Once again his hand went to his chest.

Florentino reached into his breast pocket and drew out his little vial of prophylactic magic water. "Take this, Don. It will protect you from the *mal*."

"Nonsense." Teetu waved it away. "I'll be fine. I'm going in now and take a very long siesta."

Florentino replaced the vial, but I got the feeling he knew something we didn't—something between a devout pagan and his mythical gods.

I got behind the wheel. "See you Friday."

"I'll meet you at La Fonda for breakfast at nine o'clock," Teetu said. He looked pale and the color was gone from his voice.

I left my friend with a vague, uneasy feeling. In spite of a hectic shooting schedule, I couldn't shake Teetu out of my mind. All week I was nagged by inopportune fits of apprehension. Sleep did not attend me, and early Friday morning I checked out of the Holiday Inn and was on the road by six. I crossed the border into Mexico just minutes after nine o'clock and headed straight for La Fonda and the Cafeteros.

"*Buenos días*," I called out as I pushed through the door. Teetu was nowhere in sight and I felt my heart sink.

"*Buenos días*," a sullen male choir mumbled, and I knew something was wrong.

"Why so glum, Los Cowboys won, no?" I gibed with phony cheer. I was whistling in the dark and I knew it.

"You mean you haven't heard?" the doctor replied.

My heart stopped! "Heard what? I'm just coming from the Other Side." I knew what he was going to say, and I didn't want to hear it. He started to say something, but I disconnected him before he could reply because at that moment I saw Teetu come walking in from the men's room. I felt like those times when I've been caught in violent turbulence at 36,000 feet, accepted the inevitable, said goodbye to my family, then walked into the terminal feeling perfectly ridiculous. See? I said to myself, you're behaving like a hysterical señorita.

"Ah! I see Cecil B. De Mille made it back!" Teetu stood at the back of my chair and kneaded my shoulders affectionately. "Coffee time is not the same when you're not here, *viejo*. These *cabrónes* need a moderator." I could hear the smile in his voice and it filled me nearly to overflowing.

"I'm heading for your ranch now on my top secret mission."

Teetu was in high spirits. "And before I forget, *muchachones*, Perla's birthday fiesta is tomorrow at two. You will all be there, *sí*? The calf is in the pit, the beer is getting cold, and I contracted the mariachis to play for us until they drop."

The Cafeteros accepted with alacrity and unanimity. We ate breakfast and followed the agenda faithfully for the better part of an hour: Impact of Government on Society, Banking in the Year 2000, Aspect Ratio of Brassieres and Their Affect on Conformation.

Presently the doctor came to his feet. "And now to work, señores, I have patients to see." This must have reminded the dentist, the banker, the merchants, and the *licenciado* of their obligations. We put money on the table and drifted out onto the sidewalk, still in conversation. Everyone seemed reluctant to leave the warming hearth of friendship and the small talk continued. Hector lit a Havana.

"How about Los Cowboys?"

"That *cabrón* Irwin is a miracle!"

"*Formidable!*"

"*¡Ahora sí, al Super Bowl!*"

"I have some bets to collect from my dumb brother-in-law."

Nobody seemed to notice. A car came rolling backward from the parking lot across the street and jumped the curb where we stood. It was a wild free-for-all. Hector lost a perfectly good cigar. The *licenciado*, who was built along the lines of the Basilica of Santa Verónica, was the first to react with a flying leap and a spectacular double spin rarely seen outside the Bolshoi. The rest of us scrambled like quail running from a fox on his way to lunch. Teetu was killed instantly.

Fire and Faith

"Balloons, balloons! ... Red, yellow, blue ... Meeky Mouse!"

"Shine, señor ... Chiclets?"

"The tamales are ready! ... The tamales are hot, hot, hot!"

I've never known it to fail. Make yourself comfortable on a shady bench in Tecate's main plaza, and you'll attract vendors like potato salad summons yellow jackets at a picnic. I waved them all away and continued watching the human comedy unfold in front of me like theater-in-the-round. A group of old rancheros, with terra-cotta faces and Pancho Villa sombreros, appeared to be plotting the revolution in dark voices coming from behind bushy viva Mexico mustachios. Chattering schoolgirls, perfect miniature replicas of their mothers, walked like proper young ladies on their way home for lunch in their navy-blue pinafores and spotless white stockings. The boys in rumpled khaki, sticky and sweaty, chased the pigeons or let fly karate kicks in the air.

I observed a young couple in the dark cloister of the tiled kiosk discovering the sweet pain of their first kiss.

I looked up to see a dark man drifting toward me and drop anchor directly in front of me. He was a thin man, in a black suit and a thin tie, waiting courteously to be acknowledged. He wore white penny loafers on his feet. The suit strongly implied a long history of faithful service to previous owners. The man's mouth was thin as wire. The eyes, sunny-side-up, were wide and round and pure as an angel's thoughts. But the smile was more like that of the fox in the henhouse. Instinctively, I brought my hand up and felt the outline of my wallet. That's when I noticed the thin black case in his thin hands. Here it comes, I thought. In a minute he'll be showing me an array of solid gold Casio watches for ten dollars.

Eye contact was now unavoidable. The voice was Pennzoil 10-30 "Can I interest you in a miracle, señor?" I knew it! He didn't wait for an answer. He snapped the case open. It was lined with regal purple velvet and a dazzling display of gold and silver charms in the shape of arms and legs and eyes and human heads and hearts. I couldn't begin to imagine their purpose. "How do I use one?"

"There is no limit to the possibilities, señor," the oily voice continued. "Choose the little charm appropriate to your needs and place it before the saint of your choice. You have bursitis? Take an arm. For love affairs, the heart, of course. If you don't see what you need, I have more. Look!" From his coat pocket he brought out an assortment of human organs, a pair of eyes, a cow and a bird.

My face may have betrayed a vigorous lack of fervor.

"Do you know old Don Ambrosio, the man who runs the yardage shop?" I shook my head. "Not too long ago the poor man could hardly walk. He had a huge growth on the back of his knee. Right here." He indicated the anterior aspect of the lateral miniscus of his left knee. "He had it for years, it baffled all the doctors. Poor man could hardly use his leg." He bent one knee almost to the pavement and demonstrated how a man thus afflicted might walk. It looked painful, and I started to feel sorry for old Don Ambrosio although I had never made his acquaintance. "Well, señor, one day I sold him a little leg, like this one." He held up a silver-plated leg. "He placed it before San Francisco—and go look at him now!"

"Improved?"

"Go look at him. The growth disappeared completely. I don't say to you he dances 'La Cucaracha,' but go look at him, señor. He walks as normally as you or I."

Here was a man who knew how to open with some strong user benefits and a solid reason why to buy.

"Never underestimate the power of these little charms, señor—and in Life, who knows what morning brings besides the newborn sun, eh?"

A strong close, I thought. I bought several charms to budget against an uncertain future. He took a seat next to me while he wrapped each one individually in white tissue paper.

"I see you are watching the play of life unfold here in the plaza. I have seen everything from the first kiss, like that young couple in the *quiosco*, to the last tearful farewell, the prelude to bitter parting. Oh! I could tell you many beautiful stories that began with one of these little charms you now hold in your hand—and ended as happily as a fairy tale."

I waved away another balloon man and a boy peddling plastic iguanas on a stick. I passed on the hot *churros*, but I could never resist a good story. I encouraged him to continue.

"It was right here in the plaza that I witnessed the most remarkable drama I have ever seen in my long life. It began right over there at those tables in front of the café. It's been over five years now, but everyone in Tecate still talks about Faustino and the treasure."

"Treasure?"

"*Sí*, señor, but the *novela* is not so much about treasure as it is about true love. It was another triumph for San Lorenzo, who played a major role in Faustino's happiness."

"One of your trinkets and a petition to San Lorenzo?"

"*Sí* señor. San Lorenzo is known to answer the plea of the faithful, but he is also a very jealous saint. You must never forget to keep your pledge or he'll remind you that you are delinquent."

"What kind of reminder?"

"He burns."

"He burns! How can he do that?"

"Oh, he has ways, señor, he has *ways*."

His endorsement was true enough. Any time I mention Faustino's name here in town, the whole episode enjoys re-runs for several days. I now put it before a jury of my peers and await the verdict.

The whole thing began when three young men, all in their mid-twenties, sat eating calf-head tacos at the outdoor tables in the main plaza.

"Are you going to run with the bulls this year?" Alfredo asked between chews of cheek meat.

"Of course, if you can call it running. I spent most of the run last year skidding on my face," Beto answered before bringing the taco to his mouth. He preferred brains. "The bulls last year were *big madres!*"

Alfredo and Beto were *contadores* at the Banco del Pacifico. The third man, somewhat disappointed because the café had sold out of eye tacos earlier that morning, had to make do with tongue, his second favorite. He ladled a highly volatile salsa on top and entered the conversation for the first time. "Rumor has it there won't be Pamplona Days this year." Faustino worked in the municipal offices less than five steps from where they now sat. As the *mozo mayor*, the chief gofer and fetcher, you could say he lived in the factory where new rumors were mass-produced every day.

"What do you mean, no Pamplona this year?"

Faustino put down his delicacy. "Too much damage, the merchants said. Remember last year? Bulls raging and runners fleeing death by horn through cafés and shops."

"How can I forget? I took refuge in Flaco's ceramic shop."

"By the way, anybody want to go to the fair tonight? Should be crawling with *chamaconas*!"

"I can't. I have to spend the next few days digging up a leaking water pipe in the backyard. I'm not looking forward to it. The ground is hard as bone." If Faustino was expecting offers of help, he didn't reveal his disappointment.

"Maybe you'll find money."

"I have an uncle that had a friend that was digging a hole for a well and came up with an olla, and when he broke it open, it was full of gold and silver coins."

"Everyone in Mexico knows someone who knew someone who found treasure while digging for some other purpose."

"But it makes sense if you consider our history. Between our war of independence in 1821 and our revolution of 1910, the average life expectancy of a president was around twenty-one days. Even successful candidates didn't live long enough to finish reciting the oath of office. Everybody buried their cash in those days. My own parents did."

"My grandmother still keeps her savings in a coffee can."

"I have never believed any of it," Faustino said. They paused to watch a gaggle of office girls clack their way to the fountain in spiky heels and colored stockings. Two old women swaddled in black rebosos, priceless relics of an irretrievable era, pecked their way toward the Church of Our Lady like a pair of ravens.

A little puckered-face gnome with the visage of a happy prune pushed a cart as he chimed his bells and sang his song. "*¡Popsicles . . . mango, melón, sandía . . . limón, chocolate!*" Then he added a cadenza of his own. "Buy the señoritas a popsicle . . . a generous *galán* is twice loved!"

Suddenly Faustino gulped down a thick chunk of air. "Oh my God—look!"

All conversation stopped, their words frozen on their lips. All three men sat a little taller in their chairs. Alfredo quickly ran his napkin across his upper lip. Beto surreptitiously undid an additional button on his shirt. Faustino crossed one leg over the other in an effort to hide a small tear in the knee of the tan chinos he wore. The cause of all this fevered peacockishness was the appearance of a celestial being that had just stepped out of the law offices and began to walk across the plaza. She was dressed in a fresh peppermint sundress that swirled around a pleasant arrangement of angles and curves. She was the *bella meta* of every man in Tecate, eligible or not. Even her name was a song.

"Hold on to your heart, Faustino, she's walking this way!"

"*Buenos días*, Cristina!" they called in unison.

"*Buenos días*," the heavenly creature replied.

They looked up at her face, a perfect cameo of pink nacre that inspired kisses. All three could imagine becoming tangled in the thick raven hair that gently caressed her shoulders.

"Join us for coffee."

"*Gracias*, but I'm delivering a court order."

Beto turned toward her to allow her a better view of his open shirt. "Let your client rot in his cell. Run away with me now and I will empty my heart!"

"Anywhere but in my ear."

"I love you to death, Cristina!"

"Then—quick—love another!"

Alfredo wanted his share of attention. "Well, I love no one!"

"Thank the Lord! Yours is an *acta noble*. You do the women of Tecate a great service." And Cristina walked off in the direction of her errand.

"This very night I will disclose my love beneath your window!" Beto called after her.

"The song of the popsicle peddler is sweeter to me than your serenade!" the celestial being cried over the shoulder of her peppermint frock.

The three young men remained silent for a few seconds. Faustino felt a sharp pain deep in his heart where the dart had entered. "She is so beautiful," he whispered as though in a cathedral.

"Yes, sweet face, bitter tongue," Beto shot back.

"Perhaps if you were nicer."

"A grave error. Never be nice to a woman, Faustino. Women take kindness as a form of weakness."

"I think Faustino is in love," Alfredo taunted. Faustino looked down at the cracks in his sneakers.

"Then go after her, hombre," Beto encouraged, "know the color of *calzones*!"

A ginger-colored dog with a drooly grin pulled up to their table, making it unnecessary for Faustino to reply to Beto's blasphemy. The dog ignored Alfredo and Beto, sat down directly in front of Faustino and flashed him his best smile. Dogs in general are known to have unerring instincts, but this rover was a veteran of the closing room, and he knew that in sales—You close 'em or you walk 'em. He made eye contact with Faustino and swept the flagtones with his tail. Predictably (to the ginger dog), Faustino put his taco down. It was gone instantly. The dog vacuumed the immediate area and trotted off in search of another easy mark.

"HEY FAUSTINO! The coffeepot is empty—hurry hombre, get your *nalgas* over here!" The rude imperative came from a lowly clerk who stood shouting from the door of the city offices. But when you're the *mozo mayor*, everybody is your boss.

"Have to go," Faustino said, and quietly headed toward the superior lowly clerk. "I'll see you later."

"Poor Faustino. He has the worst job, the girl he's in love with won't deign to look his way, and he's going to spend the weekend digging holes."

"It's funny, we've known him since he first came to Tecate. We were in high school, remember? And he has always been at the bottom of the bean pot."

"Remember how he always was the one sent up to the office of that thorny director?"

"I remember. And the strange thing was that he didn't do anything bad. If you remember, it was you and I who played the pranks, he just tagged along."

"All he ever wanted was to be one of us. He could be paid with praise. He used to call us the three musketeers."

"Poor devil. Every time Fate cleans out the closet where they keep all that bad *caca*, it always seems to fall on Faustino."

"Poor Faustino, maybe he'll find buried treasure."

"Wouldn't that be a lark?"

"I've got it!"

"What?"

"Let's go to a coin shop and buy a few old coins."

"You're not suggesting gold coins, are you?"

"No, no, something cheap, but dated in the 1800s."

"To plant in his yard? You evil thing!"

"*Exacto.*"

"*¡Magnífico!*"

Saturday morning two of the *tres mosqueteros* walked into Sam's Coins and Stamps on India Street in downtown San Diego. They bought four silver Mexican coins for five dollars apiece. They were about the size of a U.S. silver dollar, thick as a club sandwich, and dated between 1875 and 1880. They were stamped *Ocho Reales*.

Monday morning Beto and Alfredo were taking their morning coffee break in the plaza. Their two-innocent-guys-in-the-plaza act deserved an award. They didn't have to wait long for their prey.

Faustino came running up flushed and wheezing. "Coffee," he gasped with the last remaining breath in his lungs.

"What is it, Faustino?"

"You look frazzled."

Faustino was still hyperventilating when the waiter returned with his coffee. "You're not going to believe this!" He panted. "You're not going to believe this!"

"Calm down, calm down, what is it?"

"Yes, you look like you've seen the ghost of La Llorona."

Faustino sucked in a big breath and began in a voice choked with emotion. "I found . . . I . . . I found . . . I found . . . buried money in the backyard!" He couldn't finish. His eyes filled and his throat closed up on him.

"Sure you did."

"No, honest—I swear by the Holy Virgin."

"What exactly did you find, a couple of old pennies?"

Faustino looked anxiously in all directions, and seeing no witnesses in the immediate vicinity, opened his hand for his friends to see. "Look at this!"

Alfredo whistled. "I thought you were having a joke with us. These are real!"

"Sssh!"

"Let me see," Beto added with counterfeit skepticism.

"Yes, he's right, *Ocho Reales*, look at the dates. They're genuine pieces of eight, all right. How much do you suppose they're worth?"

"I have no idea," Faustino answered, "but what I'm thinking is there has to be more. This is only the tip of the iceberg. Logic demands that there is more nearby. I'll be digging every day now. I must swear you to secrecy."

"Of course, we're the three musketeers."

"¡Uno por todos, todos por uno!"

"Don't look now, but guess who's coming in our direction."

All three sat tall, Alfredo wiped his mustache, Beto attended to his buttons, and Faustino crossed his legs. Cristina arrived appareled like spring. Her skirt, a field of pink and purple lilacs in full bloom, swayed gently to the rhythm of her gait.

Beto was the first to speak. "Lo, the season of love is come! Tend your fields. Will the goddess of *primavera* join me for coffee?"

"What, with the enemy of chastity?"

"Me? I would pay any price, meet any *manda* for a minute with you."

"You would be making a great investment for little profit."

Alfredo couldn't stay out of it. "My dear mother wants to gain a daughter."

"Maybe you can haggle for one at the fair on market day."

Beto took over. "Name the day, *corazón*, name the day you'll consent to be mine."

"The very first day it rains *chocolate*. And now I must go get a signature on this document." And the fragrant field of lilacs drifted across the plaza.

"Come back, come back, thief—you're stealing my heart!" Beto shouted across the plaza for all to witness.

With pounding heart Faustino watched Cristina until she was out of sight, and his soul defected. He exhaled wistfully. "She is like the moon, so beautiful and so unattainable."

"You become as mute as maracas with no seeds as soon as she comes into sight," Beto admonished.

Faustino was not available for comment, as at that moment a multicolored ball rolled under their table and he went down to retrieve it. When he came up with the ball in his hands, he found a small boy glaring at him accusingly. Without preamble the child contorted his face, let out a blood-chilling shriek that brought half the plaza to its feet, and left the bronze Benito Juarez with ringing in the ears. Faustino stood blushing as the mother of the plaintiff marched up and lay claim to the ball.

Beto continued his instruction. "You'll never get anywhere with Cristina if you don't assert yourself."

"There is no room in her life for the *mozo* at city hall. It's a case of the crow courting the nightingale."

The popsicle man passed their table. "*¡Popsicles . . . mango, melón, sandía, limón, chocolate!* Tell her with a popsicle . . . love unspoken is love lost!"

"HEY FAUSTINO! When are you going to see about the toilet!" The angry voice carried from one end of the plaza to another.

Faustino rose and whispered, "If I find the rest of this treasure, I'll tell him to stick his head in and fix the toilet himself." And he was gone.

As soon as he was out of sight, Alberto and Beto fell into each other's arms convulsed with scampish laughter. When they could finally catch a breath, Beto said, "Should we tell him?"

Alfredo opened his mouth to answer. "Pfp-ffffff-pfft," was all that he could articulate, and the two young men collapsed with laughter once again.

Monday and Tuesday of the following week came and went, and Faustino failed to make an appearance in the plaza. The story of Faustino and the treasure was now on the lips of every citizen of Tecate save the preschoolers. Alfedo and Beto were now doing a little soul searching. Something was definitely gnawing at their conscience.

"Faustino has been digging up his yard for four days now. Have you been by to see what he's done?"

"I went by last night. He'll be in China by the day after tomorrow."

"Maybe we should tell him."

"Let's wait a bit. In a few days he'll give up, I'm sure. Then we don't have to say anything at all."

But Alfredo and Beto were wrong. Very wrong. The

next day Faustino came by for tacos. He was covered with dirt and more determined than ever.

"I can't stay long, I just came by to see my fellow *mosqueteros* and give you a progress report."

"You've got to give it up, Faustino."

"Yes, if you haven't found anything by now, there is probably nothing more to be found."

"I can't stop now, I've got too much invested. I've reached the point of no return. It's killing work, but if I find the rest of the treasure, I can court Cristina and life will be beautiful. And you can be sure I won't forget my friends when I strike it rich. We are still the three musketeers."

"Uno por todos, todos por uno."

The waiter arrived at that moment. Alfredo ordered cheek, Beto asked for brains. "Eyes," Faustino said.

"I'm sorry, Faustino, the eyes go early in the morning."

"Two tongue tacos with everything, then."

The waiter returned shortly and placed a paper plate containing two tacos in front of each of them.

"By the way, has anyone seen Cristina?" Faustino inquired as he attacked the first taco.

"Only from a distance. She's been crossing the plaza over near the church."

"HEY FAUSTINO! There's a cockroach in my desk. Get your *nalgas* over here!"

A taco still untouched remained on Faustino's plate. "Excuse me," he said, and went to answer the rude summons.

"We're going to have to tell him, you know."

"I know."

"But how?"

"I'm thinking, I'm thinking!"

Faustino returned in a only a few minutes and took his seat. "Hey, where's my other taco?"

"I thought you weren't coming back," Beto explained, touching a paper napkin to his lips.

"I just resigned my high level post at city hall. I'm devoting all my time to extracting that buried treasure. Well, I must run. There is much work to be done." Exit Faustino.

Another week slipped away and Alfredo and Beto were still grappling with the inner voice.

"Seen anything of Faustino?"

"No, you?"

"No, I'm too embarrassed to go by his house."

"Me too. Do you suppose he knows it was a prank and he's mad?"

"It's a possibility."

"It's gone too far to be funny. We have to tell him."

"And just what do we tell him? We had a big joke on you, Faustino, ha ha ha! It's too late for that now. We should have told him a long time ago, when he could still see the humor of it."

"I suppose you're right. We've gone beyond the point of no return."

"But, on the other hand, we can't let it go on forever."

"Let's give him until the weekend, then we'll take him to La Fonda for a gay evening of drinks and a fine dinner. Then we plead guilty and throw ourselves on his mercy. A few of those deep dish margaritas, and he'll be flowing with the milk of human kindness."

"Agreed! Friday is our deadline."

The following Friday afternoon Alfredo and Beto sat in the plaza eating tacos.

"Well, today's the day."

"I know, I already have a reservation at La Fonda."

"Are you going to tell him?"

"I thought it would be better coming from you."

"You could probably do it better."

"*¡Dios mío!* Look!"

"The Pope has come to Tecate!"

"Or Michael Jackson."

A sleek white Lincoln Mark IV, measuring just a little less than a kilometer in length, shimmered into the scene and parked at the far end of the plaza. Smoked glass made it impossible to see anything of the exalted personage this kind of vehicle is expected to convey. In a few minutes the front door opened and everyone in the plaza turned to watch a dignified *chofer* in brown livery come 'round to the rear door. It opened almost without sound and a lean figure stepped out. He was dressed in white slacks, a blue shirt open at the collar, and a soft linen blazer the color of butter.

"Who is it?"

"Nobody *I* know."

As the stranger drew near, Alfredo and Beto were nearly blinded by the brilliant flash of light reflecting from the gold Seiko strapped to his wrist. There was another sudden flare-up as the hand reached up and removed the Serengeti sunglasses.

"Faustino!"

"Where have you been?" Beto gasped.

"What what what?" Alfredo stammered without pausing for commas.

"Life is beautiful, isn't it?" Faustino beamed at his fellow musketeers.

"But but but but . . ." Alfredo was still in shock.

"It's right out of a fairy tale!" Faustino gushed.

Alfredo and Beto failed to form words, as speech is difficult when the lower mandible is paralyzed in the down position. Beto was the first to regain his faculties. "I don't know about you, Alfredo, but I start digging today!"

"We dig together. Your place, then mine—fifty-fifty."

Beto extended his hand. "*¡Chócala!*" An elaborate handshake sealed their pact.

"*Oh, Dios mío!* Look who's coming this way!"

Cristina had just come out of the law offices and was now headed in their direction. She was dressed in a pistachio summer cooler of sheer cotton. The full skirt swirled deliciously with every graceful step and flaunted a big sassy bow at the back.

All three young men suddenly sat taller. Alfredo wiped his mustache, Beto opened his shirt. Faustino didn't bother to cover one knee with another, and his linen blazer the color of butter easily hid the tear in his heart.

Alfredo opened the dialogue. "A man could fall in love on a day like this."

"A virulent disease, Alfredo," Cristina replied, "and there is no known cure!"

Alfredo wasn't discouraged. "The very sight of you gives me butterflies. I know you must feel something too, Cristina."

"Heartburn. It's remarkable, we haven't heard from Beto. Is it possible you've squandered all your wit? And you with no overdraft protection."

"Nothing of the sort. It is the prodigiousness of your beauty that stuns me into silence."

"What a shame! Admiration founded on beauty is doomed to *perdición* from the start. Men are as fickle as the weather."

"Not this man. You can bank on me like a government bond."

"What good is a bond with little interest that never matures?"

"I surrender! I surrender! *En final* the sum of beauty is virtue. I throw down my sword and beg for mercy!"

The only possible explanation open to us for what happened next is that a number of events of an intersessional nature were now in progress in the Celestial City high above the plaza.

A tall man sat looking out through the golden archway of his marbled balcony. The fact that he was sitting should in no way imply that he was at ease. On the contrary, restless fingers stroked the russet curls of his shoulder-length hair. He left his vigil and began to pace anxiously up and down the marbled halls. He covered ground as fast as his robes would allow. He was about to start another lap when he spotted his man coming toward him through the crystal pillars. The very sight of his silver wings lightened the weight in his heart.

"Ave San Lorenzo! You wished to see me, sir?"

"Miguel-Angel, my angel of choice."

"Thank you for the *confianza*, sir."

"Did you bring the files?" The question was hardly necessary. Miguel-Angel cradled a stack of folders in his arms. "I'm inquiring about a petition I received some time ago."

"The name would greatly simplify the search, sir."

"Cristina."

Miguel-Angel rifled through the files. "I have a Cristina de Alvarez who pleads for the love of young Faustino."

"That's it! I approved that petition months ago." San Lorenzo was a saint with an enviable track record, and he knew it.

"If you'll forgive the metaphor, sir, we're up to our wings in petitions."

"Believe me, I understand. Mortals seem to think we spend our time strumming harps and singing Father Vivaldi's choral music. Ours is a heavy responsibility."

"Yes sir."

"What seems to be the delay?"

"To put it succinctly, sir, every time we give Faustino a golden opportunity, he becomes as mute as a lute without strings. And we can't do anything while he's digging in that hole, and he's been at it for weeks. He should reach the Evil One by day after tomorrow."

San Lorenzo didn't answer immediately. Once again he was transfixed by something beyond the gilded arches where they stood. A beatific smile took form on the saintly countenance and he motioned Miguel-Angel to his side. "Take a look down in the plaza, I think I hear opportunity knocking."

Miguel-Angel peered over the edge as instructed. "It appears the hour has produced the man, sir."

"Exactly."

Down in the plaza, Faustino began to feel an unexplained tingling in his hands. Sparklers were going off in his heart. An unseen and unknown force pulled him to his feet, and he took Cristina by both hands. He looked deep into her green eyes and said, "I was just saying life is beautiful when you stepped up to give us living confirmation."

Alfredo and Beto were stunned into silence. They were experiencing problems of the lower mandible again.

Cristina feared her heart was going to leap out of her pistachio dress. She smiled an aurora borealis.

"Perhaps I can tempt you to have dinner with me."

"Careful! I can resist everything except temptation."

"My car is at your disposal, shall we go?" Cristina murmured a prayer and signed her IOU to San Lorenzo the moment she took the offered arm. Faustino turned to his friends. "Until later, musketeers." And every living soul in the plaza stood and goggled as the dignified *chófer* in brown livery opened the door and Faustino and the beautiful Cristina disappeared behind the smoked windows.

The Mark IV oozed away from the plaza just as a sweet madrigal wafted across the plaza. "¡*Popsicles . . . mango, melón, sandía . . . limón, chocolate!* Rich the treasure, sweet the pleasure after pain!"

Well, that's the story of Faustino and the buried treasure—or so I thought until I said to the charm peddler, "You were right, it did end like a fairy tale."

"Oh, but that is not the whole story, señor, no, the story has a happy ending."

"What's happier than finding buried treasure?"

"Finding love, señor. Long before Faustino began his dig, Señorita Cristina confided in me. 'I want something that will make Faustino look at me,' she said. 'Something that will make him take my hand in his and pronounce his love for me.' You see, señor, your humble *servidor* was a major player in the drama." The convulsion that followed was intended to be a wink. "So, of course, I provided her with the appropriate charms, a pair of eyes, a pair of hands, and a silver-plated heart. She decided to petition San Lorenzo."

"The saint that burns if you fail to meet your pledge?"

"*Sí*, señor, the very one. And she pledged a glorious novena if Faustino would fall in love with her—a serenade in the plaza in honor of San Lorenzo every night for nine nights!"

"So it was never the treasure that aroused her interest at all."

"*Correcto.*"

"So then there is more to the story."

"*Sí*, señor."

I paid the man in the revolting black suit and the Pennzoil voice for my purchases and begged for the conclusion to his tale.

The limo delivered Faustino and Cristina to the front door of La Fonda. A NASA space shuttle couldn't have attracted more attention. The happy couple entered at the height of the dinner hour. Hand in hand they wended their way through a labyrinth of voices, laughter, smoke, and the festive music of mariachis who were melting hearts at a back table. Paco, a perceptive waiter in a red vest who could recognize a couple in love as easily as a cow recognizes grass, seated them next to each other at a corner table. It was covered in a deep burgundy cloth; crisp pink napkins stood fan-folded on a white service plate. A table tent suggested an after-dinner cappuccino.

Paco handed them menus and lighted a tall taper with a flourish. "*¿Buenas noches, un refresco?*"

"*Sí*, a pitcher of margaritas." The waiter fled, and Faustino, who was still giddy from recent events, looked into Cristina's liquid green eyes. "If this is a dream, Cristina, let me die dreaming. Do you have any idea how long I've loved you?"

"And do you have any idea how long I've waited for you to look at me? Your dream is my dream, Faustino." It's altogether possible Cristina would have said more, but Paco arrived at that moment with the margaritas, and his presence inhibited *sentimientos de amor*.

"Would you like a few minutes before you order?"

Faustino nodded and they were alone once again. "Why didn't you ever speak to me?" Faustino asked in a low voice.

"Why didn't you ever look at me?" she fired back in a whisper.

"I didn't feel worthy, but now that I'm in an agreeable financial pos—"

"Shame on you! Can you think that little of me? Money, I despise it! I fell in love with Faustino. I measure you by the depth of your heart, not the weight of your gold."

Faustino was so overwhelmed by this speech that he stood up preparatory to getting up on the table and dancing "La Bamba," but Paco's quick return compelled him to contain his fervor.

"I suggest the grilled red snapper. It is fresh from the fathomless depths of the Pacific, succulent, and served with a crisp salad, or we could arrange a side dish of tender—"

"*Sí, sí*, Paco, the red snapper," Faustino agreed impatiently. Neither cared whether it was red or blue, whether its former home had been the Pacific or the Adriatic. They didn't even care if it snapped.

Cristina returned to her theme. "All Tecate knew you were digging for treasure, but its existence was of no interest to me."

"But the buried treasure was all a prank on behalf of Alfredo and Beto." Faustino then told her all about the silver coins.

"So you're poor, I'm delighted. I love you all the more! But when did you realize it was all a hoax?"

"After digging only a few days. I could tell by their behavior. What really happened was that my grandfather, who came to Mexico from Germany right after the First World War to run a coffee plantation in Chiapas, decided to go to his homeland to die. He's ninety-four. Anyway, he wanted to settle up with his heirs before he left. He settled a grand fortune on my brothers and me."

Paco arrived and served the grilled red snapper along with the crisp mixed salad. Neither Faustino nor Cristina responded to his magnanimous offer of freshly ground pepper, and Paco, being a sensitive individual, disappeared.

"And how long will you let the scoundrels dig?"

"In time to get themselves cleaned up to attend our wedding."

Cristina dropped her fork and smiled into the face of the man she adored. Faustino took her hand and nestled it in his. "Marry me, Cristina, marry me, and make me the happiest man in all the world." He leaned toward her and found her mouth waiting for his. The kiss was sweet but brief, as Faustino sensed a red vest hovering somewhere in the vicinity. He released her hand and lifted his glass. "To a long and happy life."

Young girls in love are known to have their head in the clouds when the young man they adore proposes marriage. In reaching across for her goblet, Cristina's arm collided with the candle and it landed at the center of the table. Almost immediately the table tent suggesting an after-dinner cappuccino was in flames. Quickly, Faustino swatted at the flames with his napkin, but his aim was off. He came down on the edge of the plate and the grilled red snapper fresh from the depths of the Pacific was now on the floor. The blaze quickly spread to the straw basket shaped like a little sombrero, which held the bread sticks. Without regard for his personal safety, Faustino continued to battle the blaze with his napkin.

Paco, who at that moment was delivering two *Viejo Vergels* to the next table, got an unfortunate inspiration. He threw a brandy on the flames, and Faustino and Cristina were now warming themselves at a tabletop fire.

"¡Dios mío! What is happening here!" Faustino exclaimed as he grabbed the pitcher of margaritas and poured out the contents.

Cristina crossed herself quickly and lowered her eyes in sheepish contrition as she thought of her unpaid bill with San Lorenzo. "Hurry, we must send for the mariachis."

As soon as Faustino signaled to the mariachis, the seemingly unquenchable flames surrendered. The musicians gathered around their table in a semicircle. "A serenade?" the skinny first violin asked.

"Yes," Cristina answered piously, "follow me." And she was out the door headed directly for the main plaza, trailed by four violins, three guitars, a *guitarrón*, a silvery trumpet, and a slightly smoked but happy musketeer who followed a few inches off the ground.

The Day
the Duck Sang

*I*t was a sad thing to see. Pretty Teresa Martínez was on the edge of tears. It was the worst day of the week for her. It was Friday—payday—and she wanted to cry. Poor thing.

She sat on the edge of her bed rummaging through the drawer that sat on her lap. She felt so miserable she completely ignored her *regla* and the first-day cramps that certified her womanhood. The bedroom was quiet. The only sound she was aware of was a muffled tangle of intimate voices coming from the next-door neighbor's television. She was alone in the house. Margarito was at work, Abel and Beto were in school, and she had Nito in the backyard with some toys. Anxious hands sifted nervously through layers of blouses and shirts. She hit bottom. Holy Mary Mother of God, it wasn't there!

Her heart landed in her stomach. She was sick. But her agony was brief. In the few ticks it took to bite her upper lip and push the hair out of her face, she realized she had changed the hiding place to another drawer. She threw the drawer on her lap to one side and yanked open the top drawer of the old dresser. She ripped out stockings and underwear with both hands and let them float to the floor. There, in the bottom corner, among the socks rolled neatly into balls, Teresa saw what she was looking for, a pair of blue anklets she never wore.

In the 1800s the vast majority of Mexicans had little faith in banks. They wanted their cash where they could touch it. They stashed their money within a loose adobe in the wall, under the floor, or buried it in some little-used corner of the patio. But by 1940 Mexicans, now confident of the future, decided it was time to enter the twentieth century, and deposits grew along with the booming population. Teresa, being a modern girl, opened a savings account in U.S. dollars at Banamex soon after she and Margarito were married. She had three hundred dollars and a million dreams. It was nearly the price of a small residential lot. They would build a little house there.

Then, in September 1982, by presidential decree, the banks closed their doors. When they reopened two weeks later, her dollars were government property and they gave her a little over twenty thousand pesos that wouldn't buy dirt. That's when they rented the old house with the leaky roof and the cranky plumbing. With their lack of faith in government and banks firmly restored, Mexicans are once again putting their trust in cold cash in a hole.

The blue anklets were the family savings, money against a rainy day, and lately it had been pouring. She made deposits as often as she could. It was unquestionably safer than the bank. The government couldn't get to it, the children never came into her bedroom, and Margarito, in ten years of marriage, wouldn't know where to find his socks and underwear. He would go to work naked if she didn't put his clothes out for him every day.

She turned the socks inside out and a roll of wrinkled bank notes fell out. She counted. Ninety-five thousand pesos. Five thousand short. Well, her ironing would bring in that much, and the rent wasn't actually due for another week, so that was all right. And she still had a dress to finish and deliver, and that would buy the groceries. (If she were careful.)

It was now time to go across the street and humiliate herself. It was the same thing every Friday. She hated it, but it had to be done. Quickly she made up the bed with the curdled mattress worn to the springs, she replaced the clothing and the drawers, and gathered Margarito's clothing from the old wing chair covered in shredded corduroy. A plaster of paris crucifix sprayed to affect bronze hung on the colorless wall above the bed. Dialogue from the television next door continued to seep into the room.

" . . . that I can no longer live without you. I want you, body and soul." A woman's voice, low and throbbing with urgency.

"But Carmela, your father will never permit our union. I must leave you. I must go far away. But I want you and God to hear these words . . . no one will ever take your place. I will love you until the day I close my eyes and die!"

"You mustn't! You would leave my heart in ashes! We shall run away together."

"Together?"

"*Sí*, together."

"*¡Mi amor!*"

"*¡Corazón!*"

Teresa finished picking up and ran a brush through her

hair. There was a time when I would sing while I did my housework, she thought to herself. Then she realized she didn't smile very much anymore. When was the last time she laughed? It seemed to her that she lived constantly in the shadow of the pale priest of gloom, always at her side.

She went out back to find Nito. But he wasn't on the back steps where she had left him with some toys. Quickly she scanned the small yard and saw the garage door ajar.

"Want to go visit your Tía Juanita?"

Nito came flying out of the garage. He was dressed in his favorite pile-lined winter jacket, red cotton shorts, and tiny cowboy boots. He was three and insisted on dressing himself. Teresa closed the garage door and latched it. How many times had she told them not to leave the garage open! She ran a washcloth over Nito's face and led him across the dirt road.

Teresa loved to walk in the sunshine. She was always cold. The gentle smile of the sun on her bare skin seemed to renew her spirits, if only for a few minutes. She was wearing a backless summer dress. Teresa's skin was fair, the delicate color of oyster shells, her eyes dark, and black silky hair fell below her shoulders. She had all the attractive contours of her sex and looked a very young forty. But then, she was only twenty-six.

Her sister and brother-in-law's house was no bigger than her own—two bedrooms, a bathroom, living room, and kitchen—but Juanita and Bartolo owned their house. She and Margarito didn't own anything after ten years of marriage. They never would. Bartolo's Toyota pickup was out front. She was hoping he wouldn't be home. It was easier to face her husband's sister alone. But Bartolo worked the second shift at the brewery and was home most of the day.

"*Buenos días,*" she called out as the door opened to her.

She inhaled the pleasant smell of beans simmering on the stove. It made her hungry.

Teresa was momentarily startled. A woman's agonizing shriek pierced the air at that instant, "Yes, I confess it, I love him, and I will marry him with your consent or no!"

"I forbid it!"

"I love him with all my being, and nothing and no one will stop this heart that burns within my breast for him alone." It sounded a lot like Carmela.

A woman cried hysterically, probably Carmela's mother. "My child, my poor child!"

A man's voice now, no doubt her father. "You can never marry Adrian . . . we never intended you should know . . . Adrian is . . . is your brother!" A sudden dissonant chord, a gush of organ music, and a Colgate commercial bloomed on the screen.

"Bartolo, turn that thing off!" Juanita then softened her voice. "*Buenos días*, Teresa," she sang, and scooped up little Nito in her arms. "*¿Quieres* cookie?" Nito wiggled like a puppy. He never saw a cookie at his house.

Teresa didn't know how grown people could waste their time on such nonsense. She herself didn't have time for television. They had a TV in the living room. Margarito brought it home one day. He was always bringing her gifts. She had no idea where he got it (neither did he), but it was pronounced dead on arrival.

"It must be Friday," Bartolo called out from the sofa where he lay stretched out watching the *novela*. Obediently, he snapped off the television and put his arms out to Nito. "Come over here, *payaso*."

Nito flew into his arms, giggling hysterically under the attack of nibbles and kisses Bartolo pressed into his neck. Nito finally broke away gasping for breath. "*¡Tengo que hacer pi-pi!*"

"See what you've done!" Juanita scolded, and took Nito off to the bathroom. Nito was eating a cookie when they came back.

"I can't stay long," Teresa began, "I only came to borrow a kilo of beans and enough flour to make a few tortillas." Her pale skin flushed pink to the roots of her hair.

"But it's payday, sister-in-law," Bartolo crooned. He had a keen sense of humor when not at his expense. "He'll be loaded with money when he gets home."

Juanita quelled Bartolo with a glare of sufficient voltage to fry him to a crisp had he been grounded, and he quickly restrained his humor. Everyone in the room knew Margarito would come home loaded, but it wouldn't be with money. Bartolo could easily afford the amusement, Margarito was his wife's relative, not his.

Back in her own kitchen, the painful ordeal behind her, Teresa put the beans up to cook and began to make the tortillas. She shaped a little ball of dough between the palms of her hands, rolled it out thin and round, then placed it on the hot iron. She waited until she saw the raw tortilla covered with tiny bubbles before she turned it over with fingers that learned to be quick. She'd been making tortillas since she was eight—or was it six? She thought of her mother now. "You would make a good shoemaker, Teresa," she used to say, "your tortillas look like shoe soles." The memory brought a wispy smile. The finished tortillas she was rolling out now were perfectly round and flecked with little brown freckles. They fluffed up like small balloons, and she tossed them in a basket lined with a towel. She loved the smell. Heat from the iron warmed her cheeks. It felt good. By the time she started to roll out the next tortilla, Teresa was lost in self-communion.

How long could she stay married to a loser? Forever, she

had three children. You took him for better or worse, remember? She recalled the two weddings, the first a civil ceremony at city hall, and the second in church because neither body acknowledged the authority of the other. Life just wasn't fair. You sow love and reap tears. She wondered if he would ever straighten out. She hoped and prayed. Other than his drinking, Margarito was a model husband. If intentions counted for currency, he would one day achieve sainthood. But Teresa's world came to an end every Friday. Margarito got paid, stopped on his way home for one drink, got drunk, and came home within a few coins of flat broke. Saturday was all tears and repentance. Sunday, a solemn promise, and back to work on Monday. The only reason Margarito didn't stop for a drink Monday through Thursday was that she kept him penniless.

My, that went fast. Tortilla basket nearly full. Maybe she should be grateful. He only got drunk on Fridays. She knew many husbands who got lost in drink and women every night. Some even mistreated their wives. By comparison, Margarito was an angel. He was sweet, gentle, generous, always thinking of her and the children. Maybe she expected too much.

"¡Caramba!" Out of gas. Only two tortillas to go, and out of gas! She would have to run across the street before Bartolo left for work and ask him to take her empty tank to the gas company and come back with a full one. Teresa ran quickly to the ATM in the bedroom. She might borrow food, but she would never borrow money.

In a small factory not far from where Teresa now stood stirring the beans, Margarito was stacking heavy cartons. They were marked THIS SIDE UP. He couldn't read it, but the arrows helped. He counted the cartons by poking his finger at each one to make sure he had received the same number shown on the bill of lading. Each carton was filled with electronic components. Mexican hands would assemble them and they would be shipped back to the United States in the form of transistorized clock radios. The plant was one of the many *maquiladoras* in Baja that sprouted like winter grass as soon as Americans realized you didn't have to go all the way to Taiwan to find cheap labor.

Margarito had studied electronics at a state-run trade school, but then he got married, and he had to quit school and take any kind of job he could find. A loud buzzer reverberated throughout the plant. Quitting time, and payday to boot! Margarito was preparing to head for the paymaster's window when Frank Turner, the American plant manager, flew in at full throttle and skidded to a stop in front of him. Drops of perspiration beaded on his pink face. He was in a snit. He spoke Spanish with a wooden tongue from Chicago that couldn't make the turns around the diphthongs.

"I was just told they've run out of 7255! We have any more 7255 in stock?"

Margarito didn't even have to consult the inventory, he *knew* it. "Sí, Señor Frank, we have two cartons."

Frank Turner felt better immediately. Margarito had that desirable effect on everyone. Frank Turner was looking at a round face radiant with bliss, covered in smooth brown vinyl with big merry-twinkle eyes under black caterpillar eyebrows. When the face smiled, you got the impression a whole ear of white corn got stuck in his mouth sideways.

"Margarito, you are a real champion amee-go. Go get paid, I'll see you Monday." And Frank whizzed out like a man who knew he would enjoy his weekend.

Margarito signed the payroll and the paymaster handed him a hundred and fifty thousand pesos in cash. At the door a few of his friends were already making plans. "Come on, Margarito, we're going into town and have a few."

"No, no, I have to get straight home."

"Come on, hombre, we won't be long."

"Unless we find some nice *chamaconas!*" They all laughed like naughty boys.

Margarito laughed too, but declined. "No, muchachos, you go and have a good time. I have a family, you know. My wife will be waiting for me."

"My *vieja* will be waiting too, but a man is entitled to his fun."

Margarito left them laughing and started home. It was an easy walk. Straight down the dirt shoulder along Highway 3 for two kilometers. No cross streets. When he got to the corner, all he had to do was turn right and walk two more blocks and he would be home.

Unlike Teresa, Margarito didn't live in the shade of life. He walked in full sun with a pocket heavy with cash and a light heart. He wore a white western shirt with three-button cuffs, and cranberry permanent-press pants over a frame lean as a wire coat hanger. Strands of black yarn poked out from under the wide brim of a tapioca cowboy hat. The boots were honey-colored western style, with sharp pointy toes that would make cornering a cockroach an easy matter.

His first stop was the Mini-Mercado, hardly more than a small cave, dark as a tomb at midnight and cluttered with everything man, woman, or child could need between the hours of seven in the morning and eight at night. The involuntary act of breathing in Doña Leandra's Mini-Mercado can bring on an acute attack of the jimjams to sensitive olfactory nerves. The current of air intended for respiration carries a high level of fragrant molecules, overripe bananas, musty potatoes, candlewax—Raid.

243

"*Buenas tardes*, Doña Leandra," he called out as he squeezed through the narrow doorway cluttered with brooms, mops, and a pyramid of toilet paper *en especial*. It looked like newsprint, but at five hundred a roll no one would chafe at the price.

"*Buenas tardes*, Margarito," the old lady answered from somewhere within the gloom. Doña Leandra was a kindly old lady with a creaky voice and a jack-o'-lantern grin that frightened small children. She was no taller than a doorknob, and nearly invisible behind the counter in her black crepe. Doña Leandra could have been queen of the ball on October thirty-first if that spooky holiday were observed in Mexico. "What will you have today?"

Margarito was compelled to wait until all the microscopic rod cells in his eyes did whatever it is they do, and his eyes became dark-adapted. "Give me a pack of Montanas." He peered into a glass case where colored cactus candies lay displayed like fine jewelry. Faceted gems of fiery yellow, dazzling white, pink, and orange cubes, sparkled with sugar. A filthy green housefly with the buzz of a bumblebee was throwing itself against the inside of the glass. "I'll take some of these candies for Teresa, she loves them."

"Of course, which ones?"

"The yellow, that's her favorite."

"Mine too, what a thoughtful husband you are."

"I should take something for my children too." He looked around. "What are these?" He was looking at a box filled with brightly colored animal shapes.

"Erasers."

"I'll take three."

"Four thousand pesos." Margarito paid with coins, exchanged a warm adios, and walked into the sunlight. His eyes now had to reverse the process. Margarito had company.

A small dog with striking sable and white markings appeared, and fell in behind him at a happy trot. It was immediately apparent, even to the casual observer, that this incredible animal drew from the vast gene pool represented by every breed registered by the AKC. He had the cocky, smart aleck grin of a champion fox terrier, with the long eyelashes and wiry whiskers. His body was all Doberman, and he wagged fine Pomeranian plumage. He moved with all the conceit and pride due one recently judged best of show.

Margarito was probably unaware of his companion, but the dog heeled like a blue ribbon obedience champion. His canine instincts told him that here was a dog's best friend, a man of uncommon generosity, a man with a heart that overflowed with the milk of human kindness. A man with a paper bag in his hand was a hot prospect, and any smart dog could assume his efforts would culminate in treats. He turned on the charm, performing leaps and handstands deserving of praise, though it brought none.

"Over here . . . shiny hubcaps, bumpers, mirrors, headlamps—everything like new except the price! ¡*Ganga, ganga, ganga!*"

Margarito recognized the voice. It was El Arabe, and this was one of his regular stops. They called the hawker El Arabe because his skin was nearly black and he wore a bandanna over his head. Every Friday, El Arabe parked his peeling station wagon here loaded with secondhand goods to catch the foot traffic on payday. Yellow cans of Pennzoil were stacked on the roof, rechromed bumbers and hubcaps glistened in the sunlight. The open tailgate was laden with Teflon pots and pans, toasters, rebuilt carburetors, alternators, and starters. Margarito stopped to browse, the best of breed faithfully at his side.

"*Hola*, Margarito! What will you have today, my good friend?"

"I just don't know, I don't have much money today."

El Arabe knew better. "I'll give you a very special price. Sssh, only for you!"

Margarito's loyal companion utilized this time to do some browsing of his own and leave a few notes for his friends who might happen by later.

"My boys could use a bicycle. You have a good used bicycle—cheap?"

El Arabe's face fell to his feet. "No, I'm afraid I don't have a bicycle today. I might have one for you next week." Margarito picked up a rebuilt carburetor and began to examine it. He flipped the butterfly and blew through the fuel intake. It made a clean hiss.

"Completely rebuilt and guaranteed. Twenty-five thousand—twenty for you."

"Too expensive." Margarito put it down.

"How about some oil—Pennzoil, the very best—and cheap."

"How much?"

"A thousand, for you, nine hundred. How many?"

"One can will do."

"Ten-thirty okay?"

"Oh yes. I could use a couple of spark plugs too."

"That will be thirty-one hundred, three thousand even for you."

You could say there was really nothing remarkable about this transaction, and you'd be right, except for the fact that Margarito didn't own a car. He never did, and his prospects for sitting behind the wheel of one registered in his name were not bright and shining. But Margarito had a dream, and his garage at home held enough inventory to threaten Montgomery Ward. He had faith that one day he would wake up to find the dream had come true. Margarito was simply adding to his trousseau.

By this time the little dog's optimism began to wane and he decided that to give this deadbeat the benefit of his companionship and protection for another kilometer would not repay effort. Thus he abandoned Margarito for a crumpled Hershey wrapper that smelled promising. It contained a couple of good licks. He did not regret his decision.

Margarito resumed his homeward journey in that loose gangly gait of a puppet on a string. When he came to Doña Flora's gate, he knew he was halfway to home and the bosom of his beautiful family.

"*Buenas tardes*, Margarito!" It was the friendly voice of Doña Flora, a sweet woman in the shape of a yam. She stood behind her chicken-wire fence ministering tender care to the carnations, geraniums, and roses she kept in coffee cans.

"*Buenas tardes*, Doña Flora." Margarito touched his tapioca hat and gave her nine rows of white kernels. "How are you this beautiful day?"

Doña Flora drew from a large collection of common sayings. "Like my garden, somewhere between first bud and last bloom, as the saying goes. How goes the job?"

"*Gracias a Dios* for the gringos. What would we do without the *maquiladoras*? Your garden is the prettiest sight on my way home."

"*Gracias*. I'm a slave to my garden. Men are so lucky. They have someplace to go. Then they come home to a warm house and a good dinner." A passenger bus missing a muffler roared by at that moment, erasing the last of her dialogue, so Margarito didn't hear it. But it didn't matter, as it was a duplicate of the conversation they had yesterday.

The bus left them drowning in a flash flood of diesel

fumes and dust. Doña Flora waved the gases away from her face with disgust. "Filthy things! We're forever eating dirt, and going deaf. It's like having a mouth full of chile and the water far away, as the saying goes. Give my *saludos* to your wife."

"*Gracias*, I will do that. Adios, Doña Flora." He touched his hat a second time and sauntered off.

In a few minutes Margarito was standing at the corner. All he had to do now was turn right, walk two blocks, and he would be home. But he was standing directly in the magnetic field of the Tapachula, a landmark in Tecate, offering comfort to the thirsty, the lonely, and the weak.

Tapachula was an awesome rubble of crumbling adobes with cracks reminiscent of the San Andreas fault. Dirty plywood covered broken windows. A stranger in Tecate would logically have assumed that here was a demolition job in progress and the wrecking crew was taking a taco break. The storefront had only recently been painted a garish green the color of liver bile. To Margarito it looked like the Emerald City.

He stood for a moment scratching his *nalgas*. From within the ruins came the familiar smell of tequila and urine. Strands of a tragic love song floated into the street. Pool balls clicked wickedly. He assessed the moment.

Maybe just one little sip of tequila and a lick of lime. No, no, straight home. He thought about it. Just two blocks and he'd be home with his beautiful family. He would break out the gifts and they would shower him with hugs and kisses. Just two blocks and he would be sitting at the table with a steaming plate of beans and a fresh tortilla in his hand.

But some events are foreordained somewhere in the cosmos. Napoleon was defeated in the Battle of Puebla, Cortes fell at Chapultepec, and Margarito Martínez succumbed to superior forces at Tapachula. He rubbed his *nalgas*, licked his lips, and went inside to join the society of the happy wretched.

Teresa was awake when Margarito came stumbling into the darkened bedroom. She feigned sleep. There was a dull thud when he collided with the wing chair. After living with the man for ten years, Teresa didn't need the aid of sight to know what her husband was doing. Two thunks. He had removed his boots. He was taking off his shirt now. She could hear the snap fasteners pop as he pulled them open. She heard the clink of his belt buckle, the whisper of a zipper. A sudden crash. Of course, he had tried to pull off his pants while standing up, a feat he never attempted while sober, when he possibly could have succeeded. Margarito was somewhere on the floor. He stumbled around the room and Teresa felt the bed rock as he fell in with a long sigh. The bed shook for a few seconds when he scratched his *nalgas*. He smacked his lips once or twice and he was snoring, floating away to that rosy-pink dreamland known only to the innocent heart. Silent tears streamed down Teresa's pretty face.

Saturday morning Teresa stood at the kitchen stove frying slices of bread. It was nearly the end of the loaf. Nito was already devouring his slice of bread swimming in an amber estuary of Karo syrup. Teresa was half listening to the conversation at the table.

"I saw El Arabe yesterday on the way home from work and looked to see if he had a bicycle. But no bicycle." Margarito dipped his spoon into the bowl of beans in front of him and tore a piece of tortilla. "If he had, I would have brought it home!"

"A bicycle! We could ride it to school. We could ride it to the plaza!" Beto nearly shouted.

"I would drive and you could sit on the handlebars," Abel suggested.

"I know how to ride a bicycle!" Beto shot back.

"We could ride it to the fair today!" Beto was still shouting.

"I want to go to the fair too!" Nito bleated.

"Is there a fair today?" Margarito inquired.

"Yes, and there are carnival rides, and games, and the Ferris wheel!" Beto announced at the top of his voice.

"And *palomitas* and cotton candy and snowcones!" Abel added.

"I want to go to the fair!" This time Nito screamed.

"Can we go, Papá?" Abel pleaded.

Teresa put a platter of fried bread and Karo syrup in front of the boys. "Eat your breakfast and stop pestering your father."

"But can we, Papá?" Abel continued to pursue the question.

"It's up to your mother."

Teresa had to overcome a strong urge to strangle her husband. But a good subservient Mexican wife does not threaten to strangle her husband at the breakfast table in plain view of the children. She refused to participate. "Another tortilla?" she asked in a frosty voice.

"*Sí, mi amor,* just one more to soak up the rest of the beans. God, you make wonderful tortillas." He knew he was in trouble.

Teresa ignored the compliment and put another tortilla on the griddle. She said nothing, as if by not contributing to the subject, it would end. They were all on thin ice now, even the innocent.

"Mamá, Mamá, what do you say?" they all begged in chorus.

Margarito entered a plea on his children's behalf. "Oh, let them go, *mi amor*."

Teresa was furious. Was this man crazy? She had to borrow so there would be food in the house, the rent was due in a week and they didn't have it, and she had to finish sewing a dress just so she could repay what she borrowed. And the man was talking bicycles, and Ferris wheels, and cotton candy!

Teresa wiped Nito's face with a kitchen towel and sat down at the table. No one seemed to notice she was the only one who hadn't eaten. She looked directly at her husband. "I didn't see you last night when you got home. Did you get paid?"

The smile on Margarito's face was replaced with a look of panic. "Of course, it was Friday." He reached into his pocket, brought out a wad of bank notes and put them on the table in front of her.

A bitter taste filled Teresa's mouth. She was angry and tears of frustration were near. She swallowed the lump in her throat and straightened the bank notes, pressing out the wrinkles and laying them out in a neat pile. Then in a soft voice she said, "Let's count it and see what we can do for our children today. We have seven hundred pesos here."

It was Margarito's turn to gulp. He knew there wasn't enough there to buy a shoeshine.

"As the head of the family, you should decide. It's market day. Should we go to market and buy the groceries, or should we pay the rent? Then, of course, the children could use some school clothes."

Margarito's eyes began to burn. He didn't mean to be bad. He hung his head and looked into his plate. He didn't like himself very much this morning.

"But you children will go to the fair," she announced,

and cheers went up. "Take your shine kits into town. There should be a lot of business today. But this day you don't have to bring your money home. Stay for the fair and spend whatever you can earn."

Little Nito began to wail without tears.

"What's wrong with you?"

"I want to go to the fair! I want cotton candy!"

"You're going, you're going!" Teresa cleaned him up and sent him to the bathroom. "Now you boys go and have a good time. Beto, tuck your shirt in, you look like a tramp. And Abel, get the hair out of your face. Keep an eye on Nito and take an extra pair of underpants just in case."

The boys took turns kissing their parents, first one, then the other, like frisky puppies, and they scurried out the back door.

Margarito drained his coffee cup and spoke in a low whisper. "It will be different from now on. I'll never do this again. I promise." It was the voice of a child making a promise he couldn't keep.

Teresa got up from the table and came to his side with the coffeepot. She had to support herself with a hand on his shoulder in order to reach across and fill his cup. Everything that needed saying was said in the unspoken Esperanto understood by the married couples of the world. Margarito knew he was forgiven, and with eyes filled with unshed tears, gave Teresa the full ear of corn.

Monday morning the cycle began all over again. Teresa packed a *quesadilla* for Margarito and got him off to work with nothing but lint in his pockets. She got the boys off to school and prepared herself to face another week like the last. On the way home next payday he would pass Tapachula and it would start all over again. He would come home bereft of money and memory. Saturday morning they would be broke again. She couldn't go on. Then she was forced to face reality; if they were going to make it to Friday, she had better get started on that dress. She put Nito out back and got to work.

Teresa turned on the sewing machine and began to guide the material through. She knew something was wrong as soon as the material began to pucker. She backed off, started over, when the thread snapped. Calmly, she removed the material, lifted the foot, and checked the problem. She snipped the thread, rethreaded the needle and began again. The machine hummed beautifully. Clickety, clickety, clickety—snap! She lifted the foot and found a bird nest of thread wrapped hopelessly around the bobbin. She glared at the insolent monster. The ugly yellow lettering grinned back at her with evil defiance: KENMORE. Teresa burst into tears.

By the time she went to the kitchen window to check on Nito and returned, she was calmed. She would finish it by hand. It meant she would have to buy a spool of thread and some needles. She would borrow the money from the blue sock.

That afternoon, the boys were late getting home from school. They presented their mother with tardy slips. "But why so late? What were you doing? You left with plenty of time."

"It was the dog!"

"What dog?"

"There's a big mean dog at the end of the street!"

"He comes out and chases us with huge teeth!"

"Whose is it?"

"No one knows, but he runs after us and tries to bite us."

"Well, for heaven's sake, go around the block! If you don't go past the dog, you don't have a problem."

"We never thought of that."

"Well, start learning to think for yourselves. I can't solve all your problems!"

"Can we go out and play with our friends?"

"One hour, then back here to bathe and do your homework. And tuck your shirt in!"

They weren't out the door a minute when she began to regret her impatience with the boys. She too had problems she couldn't solve.

Early Tuesday morning Teresa left Nito with her sister-in-law and started for the Mini-Mercado. She held her breath against the stench as she rounded the corner where the Tapachula stood, that is, those portions that remained standing. If God were to drop a bolt of lightning on Tapachula, Teresa would see it as an act of divine mercy. She would praise the Lord and rejoice, and maybe sing a hosanna or two.

"*Buenos días*, Tere!" Doña Flora was in her front yard with a pail of water.

"*Buenos días*, Doña Flora, how lovely your garden looks. I never fail to admire your flowers whenever I go by."

"You don't pass often enough. But I see your husband every day. I see him carrying home little gifts every Friday. You are so lucky to have such a good man."

Teresa was spared the need of a reply. A semi truck and trailer the size of a house ripped the air at that moment with a shuddering roar that would have given a wooden Indian an earache, and it was impossible to be heard. They were engulfed in a choking cloud of brown dust and black smoke. The ground trembled beneath their feet.

"I have that all day long, and all through the night. It wakes my husband, and you can guess what he wants to do.

I swear, that's all men think about! Dust and noise is what we have to live with." Doña Flora sighed.

"I can imagine you must have to dust the house every day."

"Every twenty minutes! But what can we do? The rich solve their problems with money, but the rest of us have to live with them. We're between sword and wall, as the saying goes."

"How well I know."

"We're not the kind of people that eat beans and eruct steak, as the saying goes, we know we're here because the rent is cheap enough. Still, if we weren't right on the highway, we wouldn't have the problem. But, as the saying goes, ducks don't sing."

Both women laughed at the old proverb. They talked about the weather, the cost of groceries, and housework before an open trash truck rumbled past, leaving them in a blizzard of trash. Teresa took the opportunity to say adios and continued on her way.

She walked into the dark cavern of the Mini-Mercado. "*Buenos días*, Doña Leandra."

"*Buenos días*, Teresa, it's nice to see you. I see Margarito every day. What a wonderful man you have. Other men spend their money drinking and carousing. But Margarito only thinks of his family. He never fails to buy little gifts for you."

"Yes, I am very grateful."

"What do you need today?"

"I need a spool of blue thread and some needles."

Doña Leandra brought out a cigar box and put it on the counter. "Look and see what suits your purpose, I'll be right back." And Doña Leandra disappeared into the tomb to help a woman find lamp wicks.

Teresa selected her thread and her needles. While she waited for Doña Leandra to reappear, she leafed through an assortment of color prints of various saints suitable for framing. The Mexican calendar lists well over three hundred saints—one for nearly every day of the year. Many are specialists. There's San Cristobal, who looks after the traveler. Those who lose or misplace things invoke the aid of San Juan Lumbredo to recover them. Affairs of the heart are under the auspices of San Valentin. There seems to be a patron for every human need.

Teresa held up a print of Judas. It should be made clear that this was San Judas Tadeo, author of the Epistle, and not Judas Iscariote, the infamous betrayer. Among Mexicans, San Judas is one of those specialists, and the saint of choice when dealing with problems on the order of "Mission Impossible." The bearded patron of the troubled stood in his robes, which were all the rage among saints during that epoch. He held the proverbial staff in his left hand, and in the right, a medallion with the picture of Jesus. Underneath was written a prayer translated as follows:

O glorious apostle and patron of the most difficult cases. Come to our aid and do not permit our loss of faith. Send us solace, and succor from Heaven in all our needs, tribulations, and suffering. We shall always remember your favors and never shall we fail to honor you as our especial and omnipotent protector.

"I'll take along this color print of Judas," she said as Doña Leandra returned to the counter.

"You choose wisely, Teresa." Doña Leandra directed her attention to a print on the wall. "San Martin Caballero, patron saint of the merchants, looks after my store, but for the problems of life, Judas has never failed me."

Teresa paid for her purchase and started for home. She was grateful Doña Flora was not in her garden when she went by. She had a lot of work to do.

The minute she walked in the house, Teresa placed the picture of Judas against the inside wall of her dish cupboard. She offered him a candle with reverence and repeated the short prayer. "Please," she pleaded in a throbbing whisper, "teach this duck to sing." And she went immediately to her sewing.

The days melted away like the candles she lit for Judas. Wednesday she delivered the dress and got paid. She took in some ironing, and was relieved when the boys came home from school without tardy slips. She had solved their problem, now if she could only solve her own. She paid another visit to Judas and offered another candle and repeated the prayer.

By Thursday, Teresa was a nervous wreck. Every day she lit a candle and invoked the prayer to Judas, but thus far received no indication that he was working on her case. She took in more ironing, cleaned house, and scoured the kitchen floor. She was looking for something else to clean when she heard Nito's cries. She ran out to look for him. She found him in the garage. He had taken a fall and grazed his knee. She kissed it all better, latched the garage door and took him inside. Men and children are all the same, she thought. You have to protect them from themselves, from the mean dogs and open garages of life.

She made another pilgrimage to Judas. Her heart dropped. The candle was out. Her lips trembled, her eyes filled, and a tightness came to her throat. Was Judas really smiling? Tears of joy and gratitude rained down Teresa's pale cheeks. Yes, yes! She had the answer. Judas came through! She pressed the picture to her bosom and kissed his image ferverently. "Tomorrow this duck will sing."

Thursday night she hardly slept.

Friday morning Teresa was up earlier than usual. She got Margarito off to work and the boys off to school. "Come, Nito, let's go visit your Tía Juanita." Nito interrupted the important things he was doing and came running with a smile resembling his father's. Tía Juanita had cookies at her house.

"*Buenos días*, Teresa," Juanita greeted her at the door in her robe. "You're early today. Bartolo is still snoring. Come have some coffee with me. I have a fresh pot. ¡Nito *bonito!* *¡Quieres* cookie?"

Teresa spoke in a voice made steady by effort. "I won't be needing beans and flour this morning, Juanita. But there is something I want you to help me with."

At five o'clock that very Friday afternoon, Margarito came sauntering along Highway 3 with a song on his lips. He was full of love and light and life. He looked forward to making all his usual stops. But first, a little gift for Teresa and the boys. He stepped into the Mini-Mercado and bought Teresa her favorite candy, and erasers for the boys. If Margarito had known anything about déjà vu, he could have claimed the curious feeling this experience evokes. He vaguely remembered doing this before, but he couldn't be sure. Most of Margarito's recollections were fuzzy.

El Arabe sold him a tire, almost new, and only ten thousand pesos. Margarito rolled it homeward with pride, like a boy would roll his hoop. What a beautiful day this was! Doña Flora's garden gate came into view. She would certainly notice the nearly new tire.

"*Buenas tardes*, Doña Flora, how is your garden this beautiful day?" He touched his tapioca hat, and the gleaming white kernels of his smile reached all the way to the brim.

"*Buenas tardes*, Margarito, I'm just giving my flowers some water."

Margarito leaped in the air, clearing the ground by several inches. He had to throw his arms out to avoid falling over backwards on his *nalgas*. He looked like a startled sparrow who had just alighted on an exposed electric wire. The steel-belted Firestone 650 × 14 continued in the direction of Tapachula under its own power until it wobbled to the ground in a series of diminishing whumps.

While all this was happening, Margarito regained the ability to form words. "Teresa! What are you doing here?"

"Watering my carnations, they're terribly thirsty."

"No, no, I mean *here*."

"This is our home. We live here now. Doña Flora and I exchanged houses this morning." Teresa smiled at her husband. She looked twenty-six again. "And now the truck traffic will not keep Doña Flora awake, and you won't have so far to walk."

This new information caused a temporary paralysis of the vocal chords, and the best Margarito could offer was a gurgle like that of a drainpipe in need of Drano.

"Did you get paid?"

Still shaking, Margarito put the pay envelope in her hands. She took it with more gratitude than triumph. "We're having meat in red salsa, yellow squash, and peas tonight. Dinner will be on the table in an hour." Teresa turned and headed up the path. She was singing.

Margarito glanced wistfully in the direction of Tapachula, then scratched his *nalgas* for a moment or two before he followed her into the house.

LA DESPEDIDA

"Pork tamales . . . hot and spicy!"

"Ice cream! . . . Who wants ice cream!"

"Tweeky tweeky kee-kee-kee!!"

"Beetles for breakfast, spiders for lunch. Give me a coin and I'll dine on a worm!"

We seem to have ended up back in the plaza. I certainly enjoyed showing you around my paradoxical pueblo. Look! Here come the mariachis glistening with sequins, violins, guitars, and that silvery trumpet, playing their sweet melodies dipped in tears. Listen! They're playing "La Golondrina," the sorrows of parting set to music.

Whither go *las golondrinas?*
They carry our memories to Heaven
For life is o'er when we forget

Thus, with breast overflowing, the *golondrinas* and your *servidor* say adios. We leave you now with the musical memory of a thousand sighs.

Now that you know everybody, I hope you decide to make the journey yourself. You will be warmly received with *besos y abrazos*. You certainly don't want to miss Graciela's thirtieth birthday fiesta. She is even more beautiful now than when she was twenty-four—if that is *posible*! I saw Margarito carrying groceries for Teresa on market day. He is a production supervisor and he actually owns a car. Nothing in his trousseau was usable. And next Sunday is the baptismal of Faustino's and Cristina's first—a little girl crowned with golden ringlets. I saw Concepción this morning at the fish taco cart, he was wearing a Dallas Cowboys T-shirt. He gave me a triumphant smile and a high four.

We all wait for your arrival. By now you know you can't land at our *aeropuerto*. And trains slide upon our tracks no longer. U.S. 188 is your only option. But when you cross the bridge and see the river below running merrily uphill, you'll know you're in Tecate.

ABOUT THE AUTHOR

Daniel Reveles was born in Los Angeles of Mexican-born parents. He has been involved in some aspect of the entertainment industry since his youth as a songwriter, late-night disc jockey, and producer of commercials. He has written and directed a wide variety of foreign documentaries for American television, including countries such as Africa, India, Turkey, Mexico, and Guatemala. He lives at Villa Mirasol, his rancho, on the outskirts of Tecate, Baja California, where he devotes his time to writing and playing chamber music.